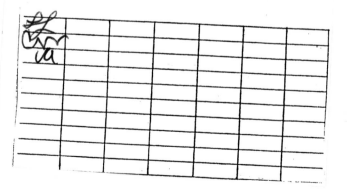

** "Did I read this already?" **
Place your initials or unique symbol in
square as a reminder to you that you have
read this title.

THE AGE OF ORPHANS

THE AGE OF ORPHANS

A Novel

Laleh Khadivi

BLOOMSBURY

New York Berlin London

Published by Bloomsbury USA, New York

All papers used by Bloomsbury USA are natural, recyclable products made from wood grown in well-managed forests. The manufacturing processes conform to the environmental regulations of the country of origin.

LIBRARY OF CONGRESS CATALOGING–IN–PUBLICATION DATA

Khadivi, Laleh.
The age of orphans : a novel / Laleh Khadivi.—1st U.S. ed.
p.   cm.
ISBN-13: 978-1-59691-616-6
ISBN-10: 1-59691-616-8
1. Kurds—Iran—Fiction.   2. Orphans—Fiction.   3. Conflict
(Psychology)—Fiction.   I. Title.

PS3611.H315A73 2009
813'.6—dc22
2008032551

First U.S. Edition 2009

1   3   5   7   9   10   8   6   4   2

Typeset by Westchester Book Group
Printed in the United States of America by Quebecor World Fairfield

To Kamran and Fereshteh

CONTENTS

. . . they have marked me—even to myself. Because I am not like them, I am evil. I cannot get my hands on it: I, murderer, outlaw, outcast . . . Because their way is the just way and my way—the way of the kings and my father—crosses them: weaklings holding together appear strong . . . The worst is that weak, still, somehow, they are strong: they in effect have the power, by hook or by crook. And because I am not like them—not that I am evil, but more in accord with our own blood than they, eager to lead—this very part of me, by their trickery must not appear, unless in their jacket.

Red Eric
William Carlos Williams

These people, the Kurds, lived in the mountains, were very war-like and not subject to the Persian king.

Anabasis
Xenophon

It is more difficult to contend with oneself than with the world.

Kurdish proverb

Book I

SOUTHERN ZAGROS MOUNTAINS,
COURDESTAN—1921

THE BIRD BOY

THE ROOF IS made of thick mud, straw and woven sticks. Each morning the boy climbs a small mound of stones to reach the window ledge and then the roof's lip and finally hoist himself to this top spot that affords a glimpse of endless horizon, the fan of a more ardent wind. *Look, Maman! Look!* Legs shrink and stretch to send the body of the boy, at four and five and finally six years, up, over and out for a moment's flight; a swift reconnaissance of air and cloud and sky quick enough to blur the eyes and bate the breath. Mountains fold into the earth and the heavens round their blue nimbus over everything, and in this instant the boy ascends. His bones are thin and brittle, arms flung out and lax and his lungs open evenly to shout. *Maaaaaaman! Looooook!* No one calls back to him; no one comes; no aunts or cousins make mention or mind of the boy who every morning jumps and jumps again. *He is but a boy*, they say. *Let the mountain air fill his lungs and the flashes of sky pulse through his head. The enthusiasms of a child are easily exhausted.*

In the end, breathless and sore, the boy cannot fly and instead must run to his maman to sit in the crisscross of her legs, where he comforts himself with the sweet taste of her milk and the steady sound of heartbeat until the bird in him is sated and calm. After the love and the drink he is ready again to walk about the village and take in the sights that repeat every day: his uncle hanging the skinned carcasses of goats and geese on the posts behind his house, messily slicing open their bellies as he smiles at the boy; older cousins stuck in games of stick fight and rock fight and fistfight turn to tease the boy with their spilled blood and swollen faces; girl cousins and aunts arguing and singing at the lip of the fountain, their arms sunk elbow-deep into the water to wash last night's rice pots and this morning's bread pans, keep him away with a simple tsk and nod of the head. At his own house the boy tiptoes to peer into the divan, where the men recline, take the pipe and keep each other company through the hottest part of the day. It is a room of rugs and whispers and smoke, and he is careful to see and not be seen, staying just long enough to catch sight of his baba's eyes, blue and far and empty of any recognition for the boy's little head that peeks just above the rim of the window and slowly floats past.

He is just a boy, young, useless and kept from the tasks and play, the chiming world of women and the dark room of men. And every afternoon he takes to the periphery of the village in search of birds to watch and want to be, birds without limitations of mamans and babas, yes and no, mountain and fence.

In the groves he marks the spry stares of sparrows and warblers for just a minute; they are too quick and low and fickle to carry the boy's interest. He does not care for the inky crows that keep company with the sheep in the pens, or the finches that peck alongside the chickens and march out to the fields.

Here he keeps his gaze fixed upward, to the ceiling of the sky, for the family of peregrines that circles high, indomitable and unsurpassed. When he spots them the boy lets loose to follow their flight with body and eyes and heart and spins about in their circle pattern until he grows tipsy and top-heavy. Stumbling, he wonders how his world would appear from *that* branch or *that* rocky escarpment or *that* particular patch of sky, and aches to fly from rooftop to mountaintop, to unfasten himself from the limits of the ground and soar in the enormous embrace of sky.

But he is just a boy. Joined to the earth by bare feet and gravity, much like all the boys who came before, he walks over the dirt and stone of the land and will turn into an old man and then a dead man and finally dirt and stone. He is a simple son in a line of simple sons, born of a maman who sings only sad songs and a baba sharp faced and proud who reminds him, with a rough tug to the ear, that he is a *lucky boy* to be tied to the land by this tight knot of aunt and uncle and cousin that will protect him from the forever fierce beat of the sun, the jagged circles of mountains and the dry deserts all around.

Still, the fascinations come first. At dusk he cannot help but run to his favorite rooftop, where he jumps and jumps until the earth and sky are a swirl and there is no up or down, no close or far. When he is tired and giddy and done, the boy lies on the roof and counts the stars as they shine out from the dusty dome, *one and one and one.* Each evening spreads over him like a satin blanket, immense and entire and yielding, to convince the boy that he too can belong to heaven and earth all at once.

THE INITIATE

IT IS THE year they take the boy to the caves. It is the year after last, when he trailed the slow-moving caravan of pulled carts and horses and men, uncles, cousins and father, down the drive to the sloped edge of the bottomlands and his baba brushed him away with his hand in the air as if to move a fly, and said: *Enough. Go home. Next year.* Now it is that next year and but for the passage of days and days little about the boy has changed. His chest is not grown or round, his arms and neck are no thicker, the digits of his age are not doubled and just this morning he walks to and from the gathered caravan with the chalk-sweet taste of mother's milk fresh on his tongue. Nonetheless, in a ceremony among themselves, the men, uncles, cousins and father, deign this to be the next year and the boy, his father's only son, will be a man in it and suddenly all the days thus far suffice. They pack him in among the supplies on the flat bed of the cart pulled by his father's donkey and his uncle's old rheumy-eyed mule and say to the boy: *Now. It is time. It is time.*

Alone in the back of the cart the boy remembers years past

when he was left alone to keep the company of girls who would tease him. *Have they left you behind again? You must not be man enough for the caves yet . . . or maybe you were meant to be a girl like us . . . come here, let us pull down your chalvar to see . . .* Chided, the boy spent days on his roof, waiting for the return of the men. His eyes scoured the landscape of the Zagros and the flats and the distant line of the horizon, and the boy wished for wings to ride and meet the men, join them or return. When they came back, only a few days after their departure, he held his breath to see them. A procession of the empty-handed—without carcass or prized ibex horns, without bazaar toys, salt or even sugar—the men who were once uncles, cousins and father returned now hollow, deflated and extinguished as wraiths; the gel and water of their eyes emptied out and the sockets filled with the bold shine of sharp glass. A procession of the exhausted and blind. And every year he waited at his mother's side, at his dog's side, at the side of the house, for the men to stumble past and for his baba to take him in his arms and then to bed, where he would lie in the web of arms as the old man muttered, *Next year, son of mine, next year,* and fall into a sleep of clutching and sweating and snoring that kept the boy curious and wanting.

Now it is his year and in preparation for the blindness the boy takes a good look around him. Alone in the back of the cart, he sits between the strings and stretched skins of instruments and flats of lavash, next to clanging copper pots and on top of rugs knotted by the tiny hands of girls who are perhaps now old women, maybe now dead women who haunt the world with these intricate patterns. The boy lies on his back to see the blue expanse. He holds his small hand up against it flat and then in a fist, the lines of his skin elaborate against the blank sky, birdless today and streaked across with white. He turns over onto his belly to press an eye between the spaces in the roughened wood slats and watch the earth roll beneath the cart in an endless succession of scrub, dirt, rock and bone, and the boy concentrates on everything above and beneath and around him, careful to memorize the look of it all.

They travel a long time through the day on a dust path that strings village to village, from which residents come forth to stand with hands idly in pockets or across the smooth tops of canes and squint at the movements of the men, to observe and say nothing. Across the day and across the land the caravan travels without stop. The boy pees through the slats of wood and takes water from the cask as the medley of men and burdened beasts moves atop the arid earth that never belonged to anyone after the Parthians (once) and the Sassanids (once) and the Mongols (once) and the Turks (just then) and the Russians (now and then) and the shah (soon), and so the Kurdish clan moves on, to own whatever piece of land they step on or roll over or smash for just that single moment of impact and no longer.

Farther from home than he has ever been, the boy feels it too, at once in possession and at once dispossessed, and so holds close to himself, hands and legs and knees to the stomach, all of it sewn neatly into a skin. Evening spreads across the sky and the procession moves on, the eyes of man and the eyes of beast now similar in a common march of figures patient and erect, that hold soil apart from sky and push the western horizon of day from the eastern edge of night. The boy sits still, sees less and less, sings and finally sleeps.

They walk until the animals slacken in their pull and the men arrive in a darkness deep and empty enough to seem not an arrival but a pause. The boy sees the nothing and senses the nowhere and the men dismount and drink and order him, *Find wood, tether the horses, arrange the sacks, go into the cave and lay down the rugs, yes, the dark cave, go.* And the boy goes into the absolute dark where the cold stone pushes all around him, full and heavy and smothering. He feels the entirety of the mountain atop him, timeless and sheathed in a thin skin of grass and moss. Inside it he is barefoot and steps on the spalled stones, compact and intricate with the details and dents of time and in a moment the cave wraps about him completely like a caul. In the dim hollow the boy recognizes no color or smell or touch but hears the ring of every sound—his own breath, the horses neighing, his father's deep laugh—as they chime within him and without. Quickly he rolls out rugs and arranges sacks and spreads blankets where he thinks to be here and there and the stone closes in until it is all he can do to sit in the noisy heartbeat of the dark, on rugs knotted by last year's girls, maybe this year's women or next year's ghosts, whose tiny hands flutter around him like bats.

In time the men come into the cave and the boy is relieved to tend to them with tea from the samovar and oil for their feet. He and his closest cousin run sticks together to coax fire and flame and the cave opens, no longer black and closed but red and centered, and the uncles, cousins and father undress to the hot orange heart. They remove layers that shield them against sun and day, women and each other, and sit naked but for the cloth tangled loosely about the loins. All around him cave carvings flicker in the new light, but the boy does not see them, distracted as he is by the sudden presence of his family's flesh: gaunt or corpulent, hairy or barren, with nipples just like his and shoulders just like those on his boy body, and remembers this to be his year and silently undresses himself alongside them.

When the cave is filled with heat a pipe is lit and passed and the men, uncles, cousins and father, inhale and exhale until the brown coals and the light of their eyes are one and the same. In his life the boy has distinguished the men by their discipline and silence, their warning and argument, their smoking and sleeping and spitting. In the lambent light of the cave, though, the men are indistinguishable, folded into a piece, a joined monad unified in motion and desire. They pick up instruments and rile their voices and together sing one song, in one breath, with one voice.

The boy tries to hum along but is distracted by the chronicles that emerge from deep in the cave walls; around him the cave walls are chiseled into animal bodies, human bodies, moon and sun. And the stone story goes: a crown, passed from hand to carved hand of figures robed and frozen, being passed, still passed, always passing, *Here, this land is yours, this land is yours, here, Parthian, Sassanid, Madig and Saladin, this land is yours.* Farther down bristle-covered boars and gigantic horses and round beasts with long uncoiled snouts walk among stalks of grain and grass toward the hunter king with his arrow and bow, toward their own capture and kill. Farther still a man in a sharp crown holds the ankles of the dead boar in his hands, and the boar, upside-down, bloodless and pierced through the neck, smiles with a twist in its lips. Women with harps in their laps, dead warriors spread out in layers of tangled limbs, the crescent moon and prickly sun and the stone story spread around the boy's head, convincing and true. But the faces—smashed off, uneven, jagged and erased—the boy understands the personalities in the carvings to be present, responsible for the evening's atmosphere, and reconciles the cold renderings in the rock with the live skin of the men who brought him here, uncles, cousins and father, who sit and sing now, full in breath, sentient and pulsed through with blood.

The Kurds have many fathers and those are three.

The boy is drawn into his father's warm lap and held tightly against loosely clad loins. His baba points up to the triumvirate of human men sculpted shoulder to shoulder in the stone. The figures, dressed in wide pants and turbans, each with a long beard of stiff coils, are linked hand to hand, shoulder to hand, head to hand in a posture of victory.

Just as I am your father you will one day father and the land has fathered us, the lines of Kurd blood do not cross but flow together from their time to ours, through those bodies and down into the bodies of son and son and father and son and king and son and me and you. We are aligned in our duty and our duty is to those three.

The boy sees a man with a sharp crown on his head, a man in a sheath of armor, a man who pushes a spear through the ground. His father pulls him in until the hairs on his chest tickle the boy's bare back and the old man's exhales wet the knots of spine on his neck.

We are the children born of Mount Cudi, where Noah's ark rested

11

after the flood, and our families are born of the animals and gardens of the survived, of God's chosen.

So he is told and so the boy hears the daf beat and the sitar strings hum.

It was King Suleiman who wanted a harem of pale-skinned beauties, and it was the djinn who captured his harem of virgins and bred the Kurds, children born of mountain shaitans and golden angels.

And so he is told.

We survived the evil king Zahak, who fed on the brains of Kurds, until one by one we escaped to the mountains and that is how we came to live in the Zagros, to drink of the snow water and eat from cracks in the rock and grow into strong men, men of stone.

And so he is told.

When you think of God, when you lay your head down and pray against this ground, they—the father circles a finger in the air and points to all walls of the cave at once—*will come to you.*

The boy leans back to nestle in his father's lap and smell the pipe and hear the chord of their one song. After a time he grows sleepy and can no longer distinguish between the vision of his open eyes and the vision behind his closed lids. He imagines himself in round robes and mottled armor, his boy face heavy with an iron beard, his head arrayed in light; father and son standing as victors atop the layers of bodies dead and flattened into the ground. He absorbs his father's breath into his back, accepts this new patrimony, gladly enters into the tight belonging of the cave and lets sleep enter and all of her entombed dreams.

In the thin light of dawn the men rise, dress, drink the samovar's cold tea and abandon the cave to walk, without conversation, up the shale and grass of the mountain in whose bedrock they slept. A gauze of cloud covers the sky and their shadows float beneath them, muted and dull. The boy holds neither to his father's hand nor to his closest cousin and rises upward like the rest: loose of limb, given to the march, the wind, to the loom of sky and drop of earth. The mountain changes from the soft ground to scarps of jutting rock and stone broken apart by intermissions of loose talus. Young cousins rush to help older uncles with offers of hands and shoulders, crooks of elbows and sturdy waists, to steady the elders against the ungracious incline. The boy too offers his reed-thin arms and narrow shoulders and is quickly pushed back by stern hands.

Na. Today you touch no one and no one touches you.

At the mountain's crest a wind blows in all directions with sharpness enough to cut men into shards and strew them about, nameless and fragmentary, across the ginger desert below. Here men lean alone against the firmament and the boy watches as uncles, cousins and father extend their arms, in the manner of birds, to keep balance along the craggy chine that leads to an even and welcoming plateau, the highest point along the crest. There they stand, hands pocketed or knotted behind their backs, to gaze at the Kurdish flats to the south or the vaulting Zagros to the east. From up high his father calls. The boy runs to the summons and is caught and kept as a feather is sought and fastened to his forehead by means of a narrow leather strap. Crowned thus, he is applauded and the men push him ahead to lead them into a deep valley from which no life sounds or flies. They descend single file, the boy ahead, jolly in this new year and new game of manhood (and possible birdhood) and they walk silently until the land flattens and the wind ceases and they come to a narrow dell of aspen saplings whose leaves flutter green and gold in the afternoon sun.

The uncles remove shoes and socks to sleep or recline against boulders while cousins walk solemnly through the grove to gently touch the thin trunks of trees only a few years older than themselves. The boy follows in curiosity and zeal, hopeful for a game, a shout, a dash through the cool copse, but is instead pushed around and out by a cousin who gestures him away.

Na na na. Not yet, later. Go. Your baba calls.

Together, father and boy walk past the coppice to a deep crevice between rocks, through a swale of seeping water, and soft moss grows atop the sharp stones. They move carefully into an escarpment where the mountain walls nearly touch and the ground juts at them from beneath and beside. In the indentures the boy sees night birds rock in a sheathed sleep as above them the sky, all day a great expanse, thins to a narrow gray blade. Aligned with his father the boy has no fear and they walk slowly to emerge from the tiny fissure into a meadow of new grass and thin streams. The boy runs to the nearest pool to drink and splash and watch his father crouch and disassemble a crude box made of rocks, from which he unearths an ax and a black-handled knife, both of which he tests on the tips of his fingers, one of which draws blood. The father pockets the knife and shoulders the ax and calls to the wet, wondering boy.

Come. We must go back. It is time.

Even before they arrive the boy can see the men gathered in a circle again beneath the trees. They are without fire or opium pipes or instruments, and because they do not sit or stand, but pace in small steps back and forth among the trees, the boy is ill at ease. His heart pulses quickly as he shouts.

Why do you stand there? Where is the sitar and the daf? Who is going to light the fire?

His closest cousin raises neither voice nor eyes and kicks the ground and the fallen leaves. The boy sees loose smiles slip out from his uncles' lips and his baba offers no explanation and gives no comfort; he grows an ax from his shoulder and a knife from his fist and the boy is no longer aligned with him and no longer cares for the game of the feather tied to his head or the ceremony of the caves and wants nothing but the crisscross of his maman's knees and shins and the sad songs that sing him to sleep.

At the sound of a sudden clap the men, uncles and cousins, take the boy by his shoulders and head and lay him down at the base of the selected tree. He is held down, by whom and how many he does not know, to stare up at the canopy of leaves that blot out the sky as hands clear him of pants and shirt and shoes (leaving the feather fastened to his forehead). When he is naked and cold the men gather around him to sing and clap as if the boy were last night's flame. They are tight and close around him and he can feel the hot air of their breath, the drips of spit that fall out from their singing mouths, and smell the musk on their skin. He opens his mouth to protest, but as in a nightmare, nothing comes. The sky above him fills with faces, a ceiling of flesh: lips, cheeks and jaws hang loose and ragged and pulled down by the force of an earth that draws all things to its center. And here the boy lies: bare and caught, lodged at the bottom of a well at whose edge men tremble before they fall.

The song stops. From all around a warmth of hands presses and the boy is touched and caressed until blood rushes to just below his middle, to the smallest part of him that only he knows and his mother knows and they know together, that fills now with a cold, flush fire that opens and closes in him again and again. His smallness stiffens and he is aroused, and the boy begins to drown in a pleasure unrecognizable but for its proximity to wild agony. Deaf and blind from the opulent touch of the men on and over his body and his smallness, the boy is oblivious to the spectacle of his father's ax aloft as he cuts apart the spine of the young tree that grows just above the boy's head. His smallness swells with pleasure and the ax falls, down again and again. Trapped as he is in the moment's wealth the boy feels no fear. He hears nothing of the fresh wood spliced above him and in his closed-eye ecstasy does not notice the black-handled blade as it is kissed by the closest cousin (who lay against another tree just last year, when the boy was left at home) then passed from cousin to cousin to uncle to uncle to father to the oldest uncle, who murmurs a single prayer, *Ya Ali*, before navigating the knife around and along the rigid organ in a cut, even and circular, that relinquishes the boy of skin and sanctuary for all the days of his next years.

With wide wet eyes the boy looks up at the faces he has always known, for he knows these men and no one else, to see their smiles and hear their song and feel their touch all over his bloodied self, and he lets fly a keen, high and sharp, full with the vitriol and sorrow of one suddenly betrayed. A burn blossoms from the very center of him and spreads through blood and organ and ear and eye until finally day and light dissipate into a clouded haze and the boy is held aloft by a clutch of hands, young and old, and his limp body is passed thrice through the new split in his tree. The men sing, certain in their ceremony, as they clean and bandage him where he bleeds. They remove the feather from his head and fold it carefully around the slack cut foreskin and tuck the offering into the split of the tree before they sew it together like maids at a loom stitching the broadcloth close. And the men sing.

Blessed is the bark by Madig to grow deep into the land.

And:

Blessed be the boy by Saladin to grow high atop it.

So they sing and so they rejoice to carry the body of the boy, this year's man, back out of the grove up the valley and mountain and into the cave, unaware in their celebration that, like the tree, the boy too has been cleaved. Here opens the first crack to let in the fear and sorrow that will fissure through the whole of his life. As a soldier he will be deftly divided through the head, as a murderer cut open through the heart and as an old man split so thoroughly that one side of him dies first, unbeknownst and long before the other, damned to serve in hell as half a man.

THE SAPLING

I AM THE boy and the boy is in me.
   Split and sutured as such I am unfit for the earth to suckle, to weave, to keep.

   One day I am deemed lumber; another day I am chopped; another day burned.

   As a tree: I am a boy and the boy is me.

   As ash: our fates will blow together in the end.

MOTHER'S FOOL

O N T H E T H I R D day the men wake at dawn and prepare for the return home. Blind and heavy from the nights of smoke and dark, the boy and his cousins work together to roll the rugs and pack the backs of animals and set out, into the blue morning, with hooves and heels seeking to match the marks they left only days ago. In silence they move away from the mountains and their carved caves and make their way across the desert floor. Ahead the horizon spreads level and sparse and above the sun rises along the same inches of sky day after day, plotted and, like the men, in correct course.

Overcome by pain, the boy rides behind in a blank refusal to keep pace with the silent, stiff men. Though he is no longer freight in this new year, he rides his own horse and holds to his own blade, the boy considers these weary bribes against what he has undergone. He keeps a cautious association with the men who saunter ahead and holds his bitterness before him like a shield. The father, who disallows such malaise, rides around his son to taunt his sour expression and jockey the boy's horse into a forceful trot that bruises his already burning loins. The boy grimaces in agony and is eventually left alone to curse his father and ache desperately for his mother's teat.

What he would give.

For a simple suckle of the warm cream he would part with his new blade. For a suckle and the soft sleep afterward he would easily give his too-heavy saddle. For a suckle, the sleep, a bit of humming and hands through his hair the boy would offer up his whole horse. Like this, morning turns into afternoon and they step closer toward home, the boy so preoccupied with the variations of barter and beg that he doesn't notice as they pass through the familiar stone wall that separates the inside of his village—hearth, women and flock—from the outside world of nomad, shah soldier and thief.

At the sight of home the men slow in their march and the boy quickens his horse to ride first and front, his eyes and heart greedy for the recognizable, the regular, the world he knew before this new year of ruse and betrayal. But upon first glance the boy sees nothing familiar of the land that bore him. They move through outskirts he has walked a thousand times, past fields separated in steeps and pastures thin with stock, and to-day, from atop his horse, all of it shines new. The boy blinks, rubs his eyes hard and slaps his face to clear his gaze of the luminescence to see it for what he knew before: dirt, rock and stream fit only for work and the occasional game, good to stomp and spit and shit on but otherwise dull. The self-aggression fails him and the land glows, resplendent with green garden beds, strong rock fences and leafless mulberry trees all irradiated with the orange sheen of late afternoon. Even the open eyes of sheep and goat and rooster wink at the boy in an offering: *This is your land, we are on it and your own dead are below it, all of us offer our lives and deaths to the man that grows within you, to nourish, yield, prosper and keep.* And the boy recognizes the direct relation to him—boy once, now man, now Kurd, now Kurdish man to reign over Kurdish land; the young suzerain, kingly after a simple cut.

The pain he has held close is gone now and he rides erect and proud and ahead of the line to lead the men into the village, where women and children run from doorways to greet them. Young and unwed girls rush alongside the boy's horse and reach their hands into his lap, grab at the bloodied bandages and laugh and click tongues in happy song.

Aufareen!

Mashallah!

A new Kurdish man among us!

Their faces, too, are new with a stark beauty. They are not the aunts and cousins he left behind, but creatures of light with white teeth that sparkle through smiles, hair that is tossed about and run down with bright ribbons and eyes that when cast up to meet his reflect the entirety of the sky's blue through them, blue with abandonment, adoration and joy. The women clap and laugh and the boy shakes hands and kisses hands and straightens himself to try to catch sight of his maman, to see her in this new year and take of her and so center himself as a man. Instead, he is suffocated by the instant celebration and cannot take his eyes off the land and the women and the village that passes him all around.

The procession comes to stop at his father's house, where a cousin runs in quickly to light the brazier and the boy's dog stands at the door to bark at the parade of stumbling men and women in song. Uncles carry the boy in on their shoulders and place him gently on a cushion in the center of the divan, where he sits to accept the gifts placed at his feet: gold rings and embroidered shirts and tins of honey candy from Kermanshah. The room fills and fills more and tiny coals are warmed and placed in small bowls attached to long hollow ceramic stems. The women push in bits of soft brown brick that dirty their fingernails and light the paste until it glows and pass the pipe from aunt to uncle, cousin to father, brother to sister and husband to wife, and the infinite night shrinks to fit in the small room, tight and entire, to close the space between man and woman, bones and blood. The men tell the women of the journey and the tree, of the boy they left behind and the new man who is returned. The boy sits and smiles, proud and lost. In his delirium he stands on the cushion and announces to the room:

I forgive you all for the cut and the blood.

I am a man in the new year and this is my village and the village of my dead and it is worth the price of a small piece of skin.

The divan grows noisy with laughter and applause and the men sing and smoke and bring with them the heavy beauty of the cave. The women sit beside them and let their heads hang and sway to the music and they ignore the boy, who grows sleepy in the thick air and moves about to seek out his maman's lap. She is not in the circle, or in the periphery where the wives lean up against their husband's backs, but just outside her thin figure is tucked in the doorway, her face tired and pale.

Maman!

The boy does not resist, cannot resist, and runs to clutch at her waist and tear at her shirt to pull for the milk without caution or shame.

The men laugh in an uproar and pull the boy off his mother and toss him, from clenched fist to fist, until he is on the cushion again and she has disappeared from the dark doorway. His baba chortles.

Na, na, na.

You are no longer your mother's fool, that milk belongs to me now.

He pinches the boy tightly on the ear and with an exaggerated stomp and smile makes a great show of walking into the doorway where she disappeared. And the family sings to this. The aunts throw their voices high and the uncles open their throats to song and night and merrily take to their houses and beds to open their throats again to the nectars of their women and leave the boy alone, curled on the cushion in the divan in a cold association of heart and liver and lungs, child and king, abandoned to a sleep filled with dreams of barter and beg.

In the morning the village sleeps through the first and second and third crows of the cockerel. Only the boy and his dog wake, and they leave the cold and empty divan in search of his maman. He walks through the streets with unblinking determination, eager to hold her face in his hands, announce his new manhood and reassure her that the babe in him will continue to devour and take.

They move toward the northern edge of town, where the women zealously compete to keep up elaborate garden plots. Here are enormous eggplants, feathery dill, pendulous squash and vines spread with cucumbers and delicate saffron flowers.

The boy walks past all the prized growth to his mother's own plot, where nothing blossoms or grows. *She is mad.* The women of the village say it and the boy has heard. *What type of woman walks over hot coals? Can't be right in the mind . . . yes, yes, she was orphaned as a girl but we have all suffered . . . who is she to stay in bed all day with that one child of hers? And the boy, left to suffer her endless sad songs, it's no wonder he runs about flapping like a bird, the craziness must be contagious . . . yes, yes, she has had a hard life, haven't we all? At least I have children from my womb and vegetables in my garden. She has only that boy and her silence and dirt . . . beechareh, still, I feel bad, she must be dried up and dead inside, just like that messy plot of hers.* They say she has no shame and it is true; the boy has found her in the wasteland before, feet covered in mud, hands long unwashed and eyes on fire with a fever that freezes through to the center of her.

Today is no different. To reach her the boy must snap through tangles of roots with his hands and kick away rotted gourds with his unshod feet and she is there, sitting as she has sat before, legs crossed, combing through her wild hair with the desiccated stalks. The boy knows to keep a distance, wait for permission, the warm open eyes, the allowance. Only then can he approach to take of the teat, just as every animal must, and hold it with one hand, or both, or just teeth, and suck until the satisfaction comes and the skeleton of his body melts into the fallow earth, heavy and soft.

Her song stops. She gazes fixedly at the boy.

So you've come again for your mother's milk, yes, jounam?

The boy nods and his maman laughs from somewhere deep inside her chest.

Well now, they haven't made you that much of a man, now have they? Running silly and shoeless in search of my teat?

She laughs again and lifts the wool shift over her shoulder and head and what is suspended before the boy is fleshy and alive in this garden of dead.

Come now, son of mine, show Maman what a man you are.

Inside the boy the new man smarts at this challenge and in an instant he is upon her with avarice, son and man, baby and boy, taking what he wants with the callous lips and ravishing tongue of a hungry whelp.

MAMAN

A GIRL WITH a basket of onions on my hip.
That is how they find me.

I walk alone beside the field, under the skies of late summer, my shawl slipping to my shoulders. They come, two men on two horses, at full gallop. When they see my skin tanned from the sun and my eyes greener than the onion stalks in my arms, they slow and stop, one to stare and the other to ask:

Are you Agha Barzani's girl?

I nod. Just as much as these onions are his onions I am the agha's girl, I want to say.

What is your age?

I shrug.

Are those his fields?

Again, I nod. Just as much as I am his girl.

And this is the path you take home every day?

It is not my home, I want to tell them, only a tent with a coal fire that blows smoke into our faces when we sleep head to foot to head to foot, three brothers and a sister and Baba Barzani, who keeps his knobby knees and chapped feet in my face, and the maman, who calls me girl and nothing else. Though they are not my family and this is not my home, I must take what they give: a tear of their lavash, a piece of meat, the every-night spill of their son's seed, for I am an orphan and their generosity is a gift, so I am told.

But I am not a speaking girl, so I nod nicely and say nothing. For a moment they look at me with sharp, narrow eyes. They stir their horses with shouts of *Yallah!* and I watch the beasts, a brown and a black, who care nothing for me or my age or my onions, run away in response to some whistle in the faraway wind.

At the well that night Zayideh whispers to me that two men and two horses came today and told her baba they found me and her baba said, *Boshee,* and that tomorrow I will be prepared. I am not a speaking girl, lest I accidentally say something ungrateful, and so I ask no questions of Zayideh at the well and ask no questions the next morning when she and the maman take me to the river, where I am undressed, wet and scrubbed raw with a wool cloth. Zayideh's hand is smooth and even and she tickles me from time to time, but I can't laugh because every minute her maman is rough and presses my flesh as if to husk off my shell entirely, to leave me more naked than I already am.

Then I am submerged, and when the waters rise to my chest and neck and chin and finally over my head, the heart inside me stops and still the maman holds me under. All I hear is the sound of water crashing on stone and water on water. A fish looks at me sidelong and swims on. I think she might kill me so I try for a scream and my mouth fills with the river and I am pulled up and dried and my skin is slathered with sickly sweet rose oil and I am dressed in thick skirts of bright colors and one woolen shift after another to cover my flat chest. Zayideh combs my hair and the knots come out in clumps, and she tosses them into the river and onto the ground until I am light of dirt and skin and hair, so light as to be nearly empty, a girl taken from herself and given into the river.

In the afternoon the horses return with the sun in their eyes. Their men ride to where I sit toasting seeds at the fire and look down at me, one with a smile and one without. Baba Barzani takes them into the tent and yells at me to prepare the tea. Zayideh pinches my waist and whispers in my ear.

Make it strong. You might be wed yet.

I am alone with Baba Barzani and the two men in the tent. I heat the coals beneath the samovar, fill the basin with water and drop in the leaves. I watch them spread across the surface of the water like lace and listen to Baba Barzani tell them the story of how my family died. He explains, though he never saw, that my parents had been shot first, the shah's work, of course, then sliced and put into the fire that ate up our house. I was found in the pen, clinging to sheep.

I was forced to take all of their animals in the pen, you know, save all of their livestock, bring them home with me, and the girl came along too. And how she screamed those first nights! Ay Khoda! She hasn't spoken much since, thank God.

Here the two men nod and sip their tea and crunch on the sugar rocks. Baba makes no mention of the work his sons have done with me, or even of the work he has done, in the tent at night loud enough for the maman and Zayideh to hear. Instead he tells them again and again:

She is a pure girl. Clean like the river.

Cleaned by the river, I want to say, but it is true, I am not a speaking girl. If I was I would tell the two men I hid behind a pile of blankets when the soldiers came and demanded tithes, taxes for the herds, payment on the land; my baba refused them and said, *Your shah is not my king, this land belongs to the Kurds.* I would tell them how the soldiers laughed and one took him by the hair and held his face to the floor and the other three threw down my maman and said, *I am sure the shah will be happy with some of the jewels from her purse.* From my spot I saw the black feathers on top of their shakos quiver from side to side and watched the toes of their boots carve holes into the smooth dirt floor I swept each day. I listened to my baba scream horrible words at the men and then scream no words at all and in the end mumble his prayers and pleas with a mouth full of spit, tears and dirt. After they each took a turn on my maman she was a limp thing and the soldier carried them both into the yard and shouted, *What good is a Kurd who can't pay? What good is that to the shah? No good, no good at all.* I ran into the pen to hide between the smelly wool of the sheep and ewes and watch all the quick moments of the kill and the long moments of the death and wait for God to turn me into a lamb so that I could disappear from my own flesh.

The two men in the tent drink their tea in silence. Outside I hear horse hooves stomp on the grass and the blustered breath of impatient beasts.

Chai? I ask of the men and the men shake their heads. One of them grabs my wrist and inspects the palm of my hand. The other runs the tips of his fingers across my forehead and jaw.

Koshkel-eh, they say to one another.

She will do, they tell the baba Barzani.

The baba coughs.

She comes with nothing, no dowry; she is an orphan girl, pure, but an orphan . . .

I am told to bundle a few things and sent out of the tent and Zayideh helps me and teases and pinches me all the while.

Tomorrow you will have a baby and your flat chest will swell with milk just like the ninny teats do.

The maman sits crouched at the fire, flipping the bread from side to side, and says nothing as I get on the horse and wrap my arms around the strange waist. Baba Barzani says nothing and stands outside the tent with his hands clasped behind his back and we move slowly out and away from this home to the next. Zayideh shouts and claps behind me.

Good-bye, goat girl! Khodafez!

I ride with the man who touched my cheeks and jaw and the spine of the horse shifts beneath us with each step of its heavy haunches. The afternoon lasts long, and we move toward a sun that empties itself into the sky and onto the mountains and rocks and covers the land in a thick honey gold and then a dusty bronze and then disappears. I am asleep when we stop and the man lifts me from the horse and takes me to a sturdy house, not of cloth or canvas, but stone and mud, and lays me down on the motaq. I feign a deep sleep as my shawl is unwrapped and my shifts undone and all my skirts taken off until I am cold and shivering. He is on top of me with a body of muscle and hair and it is not a quick or quiet thing like in the tent with the brothers, but a prolonged deed; one movement that lasts through the long night. I feel a heat spread and pulse inside as if I was nothing but heart, no stomach or lungs or head, just a hot fast heart. The man takes me and turns me, now on my stomach, now on my back, and I am rotated in slow revolutions like planets and so I rise out from myself to float above the man and the house, amidst the pockmarks of stars in the night sky, to watch and wish for the red slit of dawn to cut open on the horizon so I may again sink into myself, to sleep and dream.

That is when I knew you first, jounam, boy of mine.

That is when I felt, in my bones and blood, that I, orphan girl with no belongings, girl with the basket of onions (not hers) who stood on the ground (not hers) with hard bare feet, was to possess a soul of her own; a son (mine) born to me, the mountains and the day.

Now you stand before me to beg for milk and I want to say yes and yes and yes again, and hold your soft-haired head to my breast and sing my song to you, but you are no longer my boy, but a man, their man. I am bitter and furious that my one possession has absconded so easily and my garden dies around me and in me and in vengeance I will whisper in your ear: I knew you when you were a nothing. Not a Kurd. Not a boy or a girl. Not even your father's seed and not the beast in my belly. I knew you when I planted fields that grew greener than God's eye and the birds flew in ovals above to admire my work. When my mother screamed and my father spit and cried as the Kurds were cursed I knew my simple body would birth a doomed man, just as the green-eyed girl alive as the summer fields would become this woman before you, barren and rotted; we are part of the cycle of land and love, have and have not. Here, I have you, jounam, to hold and rock, to suckle and scold, to slip through my fingers in this next year to leave and join the rest. Go. Follow your men from one silly battle to another; claim this pebble-strewn plot or that and know this land grows and dies with little care for the men who try to hold it. Drink, my thirsty boy, drink. Take of my teat and your cut skin and your smoking pipe and your silly steel knife and pretend a man marches in you as the earth herself slips out from beneath you. Drink, jounam, drink as your motherland sours and dries.

KITES, TRINKETS, BOOTS
AND BIRDS

T HE SEASON OF his initiation passes from winter into a cool barren spring. The boy takes to his new life with vigor, as it is a good life, full with allowances and nearly endless permission.

Of chores there are few: clean out the samovar in the divan with fresh water; keep the men's pipes oiled and ready; take his mare to pasture every morning and afternoon. None is more important than his Friday morning obligation to choose the an-imal slaughtered for the Friday afternoon feast, to pick which watery eyes, which bleat, which open breath of life must pass now into an instant death; to stand unwaveringly before his butcher uncle and decide on death itself without sentiment or visible deliberation.

Of duties there is only one: to keep watch. He has been taken aside and told, by uncle, cousin and father alike, *The shah comes with tanks and armies of horses and men. Keep a careful lookout for them. They will be of a frightening size, but do not scare, run to give us warning and all will be well. This is our land and the gods of it are on our side.*

No longer allowed his morning jumps from the roof, the boy perches, bird-like and still, on the highest hill in a constant survey of the continuous sky and the Mesopotamian flats and the horizon where they meet. He knows nothing of battle and passes the morning hours imagining the oncoming cavalcade of horses that breathe fire and smoke, his strong scream of warning, the shoulders that will hoist him up to celebrate his bravery and sharp eyes. By afternoon he is hot and distracted; his thoughts are full of air and wind and view, the count of passing birds, the shapes of flocks and their elegant escapes across the sky. Evening comes and the boy descends into the village, where he reports duteously that the horizon is empty and without threat in any direction. For this service he receives a warm hand to his back from his baba.

You must have lucky eyes, boy of mine, to keep such strong soldiers so far away. You will make your ancestors proud.

Of permissions, there are many. Now he can slap the younger cousins, the ones who have not yet had their year in the cave, slap and laugh and pull on their foreskin with taunts of the pain to come. He can ride away on a horse, any of them, as far as he wants, to traverse the distant edges of the mountains and return home with trinkets of traveling salesmen, the doves of magicians, kites made by the old bahktis.

He can travel aimless and free but must return to take all of his baba's commands: *Clean the pipe of grit, wash my turban clean, dig for the wax in my left ear!* In turn, the boy has the permission to command his aunts and girl cousins alike: *Food! Drink! Now!* Though he demands of his maman like he sees the other men demand of their women, the boy is careful to keep himself close to her, so to take from her the milk he feels his new man needs. Without chiding him she allows it, always and only in her dead garden, where they are found by his baba, who doles out a hard smack for the transgression. And so it is. For the sake of these permissions, duties and chores, the boy must haughtily abjure the warm milk and heartbeat and sever the liquid thread that ties the boy to mother and mother to land and land to the bodies of all the boys before, and so close, the heart of the child, ventricle by ventricle, until the organ's sunken shape is inhospitable to any innocence, folly or blind love.

Now the boy wears the thick scarves around the loose pants, heavy shirts and a turban tight about the head. He moves around the village with an untested strut and puff of his chest and the men applaud him while the girl cousins laugh. Every afternoon he walks alone to the ice water stream just above the village to swim, as instructed, in the near-frozen rush that pierces through him like needles until he has to sit, knees pulled up to his chin, and sob the hot tears that cover him in a lukewarm sadness. Once he has cultivated the cold heart of the Kurd the boy walks back to the village to be one man with the rest; to sit in the divan and smoke the sweet brown paste and listen and nod at the stories of battles won and land gained or lost, to grow sleepy but feign joy; to smoke and cough and drink and vomit and sing and cry into the night until the distinction between everything and everything else dissolves and the boy, laughing, is father and dead grandfather, past and present, table and turtle all at once.

★   ★   ★

Long before dawn the boy is shaken awake and told to dress.

Hurry. To the divan. The courier has come.

The boy follows his cousin, his head still murky with dreams.

The room is full of men who smell of sleep, wives and warm beds. They gather in a circle of serious faces to listen to the whispered story from the courier's mouth. The boy sits with the rest and stares at the stranger among them, a thin man with dusty skin and a turban wrapped tight and high around a face washed over with death. Too tired to understand, the boy leans on the cousin next to him, who listens rapt and wide-eyed to the tales: charred fields, tanks propelled by captured thunder, aghas' angry faces hanging from gallows made of sturdy teak. The courier speaks of villages smothered: Bana, Hawraman, Orumiyeh, Sanandaj; households robbed of gold and goods, ransacked and then wet with gasoline and burned while the families were bound and forced to watch the pyre of their home. He continues on, eyes downcast, to tell how the hero Simko was captured, tortured and tossed to the street to scare the Kurds and deem their call for country foolhardy and counterfeit. The courier pauses for effect, for breath, and the cousin incessantly elbows the boy.

Vay, vay vay. Now we must fight! Are you hearing this? We must go!

The room is alive with panic and joy and the boy wakes completely from the courier's nightmares to find the faces of the men turned and contorted in a manner unfamiliar to him. They begin to move and jostle about the room like different limbs of one angry organism and the boy is kicked and pulled and nearly stepped on. He grabs about his insides for the man that supposedly grows therein and finds that a sensation of bravery sizzles in his gut, born of the fervor in the room, and grabs his cousin by the shoulder, to shake him and cry.

Yes! We must go! To defend the land for the Kurds! Yes!

The courier continues with the names of passes, the numbers of horses, the hidden armories and on and on. The boy stands to listen to the messenger, who paces in front of the window, slowly revealing details and plans. Behind him day breaks over the eastern mountains and thin yellow light floods the divan, filling the cracks of the men's worried faces with gold, like a promise or a prize.

The village comes alive. Everywhere arms reach to empty supplies of food from storerooms and cellars and pile them in a center courtyard where a spit turns two dried and bloodless calves. The knives are unburied and cousins take to the blades with hot oil until they glisten and wink, while uncles push bits of bridles into horse mouths as penned-in mules and hinnies watch with indifferent eyes. Women, wives, sisters and girl cousins, run about and cry, *Khoda! Khoda! Khoda!* with drawn faces and moist eyes. They bustle in kitchens, courtyards and gardens to grab and pack for their men. They clutch cummerbunds and stirrups and wail.

Khoda! A quick return!

And:

Khoda! A victory against the shah, that treacherous djinn, ay Khoda!

Older aunts chant their suras feverishly and young girls drop peacock feathers into the saddlebags of their unwed cousins. The maidens laugh and throw bright-eyed smiles in the faces of tomorrow's husband, lover, father, and promise them:

Jounam, I will wait for you, I will wait.

Come back with a gold coin, a soldier's tin hat, a victory trinket for us to build a home around.

Victory is the spice of love, don't you know . . .

The women wail and move through the morning filling sacks with supplies of lavash, fallen fruits, sweetmeats and tea; filling ears with cries and plaudits, hands with locks of hair; all the while careful to fill the veins of their men with braveblood enough to last for the journey and the clash.

The boy works alongside them, packing and gathering, and fear tickles all over him like a painful itch. Now and again he pauses to stand and feel through the soft soles of his sandals for a tremble and then flattens himself to feel for the vibrations, and still, nothing. No tragedy reaches him through the crust of earth; he hears no shouts calling the warriors in the direction of the dying. He wants to run to the divan and break the courier's sleep and make sure the hero in him will be born, that there will be battle and victory and his baba's pride, but he is caught by arm and neck and commanded by cousin and uncle and father.

Sharpen the blades! Yes, even the scythes!

Pack the bags with rice! Chai! Toorshi! Morabah!

Fill the casks with water! All the water in the well!

At the well the boy drinks and drinks from the cool wooden bucket, gulp after gulp, but cannot swallow enough to wet over the dry desert fear makes of his mouth. Thirsty for something else, the boy forgets his duties and runs about to find his maman. She is nowhere to be seen. Not buried underneath the blankets on the motaq, at the river's edge or in her dead garden, and the boy cannot see or think through the gaseous dread that covers him inside and out like a cloud. When it is time he is found and easily snatched up by the hard hands of his baba, which hoist him onto a waiting mare. The old man admonishes, *Eh, I thought I brought home a man from the caves, a brave Kurd . . .*

The men leave the village in a line that snakes behind the slumped courier. The cries of women follow them until they reach the road, where the sound folds in with the wind and fades. At the crossroad the courier pauses and the boy watches dusk empty itself into the bottomlands and cover the earth in a blue mist. His mare shifts foot to foot but the boy sits in a daze, occupied by the chore of driving the fear back inside, the scare that beats through him in a fluid pulse, potent enough to keep loose the bowels, tenuous the fingers and waterless the mouth. He reaches into the front of his pants to feel the wound of the circumcision that is now almost healed and tries to remember the man he has been made into: a Kurd to sit straight backed and stern and listen carefully to the call of the land. The courier steps quickly to the east. The men heel their horses and orient themselves toward night. The boy's mare jumps out and down in rhythm with the rest, his rider nervously fondling his broken piece with one hand and clutching at slack reins with the other, quietly muttering, *Maman.*

For one night and the following day the line moves east. In the silent windy dark through to the arid day the boy keeps close to his father, who shouts constantly.

Raise the reins! Keep pace!

Sharpen your back! Look, son, there, look!

He points to a jagged outcropping of stones in the shape of a broken wall.

There is the fortress of the Bistoun, where we were victorious against the Umayyads and the Sassanids. That is where the Kurds held to their land, and look how it still holds to itself.

See? Over there—

He points again, this time to a rock-strewn road that juts off the trail.

That is the path to Nurabad and the river Cam-eh and the bone fields of Luman, where the Ottomans left us dead in the sun, for the birds to eat out our eyes and the heat to melt away our flesh. Only now has the earth begun to take in our bones. Look—

He points at the faint seam of mountains that sew together the land and sky.

That is where the Kerand live. Watch out, boy, all their daughters have olive-colored eyes . . .

And look here, and look there . . .

The boy does not care to focus on his baba's demands to stare at the ruins, empty of glory, and to spite him turns eye and ear in the opposite direction, where he spots a figure—a quavering hallucination of perspective and temperature—a specter soldier of the unclaimed lands. The boy narrows his eyes to make out a man tied together with windswept tatters, his legs split atop a solid horse, the two bodies as shaped and still as clay. The boy is certain they have come upon some fettered symbol unearthed and planted on the surface of the desert to anchor down the nests of ever ascending dead. The boy makes no mention of the vision and the men continue their sleepy march and his father keeps up with decries of: *Here!* and *There!* Eventually the horses themselves come to a halt, undirected and on their own, before the figure and his beast. The animals shake their skins and neigh and the specter soldier raises a bandaged hand. One by one the men fall asleep where they sit and slump on their horses, closed eyed and limp, as if under a spell, and for the first time the boy is calm and unafraid. The specter soldier turns and leads the men off their path east toward the unknown south and the beasts follow one by one, carked by sleeping cargo, with no reservations in their natural minds.

The wrapped man leads without staff or gesture and after a time they move up over barren mounds of sand and the horses must high-step, a foot a foot a foot, to keep their muscled masses in motion, to stay above the sink. All until the animals sense water, which they come to in time, a depression filled with viscous mud, where the horses pause to drink while the men fall off them to wash their faces in the muck and mount again sporting masks of dripping sand. The specter soldier keeps pace at the front and the boy, who is not at all asleep, rides to meet him, to stare at the scarves of dark fabric wrapped tight around head, neck and arms. There are slits for eyes that look only out and everywhere else the man is encased. The boy seeks out some hole, some space beneath the scarves, to reveal a slice of skin, to know the man as a man, but there are no disclosures. A sweet smell of rot seeps from beneath the rags and the boy's mare steps back and away. The caravan moves on.

In the afternoon the sand is whipped by the wind and the horses tilt their heads and close their eyes to the sharpened air, follow head to tail to head to tail in a simple blind pull while their sandmasked men sleep. The boy wakes in the cool of dusk to see the sand has turned again to hard earth sprouting with sagebrush, cactus, lizard and creek, while above one star suckles the night sky. The march of horses, men, father, courier and specter soldier move forward into the dark until they reach the ledge of a great crevice, a deep and even cut into the earth's crust. The boy peers over the edge to find a city aglow, of domed gypsum and carved onyx porticoes, and he shakes his head once and then twice, certain the city is his head's manifestation of the day's heat.

The specter soldier dismounts and walks ahead and then down into the canyon that yawns before them and the men shake their heads of sand and sleep and descend with the same easy and unsuspecting step that carries them every morning from warm bed to cold outhouse. The boy follows and his mare goes to join the other steeds that sit on their haunches at the precipice like a pack of obedient, oversized dogs. They descend switch-backs in silence and the boy, distracted and stunned, forgets the morning fear and the afternoon heat and takes in the city steeped all around him. There are fountains and courtyards, streets of smooth alabaster and azure mosques. Everywhere span banners, from rooftop to rooftop, window grate to window grate, orange and red cloth spread about like the leftovers of some sumptuous celebration. Otherwise, there is silence and the streets of the sunken stone town unravel one after the next, empty and lifeless, with the exhausted hush of a storm survived, a calamity come and passed. The boy rushes to keep up with the men, slipping once or twice on the worn steps.

At the first crossroads a body hangs, bloated and strung by the neck. In the easy evening breeze the exploded eyes and distended tongue sway from side to side. The men pass beneath it without notice, but the boy stops to look. The lack of life does not interest him. He sees it in the fields around his father's house and in the fields after an animal lies down to approach death, moaning in invisible pain. He has even seen it in his own room, in his own bed, the morning he woke next to the blue body of his year-old brother. In the boy's life death is a regular thing; it is the boots that fascinate. They dangle before him at eye level, structures he has never seen, and he stands beneath to-morrow's carrion to hold a hand out to the leather and laces in curiosity and want. They are severe encasements: hard and im-penetrable and leaden as shields, as if to press ground away from body, skin from surface, earth from sole. The boy feels his own feet, clumsily shod in canvas and hide and separated so barely from the ground beneath he can feel every pebble and divot in the stone streets of the ancient city. Bravery is in these boots, the boy is sure; if he wore them, all battles could be won. Hun-grily the boy reaches out to touch the boots and feels a quick wind snap from the mouth of a dog that circles the swinging body in a devoted pack. Blood drips from the tip of his finger and he lets go his fascination and runs to find the line of men, leaving the boots behind, eager to imagine the possibilities of their strength.

Before a plain iron gate the specter soldier stops and shouts, *Bohzkohn!* The rusted iron hinges squeal and one by one the men—uncles, cousin, father—disappear dutifully under the watch of an old man who mutters, *Yallah! Yallah!* They are taken to an interior courtyard where rugs are spread and a cop-per samovar steams at the hands of a girl in a flower-patterned kerchief. Overhead, the moon is a half thing and they sit in the laced night-shade of a rangy ficus, the boy among them and

the specter soldier between, and they are silent, unsmiling, sipping their tea until the last drop when the old man calls:

Rostam!

An adolescent appears shouldering a canvas sack.

There.

He gestures with his hand to the center of the circle.

Put them there.

The bag is released and the contents land with a curious clatter. The men are quick to draw the rifles out, to examine their
long narrow caverns and delicate crescent-shaped triggers and
smile. Rostam, gone, now returns with boxes of small shiny
bullets linked together like decorations of gold, bridal dowries,
beads for prayer, and the men don them as sashes around their
shoulders or cummerbunds about the waist. They take again of
the tea and rise to leave, the boy with his own sash and too-
long rifle that he uses as a walking stick. The specter soldier stops
them with one raised hand.

*They are from the dead soldiers of the shah, those responsible for the
silence of our town.*

*Take them, make a noise so the shah will know the Kurds are not
defeated.*

He sits again, exhausted, and signals to the girl, who aban-
dons the samovar and kneels before the old man to unwrap the
rag straps from his face. Round and round she walks, soft footed
and in song, disentangling him from his bandages. The men
stay to watch the revealing of welters and burns that shine out
wet with blood and pus. Naked but for this skin of scars, the old
man raises his arms for the girl to apply a white salve that she
pushes from the sharp spine of a plant and rubs onto the gore

of what was once a muscled torso, a sinewy shoulder, a broken-featured face. The specter soldier rocks from side to side, his arms lifted, in what devotion or surrender or pain the boy does not know, and hums along to the kerchiefed girl's tune. Whatever bravery the boy claimed dissolves and churns heavily at the sight of the gore until he is nauseous. The men take their leave and walk through the iron gates, each stopping to clap the boy on the back. *Eh, if I hit a little harder maybe I could slap some of the green off your face.* The men joke, happy with their sudden bounty.

They emerge from the crack of the earth, mount horses and ride away from the sunken city. In the iron wash of sky a few stars, disparate and unstrung, blink down at the caravan with their dusty sheen. The boy lags at the end of the procession and thinks of the boots and the skin of the specter soldier and the empty sunken town. His father leads the line, strapped across the chest and back with half a dozen rifles that fan out from his figure and cut his silhouette against the horizon, jagged as a spur.

Ah, and there! Look! The rubble in the distance. Our castles of Hoshap and Bistare, where we fought off the Mongols and the Arabs with the valor of a million men, just as now we go to fight the shah.

The boy does not listen or look and instead raises his head to gaze at the sky, where a cast of falcons, six or seven by quick count, spins slowly around the itinerants below. Peregrine, like the men who wander the age-old land, they move with an infinite glissade, carving rounded shapes into the surface of the sky. The birds take all of the boy's attention.

And look . . .

But the boy cannot, for his neck is craned taut and straight to see wings that jut out and then disappear in a pulse, a stroke, a soar that takes weight from the boy's body; and he is light through the chest, through his head, and nearly aloft. Made of wings and wind, the birds aviate in arcs and dips above the distressed land, above the fissures of stone, its explosions of magma, the tension of its wood and wire fences and the evanescent demarcations of time, fury and blood to which his baba points.

And look, here . . .

And look, there . . .

But the boy does not, for he is trying to fly. With his chest opened upward he pushes his face deeper into the beam of sun and wishes for his thin bones and narrow shoulders to aspire among the chaotic open-aired thresh of wings, to fly high and above the hemmed land and sweep aloft the delineations marked out for him, on him, into him.

BIRDS

O F EARTH, WE SEE ALL.
    Though our ears are empty and our feet frail farces,
our lungs breathe the best thin air and our wings rise and fall to
draw circles in the sky. We fly interminable; omniscient; above
rotations of earth and time.

Of earth, we see all.
    Below, the many spines of Mesopotamia: her plates long buck-
led into mountain ridges, hoary and high; rivers and streams,
silken kraits that line the land in silver and blue; the undulations
of skulls buried beneath the desert floor, one after one after one,
like the nodes in history's back: benighted, elapsed, in dissolve.

Of earth, we see all.
    Below: the scales of a scorpion, the whiskers of a grouse, the
freckles of sheep that move across the green hillsides. Below:
the sandy substructure of ancient wells that rest in the shadows
of treetops whose roots and trunks they water slowly over the

ages. Below: a desert pocked by brush and crater; the unmanaged dunes; the swales lush and green; a defiant nature.

Of earth, we see all.

Below, the human effort: to sow, to order, to reap, to flame, to farm, to slaughter, to sex, to sit and to stay, to move and to horde, mortal and unresolved. Below: the harnessed wood; the tamed stream; the crumbled ruins strewn and screaming about the surface like a million mouths of broken teeth. Below: a madness for marking.

Of earth, we see all; we are the eyes of God.

Below, the caravansary: a march of men in a string, like ants, thirsty and maddened to possess the mound. We have seen the march of men before: Chaldean, Greek, Parse and Aryan. All with the same two limb legs and two limb arms, eyes to witness and water, ears to hear and hands to clutch and caress. To us they are but one man, the same man, a man the same as the ant in a constant march and march and march.

Of earth, we see all; we are the eyes of their given God.

Below, the boy in the caravan gazes up to the swirl of us with a sterling desire, cursed, as he is, to the gloried ground.

THE MIRROR WITHOUT SILVER

B Y AFTERNOON OF the third day the men camp in a cool ravine where a thick river cuts into the earth with such ferocity of sound and rush the men are mute at its bank. The boy climbs in to wade ankle- and sometimes knee-deep in a torrent as swift and unforgiving as any he has ever known. He watches the men invigorate themselves in the cold waters, slip on the mossy stones, swim against the strong current to emerge cursing, dripping, smiling and anew to laugh at one another and lasso wet turbans through the air. With puckered hands, swollen ankles and numb feet the boy reaches into the churning flow to catch and uncatch the slippery carp that slick themselves on his feet and legs as the men take to the sandy shore to lie in the warm sun. Even the courier sits serene in the shadow of a stone ledge to suck at a long pipe and watch the men become boys and listen to the din of air and water drawn from high above. The boy watches him and wonders if the courier's call to fight and tales of terror were but a secret to deliver the men, without shame, to this halcyon riverside.

At dusk they see a figure of an old man, a stunted mule and

a rickety cart on the ledge above the ravine. A voice shouts down to their gathering.

Have you space for an old wanderer?

With claps and cheers the men respond.

Come down, this is God's earth, come, come down, old man.

The humble caravan descends down into the canyon with such a clatter of copper and glass and bray and creak that the river herself seems hushed. With a nod they make their way upstream, where the mule takes water in the shallows and the old man undresses and bathes. All the while he is hungrily eyed by the men, uncles, cousins, father and courier, who watch with faces that plea.

Tell us.

Tell us.

You know, so tell.

The old man sings to himself and cups handfuls of water to throw onto his neck, into the pit of each arm, through the holes of mouth, nose and ears. He shapes both hands into a bowl and fills them with water that he dribbles across the spine of the mule. He is a happy old bahkti, the boy thinks, to travel the desert with fantastic wares, lungs full of song and jokes and a mind privy to the fates of men. Uncles, cousins and father stare impatiently at the old wet man and his wet mule. Silently they plead.

You have come to us on the eve of battle. So tell us.

And:

You know, so say.

Clean and cool, the bahkti chides them jovially with tawdry jokes from his collection: an unfortunately placed scorpion bite;

the travails of a certain woman born with the parts of a man; the story of the Lur herder who, in the act of affection, lost his prized part when the donkey jumped at the sight of a mouse; and on and on. Only the boy and the bahkti laugh. The men leave the riverside and walk up to the camp. Happy with his new company, the boy reaches again into the deep pools for fish.

To catch the carp you must fill your hands with anger and force, finger to finger to finger, five and five across. At the first touch of the scale or whatever passes—an eye, a gut, the last tail fin—you must grab and press with extraordinary force and no thought at all.

The bahkti sits on the smooth river rocks, preoccupied with the activity of cleaning his ears. He sticks a gnarled finger into his ear hole and explains:

You must pierce.

The bahkti pulls out an orange waxen lump and shakes it at the boy.

The fish know you are not keen with that clumsy clapping.

The boy submerges his arms wrist-deep and feels only the stones and water and then the flesh of a fish that he fiercely grabs and punctures as it passes through his hands. From the swirl he withdraws a carp, mangled, bloody, spirited. He continues to press and feels his own fingertips drain the life from the cold wet body until it falls limp in his hands. The bahkti gives out a demoniac laugh and licks his waxy fingertips.

Aufareen. Aufareen, boy. Come and choose a prize.

The boy follows him back to his covered cart, where the floor planks are loosely hewn and all manner of dirt and dust covers the contents within: a bell, a string-limbed doll that moves at a tug, a gourd filled with seeds to sound like rain, eye masks of clear dark glass and twine. The bahkti fingers them all, leaving behind the clean streak of his touch. From a canvas wrapping he removes a jagged piece of blackened mirror and hands it to the boy, who examines it to find fragments of his own face: the lip and the nose, the blinking eye and the brow above, the red mouth full with tongue and tiny teeth.

It is sharp, but it is yours. To break it is a certain curse.

He is careful to carry it first in his palm and then in the folds of his waistband and tells no one of the lesson or the gift.

In the evening the men feed the bahkti and offer him the best of their smoke and arak and gather to wait for their fortunes. The old man sings them songs of the famous Kurd warriors, tales of the brave Simko who hides in the mountains with bands a thousand strong and ballads of the pretty blue-eyed maidens who live in the cracks of the Zagros, sequestered and pure. The uncles and father recognize these as stock tunes and ask directly:

What of us, uncle? Where are we to fight and when?

The bahkti clears his throat, pounds on his duduk with one hand, plucks the sitar with the other and sings:

It matters not, the fates revolve.

Like the earth and the moon and the sun.

The fates revolve.

What was your father's victory is your loss and your son's triumph, his scion's tragedy.

Ask me, and this is all I can foretell. Lay didi la la. La didi la la la.

The boy hears none of this and lies stomach down on his sleeping sack to gaze and gaze again into his own eyes, green ovals unfamiliar and flinching, open and endless with infinity to rival the black cosmos above.

For days they bivouac alongside the river and wait for a sign. The bahkti has long since gone and the courier no longer leads and the boy grows bored and impatient. He follows his baba about and begs.

Now, Baba, now? Can we go now?

His father is taciturn and says nothing to the first few inquiries and then finally replies.

It is not for us to choose. We must be told.

Days pass and the itch of excitement dulls, and the father grows irritated at the boy's sullen face and sends him, with a cousin and a bronze coin, up and out of the ravine to find a goat for sacrifice. The father orders the two boys:

Go find a nanny and we will offer her up, blood and spirit, and wait for the telling, for the command.

The boy and his cousin walk toward the great green slopes with little idea as to where such an animal exists. The boy takes time to explain victory to his cousin, as he has come to understand it, as he has invented it.

There will be ribbons and fireworks and all of the girls will kiss our hands and heads because we have made the land safe for them and my maman will be happy enough that her garden will grow all around her and then I can get a little drink . . .

In the early afternoon they stand before a house of white mud from which a man emerges, without summon or call, and takes the boys to a pasture of soft clover and daisy clusters, where a flaxen-haired nanny chews coolly on the earth's sweet cud. A length of rope tethers her neck to a post beaten deep into the ground and at the sight of the man and the smell of the two new boys the nanny nags just once, loud and guttural, and runs to dash away but is caught by the solid rope tied to her neck. In an instant she is raked backward. The boys approach and again she lurches forward with an ornery and defiant pull and again is restrained. Between each yank the nanny pauses to smell the malfeasance on the two new boys and dodge their death message again and again until finally a rock makes its way to her head and she can no longer pull herself from the stake or pull the stake from the ground. With neither bleat nor tug she follows the two boys back to camp, her eyes dazed with admonition and omen.

At the camp the boy's father inspects the nanny with disdain. He looks once at the goat, and with her honest and impertinent face, she looks once at him. The father shakes his head.

There is too much life in her yet.

Neither the boy nor the cousin understands for what misdeed they receive such fast slaps about the head and in their surprise they forget to cry out. The father walks away from them angrily to tie the nanny to the ravine's sole tree, where she can reach neither water nor herb, and the boy trails behind to hear his father's mumbles.

She is a bad omen among us.

Ya Ali, pardon us for such a hasty, untame offering.

Ya Ali, pardon us, please.

When the sun sets the boys tie the she-goat by the ankles, front and back, and carry her to the fire where the men wait, sing, smoke and hold out a bowl crafted just that day of hardened river silt. Even upside down, after a day of bray and bleat without water or cud, the nanny flicks her tail and head with strong snaps and twists her torso in flagrant jerks, her buoyant body one gesture of loud declaration. The knife at her throat is a thin thing, a quick thing, and the blood flows first in spasms and then streams, and the final sounds of her life are drowned by the men's song. It is an unfamiliar song, one the boy has never heard, a series of names intoned again and again, and the boy takes to his bed away from the feast of red drink and red meat and the drone of that same song. He blinks in the night and waits for the men to sleep and for silence to cover the camp like a heavy blanket. Tonight he is tired; the day has been long and unwieldy and the boy has no energy left to discern between celebration and lament.

BABA

Ay Khoda, I am a listening man.

We hear them first in the wind; long songs that whistle *youuu youuu youuu* and tease us out from under our women and away from our warm fires and off the spines of wearied jacks. Easily we are pulled from these lives and strung about this enormous earth as servants to your sound.

And we follow, ay Khoda.

We follow the choruses sung to us by the wings of birds, the tick of rain, the puzzle pieces of cloud left in the sky at day's end, and we come, Khoda, we come to your commands. As you called my father before me and call the father in me now and my son who is now at my side, we have all listened and yoked our unknown fortunes to your desires.

In my life I have joined the men to walk the hot desert flats, climb sharp mountains' edges, and live in caves so to better hear your summons. To better rid our land of outsiders: Russian, Armenian, Turk, Qajar, and now this new mock king. Battle after battle the Kurds have rushed to defend this land, all at the beckon of your call. To hear your call is to obey. We listen for the sake of our lives, the lives of brothers, sons and unborn alike. It is fear that sacrifices the land and love that holds it close, so you have called, ay Khoda, and so we obey, obey, obey.

Twice now I have come to this ravine. Once when I was a boy like my own son—who is still malleable of heart and head, though he masquerades with a firm age—and now once again when I heard your call in the courier's voice. Each time we gather ourselves in obedience, neither conscious nor considered but made of movement and memory, and each time we find ourselves swallowed in this depth, this chasm of shrub and cut red stone, to wait for your command and brace for the battleblood to beat within.

That first time I waited like my boy waits, unknowing, and I listened to the uncles tell me I must steel my boy heart and boy breath, for when the battleblood comes there is only black fury for sight and death drone for sound. I waited patiently for you then, ay Khoda, and for days, nothing came. My father and uncles smoked and threw dice and waded in the river like children. We sang to you every night and every dawn I pressed my head to the earth to hear a sound and the men laughed at me, *Foolish boy—what if it comes from the sky, what if it's in the wind?*

I was taught to receive without expectation; and so you came from the sky in a murmuration of the smallest birds that landed on our shoulders and heads, and we emptied the ravine to follow them up and out to the desert floor. Flying before us we could see Mohammad Al-Din's men and their cloth tents spread across our land, easy and unaware. And we rode in to take of their horses and their camels, their gold and feathered hats. We rode in beneath the flurried, chirping starlings as bayonets broke in our horses' ribs and we fought with empty hands; to pull the tongues from their mouths and push their eyes into their heads and press in the soft skin of their necks until, face by face, they fell. And you were with me all that time, ay Khoda, and I was just a boy with blood on my hands and the sense of you in me much more than a sound in my head, more than a song in my ears; an enchantment entire.

And here again we have come to wait for your call and the boy I was then lives in my boy now, with his own impatience born of a mix of fear and courage. He wanders our riverside camp in constant query: *When do we go? Where do we go? How will we know?* How am I to answer, ay Khoda? How do I teach patience to my beloved? He is but a boy, full of fanciful ideas and too long at the breast of his mad mother's milk, but he is my only and I have loved him with all of my living self and all the dead I carry in me. All that is left for me is to teach him.

Teach him to be a listening man.

A man patient to you.

In blind duty like the rest of us.

The boy lies awake each night to look up at the stars and seek out a sign, and I cannot explain that here we've been cast, with no course or recourse, to wait, growing bored, hungry and vainglorious in imagination alone. Many days have passed since we left our women and wives, ay Khoda, and though we sing to you each night and clap our small hands to the ceiling of stars and wait for the thunder of your two palms, or the flight of owls, or the whistle in the wind—nothing comes. My boy listens to the men, who have grown disquiet, and asks me:

Do the gods have us wait here while somewhere our blood burns?
Baba, why do we wait?

Amu said that while we sit cross-legged in this ravine day and night
Kurd blood, mamans' blood, burns and burns and we do nothing. So
I send him and his eager cousin to seek an animal for the
slaughter, the blood sacrifice that always brings you near, and in
his return, ay Khoda, your call has come.

And: I am a listening man.

And: I am an obeying man.

To hear and obey you are one and the same. When you sent
sign in the body of the goat, I cursed the boy and tethered
the beast far from the men, who would know with one look at
the overalive eyes of the nanny that the enemy is near and
strong. I kept the beast away until moments before the kill, to
spare the men this truth, but they recognized it nonetheless and
we have taken your omen in stride, without complaint or plea,
as this will be our land long after we are gone.

We are listening men, ay Khoda, and if this is your command,
so be it. Our minds are not made of matter but of the echoes of
your desires, and we are obedient men, ay Khoda, and I a willing
father among them, prepared to lead my one son into an unfortunate battle, the two of us ready to attend death's call.

THE NIGHT ESSAY

WITH BELLIES FULL of goat meat, the men rise at
dawn, empty camp and travel up the steep ravine walls
and across the same grassy planes wandered yesterday by the
boy and cousin. The smooth flats give way to slopes jutted with
boulders and the men dismount and ascend into a soft mist that
hides the sharp rocks all around. They maneuver through cracks
and along switchbacks that elevate them to a vantage point beneath a sheltered and craggy peak, where they remain, secreted
and all-knowing, like the gods they call to in their everynight
prayers. Here they perch to afford a view of tents, men and black
machines that rove about the green plain below, small and shifting, measured and disoriented, like citizens awoken to an unfamiliar country.

At night the group bivouacs in the talus slides between stone
peaks and their shadows. The men arrange samovar and pots
and feedbags in the loose pebbles as if arranging accommoda-
tions in a luxurious divan. They set up no tents and light no
fires and sing no songs and play only silent games free of raillery
and maintain an invisibility so pristine the boy wonders if they

exist at all. He questions nothing though, for since the sacrifice and the slaughter the men have moved with somber and absolute rectitude, as if taking orders the boy cannot hear. For two days they camp, eating only salted meats and drinking cold tea and regularly climbing up to the peaks to catch sight of the shah's men and crawl down again, expressions unchanged. At night the men sleep bunched together in tight knots below the warm bellies of the horses, which shift from side to side in the steady saunter of their equine dreams.

One afternoon six caravans of men arrive in succession, turbaned and armed, to join the congregation already gathered. They embrace and speak and smoke and make camp amidst what is already established. At night the boy steps carefully about them, for he is unable to tell his own cousin from another cousin, his uncle from another's father; his men are now so mixed with strange men that in the dark, all the faces meld into one. To fall asleep amidst them on that first night, the boy gazes into the mirror given to him by the bahkti and takes the reflected image as a brother, his homologue among the arrived, to whom he whispers the secrets of the bravery and fear he juggles within.

We march forward, for we are Kurds and this is our land. The men of the shah may look strong, but Baba says it is not the right sort of strength and they will be defeated with one blow from my new gun.

The boy nods and his reflection nods back. The boy goes on.

We must push the soldiers back off our land so that there can be smiling mamans and sweet tea and days of uninterrupted play.

The reflection smiles at the boy.

Yes, our land. My land and yours. I've no fear in me at all.

The reflection is still, serious through the eyes and about the mouth. The boy nods to make sure it is in fact his replication and not some other world of boys like him, scared and silent. The reflection nods back.

That is correct, no fright at all.

Well before dawn on the fourth day the men rise in unison and relieve into cupped hands their night's liquid, which they splash onto their faces. In the early blue light they do not eat breakfast or bread or even dried meats and mulberries, and the boy grows hungry and cannot find a face familiar enough to complain to and so scrounges about the empty burlap sacks and finds nothing. As if to tease the hungry boy the men take turns with a knife and cut a line across the palms of their hands and squeeze blood out from their bodies into a tin cup that follows just behind the knife as it is passed from man to man; they drink and are nourished. So it goes for the morning and the afternoon. The forty or sixty or eighty men obey the silence and pour of their life juice into a cup and imbibe it easily, as if it were a glass of tea. The boy makes the incision himself and the gash sears less than he expects. He clutches his fist to watch with glee as the ruby drops join the rest and hungrily drinks the warm viscous fluid like a noonday soup.

At dusk, when the sun stretches into a thin line and the red line of blood has passed into and through all the bodies of the men, they descend. They leave the encampment, each on his own horse with his own gun, and footstep carefully down the shale and whetstone of the mountain. There are more horses and men than the boy can count and they follow, one after the next, in a long line that looks from the bottom like the mountain's own vein. Once down on the plain they take cover under the navy coat of a moonless night and walk toward the steady flicker of the shah soldiers' camp, keeping their long-barreled shotguns and rifles laid perpendicular across the necks of their horses. Drunk on the night and the warm wind, the boy marches along gaily, his eyes trained to the fires that burn on the far distant sphere, open and inviting, as now he is in a line of warriors to war, in love with the land that spreads out around them, for tonight it is his to claim.

The boy can feel his baba's eyes seek him out in the crowd. The father searches for the son and catches sight of him at the end of the line, where he stares into the night with a focus resonant and clear. His posture is sturdy and there is little left of the nervous or uncertain child. The boy watches his baba turn to lead in the front with a satisfied expression and knows he is a glad baba, happy to offer history a hero.

They approach.

From the periphery of the encampment no sentry stirs or yells *Kurd!* and the men enter with speed and raise guns and bloodied fists in the air but make no war cry and wait instead for the sounds over which they have no control. The garrison's young soldiers barely move from their fires or out from underneath the blankets and they are easily overtaken by Kurd riders vested in sashes of bullets that shine brilliantly from days of diligent spit and polish. Not until the first shot, a misfire from the hands of an old uncle, do the soldiers scatter into tents and supply piles to regain holsters and bayonets and rifles and redirect their confusion forward, into the chaos.

★   ★   ★

In a minute, an hour, the night entire, the boy, long fallen and aimless on the surface of the nightmare, wanders to witness soldiers and men entangle in rigid links of human flesh, and he bawls in the spaces between burning tents and motionless machines. From triangle openings in canvas huts, soldiers aim and fire and hit horses that stumble and collapse in heaps. The men who rode atop them scramble from underneath the crushing slab and the boy watches one after another fumble at the triggers of rifles and pistols not even once cocked. Shots are fired, aimless and ill-guided, only to disappear into the night or pierce the muscle of a dead horse. Eventually the men, uncles, cousins and father, abandon the combustion of the weapons and take them as steel staffs to open the faces of soldiers, with brutality enough to bring forth blood. They exploit whatever surprise remains of the attack and raid tents to drag out the unbelieving and the fearful, to force heads into fires and pummel the raucous globes of flame until extinguished. But the soldiers are intact, unfazed, already part man and part machine, and raise their rifles like arms and fingers and fists and take to the easy rhythm of fire and shoot, fire and shoot. And what the men perform with cries and shouts the soldiers perform with automatic efficiency: to aim and pull life out again and again with a mechanized dexterity and repetition so thoughtless that in the disorder and bloodletting the Kurds, adorned in useless ammunition, now accept bullets from the guns of soldiers trained in nothing but the aim and fire. All around the boy there are sounds of falling, the fallen and cries of:

Khoda.

Khoda.

Ay Khoda.

The column of Kurds has dissipated and the boy wanders, unattached, through the battle to see only what the fire allows: the copper buttons of jackets, the shined black soldier boots, the sheen over the eyes of the men—uncles, cousins, father, soldiers alike. From the corners enormous beasts, made of heat and exhaust and throttle, move slowly across the camp, dropping soldiers who shout commands and organize themselves in rows to kneel and shoot. Older men in uniform stand back from the action, crops at their sides, and watch from under stiff-brimmed caps, their expressions blank and unconcerned. The boy walks on, unfazed and deaf.

In these short instances and insufferable spans the boy lives through a night forgotten by history, where the men of the land and soldiers of the shah take to each other with bullet, knife, curse and bludgeon to craft a single composition; the precise choreography of flesh puppets, strung to a thousand stars and pulled as sparring lovers, to and from the flame, to and from the gouge, to and from the stab and shot, their beating hearts like magnets charged to the opposite pulls of victory and death.

For shelter, for sleep, the boy lays his body in the desert dirt alongside the carcass of a stallion. He lies face-to-face with the collapsed beast at the very moment of the horse's death and the boy is the last vision caught by the black equine eye before it sweeps back, glutinous and glib, into the carved head.

What the stallion sees in that intimate infinity will be foretold over the time of the boy's life and the life of those he spawns and the lives to exist over and after this one: a boy lies to sleep in the desert dirt; lies to faint; lies to die. Around him fires burn in triangles and pits and over the round curves of flesh. Everywhere in the lit oasis hungry djinn burrow down to Azrael and ghosts rise high among the dead strewn at the periphery.

The father searches for the son.

The father searches for the son.

The father searches for the son.

The son lies in the desert dirt to sleep, lies to faint, lies down to die; to remember and forever forget what the equine eye sees in its last sight: a boy seeded with a shame enough to burgeon and grow and take lives of its own. The father searches for the son. The father searches for the son (the son rises to the call and shouts in soundless dream talk, *Baba! I am here! Behind the black horse! Where are the uncles and the cousins? Why do you lie and lead us to this death?*) The father searches for his son and finds him dust covered and upright behind the corpse of a horse and reaches a hand to reach out for the boy and takes instead a bullet through the center of his palm. A soldier laughs and mutters, *Kurd,* and drops his weapon and takes to the father in a meticulous rage to kick his fallen body, unravel the turban from his head and plant boot after boot into the shattering skull. The father cries out nothing at first and then:

Please. Please. Please. And with his one good hand tears at his hair like a woman.

Please, I beg you. And his moans are high-pitched and sniveling. The boy silent-shouts at his father, *Baba! Baba! Why do you beg? Baba, rise! Rise! Rise! Rise so that we too can be carved in the mountains' stone, father and son, Kurd after Kurd . . .* But the soldier is an automaton made not of night or earth, but of a machinery bleak and unstoppable that takes boot to head, boot to head, boot to head, until the face on the floor is covered with a bloody veneer; unrecognizable as father or son, uncle or cousin. It is in that moment the dying stallion sees the shame fester and feed in the boy, as the boy too would like to kick at the father, to thunder-shout, *Rise! Rise! If this is ours, then rise!* But instead the boy chooses to never remember, and thus never forget, and keeps the crushed face of his father secreted in a damp purgatory of forget and never-remember, to rove destitute as a ghost through the living days of a son who can never forgive.

A boy lies in the desert to sleep, to dream of boots, thick and strong and without the holes of history, that he can wear upon his own small feet to keep the feel and pull of the earth pushed back and away.

THE BAKER'S SON

LISTEN, I TELL the Kurd orphan. Do you see that cadet over there? The one with the sandbag cheeks and big behind? He farts so massively in his sleep that you will want to pinch your nose tightly and breathe only through your mouth. Like this. I hold my nose with two fingers and let my jaw hang open like a mule's. See? Some of the boys think you can still taste his stench, but don't believe them. They complain about everything. What's to complain about? I say. We are all here in this sweltering nowhere, our food is deliciously rotted, the morning tea smells like my baba's armpits and we have to go around slaughtering the likes of you all day and all night in the name of some imaginary king. A soldier's dream, wouldn't you say? The Kurd orphan stares, unsmiling.

The sergeant brought him to my tent at dawn, explaining the obvious: he was a Kurd boy, he had survived the night, the massacre of his barbaric father and uncles, and by the shah's orders, captured orphan boys are instantly conscripted. As he talks, the sergeant holds the Kurd boy by the neck with one hand and picks his nose with the other and orders me to tell him the story of my own glorious conscription. Even though the sergeant is a fat man with thin wits who regularly sickens me with his oily face and rancid burps, and even though my head still burns from last night's battle, I oblige. I tell the Kurd boy only the choicest bits of my story: the day the shah's soldiers came to my little mountain town of Ramsar and all the village boys ran to join, eager to align themselves with the majesty and force of such a regal army. And the soldiers still burned down our madrassa and my own baba's bakery with its stores of wheat and flour. But we were determined to join, at least from what I can recall, because with one hand I clung to my own maman's teat and with the other hand I reached for the gun they held before me. Yes, I think that is how it went. All the young boys were willing and ready and though I still have scars from the bayonet blades on my arms here and here, they are proud scars, Kurd boy! The soldiers told me they were marks of my forthcoming manhood. And just like that we were gone and I have not seen my family or that rocky village since, thanks be to our great shah.

Uhh-huh. Our great shah.

The sergeant nods in his stupid agreement. The Kurd boy makes no sound or gesture. I continue, detailing the joys of the barracks, the never-ending elation at our all-day and all-night marches through deserts and mountains abandoned by Khoda himself. There are mornings you will wake to the beautiful songs of birds. I make mention of the comfortable beds, kind commanders and the honey we were given every morning with our bread and cheese.

Don't forget to tell him about the walnuts.

The sergeant pipes in, switching from one nostril to another to dig deep and listlessly while listening to my tale with rapt attention, each bloated eye watery with hunger and imagination. Yes, walnuts! I tell the Kurd boy. Enough to fill both hands. Crunchy and sweet and laced with tiny ants that make them even crunchier and sweeter! Then there are wrestling matches just like the ones you and your brothers had, I am sure, if not better, where the commanders watch and smoke and bet on the strongest boys and watch happily as the weakest boys cry. And the uniforms! Comfortable and cut to fit, itchy and still smelling of the Russian Cossack who last wore it. You will find yourself booted and tall, strutting about just to hear the rhythm of the spurs at your heels. A gun of your own, a knife of your own, a hat that might match your head, all gifts from the magnanimous shah, our father and true commander. *Yes, magnanimous. Yes, our true commander.* The picking sergeant murmurs as if in a trance.

Animated beyond belief, I go on. Have you heard of Tehran, boy? We are greeted like heroes in Tehran. The city where the lamplights burn all night? Where the women rush to you, Armenian, Turk, Azerbaijani, to touch the buttons on your uniform and the brim of your hat and offer themselves to you, though they smell like rotten fish. Where you can walk from street to street receiving greetings and gifts like a king and every commander and cadet you pass salutes you like family. Pure popularity, I assure him. The lies exhaust me and I close with a flourish. Service to the shah is an honor full of rewards you cannot even imagine! Today is the first day of your blessed existence. Befaymin! With all my heart the army of the shah of Persia, soon to be Iran, welcomes you!

Aufareen! Aufareen. A thousand years for this shah and his Iran!

The sergeant removes his finger from his nose and hand from the boy's neck and claps deliriously, like a deaf child, with his eyes closed and a wide smile across his face. The Kurd boy stares at me with his clear eyes and unscarred face. He understands none of what I say but keeps his gaze fixed on the shapes of my lips and face as if to determine what I intend.

When the sergeant has left us I find a long rope and tie a loose knot around the orphan's ankle and another around the center pole of the tent. We lay down together on my cot and I whisper to his frozen face: it is not as bad and some days it is worse. He stares at me. He is a handsome boy, no more than ten or so, green eyes, with a curved mouth, supple and red. I fall asleep with his warm breath in my face. I wake in the unbearable heat of the afternoon to the sound of laughter filling the tent. Loose of his knotted leash the Kurd boy stands before me wearing my discarded boots, the laces wrapped clumsily around his shins, his face split in the smirk of a maniac. The other soldiers egg him on.

Show him. Show him. Show Karaj your new trick.

The Kurd boy grins and runs out of the tent and into the searing afternoon, runs among our tanks and tents, trips and rises, falls again and rises again and comes to kick the body of some nameless remnant from last night's massacre. He kicks it again and again and stumbles back to me with the same delirious smile. The soldiers laugh and taunt.

The sergeant will be pleased, Karaj, you are raising the perfect cadet.

I drag him back into the tent, lightly smack his grinning head and wonder if such instant orphaning and instant adoption will beset the Kurd boy as a blessing or a curse. Either way, he is my brother now and his jovial face fans my hot mood. Listen, I tell him. See that soldier over there? The one with his rifle across his shoulders, the serious-looking one? Every night he wets himself in his sleep! Can you believe it? A grown soldier of the great shah! Pissing like a baby! The Kurd boy smiles and I smile too, like two brothers sharing the same joke.

DISBANDED

THE TENT HANGS in a series of soft drapes drawn up to a round apex. From the opening a solid yellow trunk of sunlight shines down. The boy sits cross-legged in the dark and watches suited men walk into and out of the slash of light in steps just long enough for the brilliance to flare their bronze buttons and lapel metals. The boy has been in a dusty dark like this before; in his disorientation he cannot help but confuse the memories of the cave with the memories of the massacre. It is early afternoon and hot and the boy's allegiances mix randomly as he sits restless, with the zeal of a novitiate lost, in the center of the shadowy tent, eager for the flavor of this new world's song and clap.

A hand appears in the shaft of light, disembodied by the dark, and holds a severed head by the hair. The smear of life liquids: mucus, blood and dry salted tears glisten in the dusty sun and the head twirls neatly in one direction and then another and comes to stop and face the boy with a long-dead stare. The jaw drops with a small jointed snap and a plum-colored tongue falls out, swollen and thick. A voice from the dimness asks the boy in his language:

Is this your baba?

The boy nods and shouts, ecstatic.

Baba!

The boy looks directly into the open eyes and announces:

I wear the boots now too! Look!

The purple tongue shines in the light and the boy, embarrassed for his baba's ridiculous face, tries to stuff the muscle back into the mouth to give some order to the disgraced animal. All around him the darkness laughs.

And now what of us, Baba? What of the father and the son and my son and the kings of this Kurdish land? Now what?

—

Baba?

The desert wind blows hard and the walls of the tent arc inward to shrink the cavern and gather the men and the boy in an even smaller darkness. Over the top of the opening the gales drive with such a force as to create sound like the breath of lips over the rim of a bottle, like a whistle from the dead in one note: high, lucid and pure. In a jolt the disembodied hand yanks at the congealed mane and the head is gone. The boy waits, perhaps for the rest of the body, perhaps for an annealing where everything comes together again, alive and attached. A man in uniform crouches beneath the light and calls to the boy in his own language.

Come near.

The boy walks close and craves to touch the man and his shaven face and his sharp hat, but instead the man touches him: his cheek and jaw, the line of hair along his head, the roundness of his shoulders and flanks. The booted man stands to search

74

through his pockets and draws forth a trinket: a figure of wood and string painted to look like the boy himself, legs and arms and a helmet of brown hair. With deft and nimble fingers the man manipulates the strings and the wooden boy walks and raises his legs, lifts his arms and kicks at the air with his wooden feet. The toy dances in front of and atop the boy, prancing from shoulder to head and down to shoulder again. The others in the tent look on, uneasy and suspicious of their captain's sudden delight. The boy snatches the wooden figure that crawls on his head like an annoying insect. The captain laughs and says in his harsh accent, *Go on, keep it. I have pocketsful. They dance at your will. Good puppets always do.*

What water he receives comes from canisters and tastes not of mossy river rock or wooden well bucket or dried animal skin but of metal, sharp and acrid in the mouth. What food they give him—salted meats and bowls of rice—cures the hunger for only a few minutes before he retches the lot of it in a viscous spread at the soldiers' feet. For the first days he is tied by a long rope loosely affixed to the center pole that holds up a musty, damp tent, and for those days the boy keeps to himself, shits in a corner and wets his pants. When awake, uncertainty overtakes him and the soldiers, booted men all of them, move about like specters to smile, poke his cheeks, pull down his soiled pants to look and laugh and smack his parts.

The boy makes eye contact with all of them and one of the soldiers, who closely resembles his oldest cousin, Nivad, gazes blankly back. The cousin and soldier are of the same age and have the same deep cleft in the middle of their chins and curled hair. The boy is quick and thrilled to shout, *Nivad!* Immediately he is slapped. But now he is desperate and convinced (and loves his cousin, who always kept a smile tucked away at the corners of his mouth and once sewed a kite for him) and remains adamant enough to shout again: *Nivad!* And he is slapped again by soldiers who mimic his desperate one-tone plea, *Niiii-vaaad* . . . The boy cannot help himself. If this is Nivad then they are not dead, not the uncles, cousin or father, and he follows the familiar soldier from tent to tent, meal to march, until all the soldiers, identical in height and dress and voice, form an army of Nivads.

In these first days the mind of the boy turns to madness.

He runs from one to the next to tell them that their uniforms are merely costumes they can now abandon to become Kurds again, his Kurds who have been victorious against the shah and now must find his baba's body, *quickly*, and sew on the head, collect a few pairs of boots and start the trip home. Again he is slapped.

Days pass and the boy is calm and hysterical in turns. After a time the army takes him for its own as he is quite obviously a Kurd and an orphan and a fool, their loot from the land. He is untied from his leash to serve as the errand boy and quickly becomes the captain's favorite. Every evening he is allowed to sit on the old man's lap and play dutifully with the puppet as the men play dutifully with him. On the day of dispersal the regiment collects itself, machine and man alike, to move north toward the mountains of Sanandaj in a line of tanks and horses much like the lines the boy has known.

The day is hot. The sun rises straight above them and lizards and snakes scuttle to shade as the army walks slowly out from the valley of the massacre and the boy rides on the captain's horse, nestled between the old man's legs. The party passes the pile where Nivad himself lies atop the men: uncles, cousins and father's headless corpse in a mound of the boy's own flesh left to rot and disband at the prick of desert heat and vulture beak. The boy keeps fixed on his puppet, his dirty fingers and new boots, and does not raise hand or eyes in the direction of his fallen family. They move slowly into the first pass heading east and the mountains take them in, the desert behind them left to the shadows of sun and moon.

Book II

NEHAVAND BARRACKS AND THE
TOWN OF SAQQEZ, PERSIA,
SOON TO BE IRAN—1929

NEVERMORE THE BOY

THE GARRISON IS secreted between two long mountain lines, deep in a vale, continuous and immense. Whatever elements pass into and out of the green basin do so under the jurisdiction of the stone stacks: what sun there is shines briefly between midday and one when it passes in a quick arc from one peak to another; what wind blows hard and direct, strong enough through the corridor to knock off caps and disturb card games. Even the rain falls straight and hard as if pulled, string after watery string, by the greedy hands of the buried dead. The one road in serves doubly as the road out.

He is caught in the captain's favor and stays each night in the officer barracks, where he washes the old man's feet with rose-water and powders them over and under with lilac talc. In this year he is a steadfast favorite for taking the beatings and caresses and develops an ever-growing fondness for touch such that he starts to hold still his head for the slap, open wide his mouth for the suck and keep stiff his whole self when the captain's pistol presses into his temple in a game that makes the Armenian whore laugh. And he is a diligent pet boy to hold that same pistol to the neck of the Armenian whore as the captain labors above and behind her with the enthusiasm of a donkey.

In his new life he is a cautious boy and hides behind the wide hips of the whore until the captain goes to sleep. Her back is pale and covered in a thin layer of hair and he pushes himself up to her and closes his eyes to imagine Maman on the other side, her breast and face and fingers. The whore helps and pushes her back and ass into him and the boy burrows down in her warmth. When the old man is finally snoring the boy crawls over her big body and curls his tiny body into her belly and breast and takes one enormous teat in his two small hands and holds it to suck at the dry nipple, to imagine and delight. He keeps at this the whole night, the whore asleep before him and the captain snoring behind him and his orphan heart beating steadily between the two, happily awake for this fantasy of Maman and Baba and love all night.

At dawn the captain stirs and the dream ends. The boy releases the body of the whore and moves quietly to the cot on the floor where he is supposed to sleep. In the first hours of the morning the captain and the whore stir and he cannot help but cry. Pushed off the bed, away from the heat of their bodies and the friction of their fucking, the boy is more than alone, he is without, and he shivers until dawn, when he wakes the captain and begs for his command. The captain murmurs orders in his half sleep: *Eh, Kurd boy. Find my boots. Bring the chai. Scratch the bottom of my back.* And the boy gobbles them up, delicious as cherries, and marches about from task to task, certain of his place in the world. Like this, day after day for the first year, he is shorn of the boy from before and cannot remember the pieces of that other life—heartbeat, sapling, cold carp—so that even the mother tongue grows sticky on his lips and he answers to all calls with the crisp Farsi: *Yes yes yes.*

Another year passes and he becomes a good boy in it, still nameless and orphaned and so preferred because he is an *idiot Kurd* who runs to the warm deep pleasure of command like a happy dog.

The pipes, on your knees to light them.

Lay out the motaqs.

Embrace me here and here, yes, there, hold me tighter, you mountain ape, until sleep comes, my darling, darling boy.

And he is ordered about to do and do and do and the boy does, jubilant to be at beck and call. He serves captain, lieutenant, colonel and sergeant, who crave his green eyes and his soft face free of hair and his hands that are not yet rough, who cling to him in boredom and battle chaos alike as he is the choice boy: fatherless and motherless, so pitied and treated to fat from the stew, sweet lumps of sugar, necklaces of copper bullets; so spoiled. Easily and every day he is loved of a necessity (theirs and his) in slaps and suckles all the same; a love for the daylight world (in calls and commands) and then a love at night (in clutches and embraces) held close as a pet; a village girl; a much missed mother, cousin, sister.

Afterward, sleep comes to the orphan boy, deep, terrifying and plagued by dreams that spread through him like greedy tendrils of a zealous vine. The boy finds little rest. Of the varieties of night tortures he prefers most the dreams of song and drum and men gathered in his baba's divan. And though the dream leaves an ache behind, the boy would prefer this reminiscence to the more common nightmare of his village as it is plundered, the fields set on fire, the granary ablaze, the pens burning with the skin and hair and eyes and hearts of animals that he loved as pets.

In these dreams the men who cling to him in their sleep are always the culprits. They are monstrosities unto themselves; their noses running with thick, vile mucus and hands far larger than their grimacing faces. They march through his Kurd village and take the women and stuff them heartily into their monster mouths. The girl cousins are snapped three at a time and some of the oldest aunts are spat out and stepped on. The boy runs about, miniature at their feet, trying to distract them with offers of chai and massages, and even kisses where they want them most, *Anything, Agha, just put down your bludgeon . . .* The monsters move through his village, unaffected by the pleas of the boy with the size and stature of a flea, and come to sit around a fire they feed with his baba's instruments, clean out their teeth and belch. *Kurds are a bit too salty; next time, with rice.*

The boy wakes to an insanity in which he is unable to separate dream from actual day. He rushes about the camp, set and determined like a maniac, to serve the soldiers whatever they ask, to take their insults and demands and keep them calm to spare his village and its women, youngest cousins and oldest aunts and maman alike. They are the long-lost faces of a home he can only conjure now in tortured dreams.

For two years the orphan is stuck in this service, mindless and numbing, until finally the inexorable hardening occurs. Without any effort the body of the boy changes, with flesh less ample for the grab and smack, indecorous bristle to cover the face and all over a general roughening of what was once supple and soft. Thirteen years now, the boy grows inches in months and the commanders shrink in his presence. Soon he is their size, if not more, and they do not touch him or even speak to him, as he has grown handsome and strong and full with a pureblood they cannot claim. The boy is relieved of his darling days and, like a chick to the nest, tossed in the passel with the rest; a plebe in the great army of the shah. The cycle of home dreams comes to an end and the boy sleeps on a dusty cot and dreams nothing but black and occasionally of birds as his body pushes out of the skin that held his maman's son.

He is given a uniform of his own to match the uniform of the commanders he so admires. A jacket of dark beige with buttons to cinch tightly in the front, epaulets that snap at the shoulders and a collar he turns up to make his neck look strong. The pants are similar in color, sharp-creased down the front, with wires that loop from the hip to the knee on the outer edges of his thigh. His boots are tall and stiff and he vaguely recalls wanting them from a time before. They have more eyelets than he can count and he wears them underneath the wraparound spats that fit the narrow pant leg into the boot and boot into the spat, everything taut and slim like the shin of a horse. He is keen to insert, tighten, wrap; eager to appear well fitted by this new uniform, this second skin of the men who are now his men, that he will wear in one form or another until the day of his burial. This first uniform is impermeable, an armor of thick Russian wool to defend the young boy, not yet man, no longer son. He wears it around the barracks that afternoon. His skeleton pulses forward in the casing and his shadow is a wide, fearsome thing and he is happy with the wholehearted suffocation, the elated excision of the boy beneath.

And so: born at the age of eleven, to the Honorable Shah Reza Pahlavi.

And so named: Reza Khourdi

Age: Approximately 12–14 (undocumented tribal stock)

Eyes: Green

Other: Birth mole on right cheek (apricot shaped)

The attaché from the Ministry of the Interior in charge of new citizens is tired. A seemingly endless stream of unnamed orphaned cadets stood before him today, sad eyed and too small for their uniforms, and naming them has made the old man sleepy. The first name is easy; it is the first name of the Most Imperial Majesty Shahenshah Reza Pahlavi I, and with it the boys join the low ranks of same-names, an instant empire of agnates born to the new nation. The second name is simple protocol as well, regional, with reference to the tribe of origin, in an effort to demystify the sacred identity and fold it in with the other tidbits of the bureaucracy and state. The attaché lifts his head from the sloppy floral script that deems all of this so and lets his tired eyes fall on the cadet in front of him. The orphan boy does not look away. He is handsome and his soldier suit is a good neat fit. The attaché stares dreamily at the cadet's tile-green eyes. They are clean through to the black pupil, and bright, and the attaché recalls a girl, two rooftops over from his Tehran home, who hung laundry each morning on invisible lines stretched across the sky while children screamed at her, *Parvaneh! Parvaneh!* and she ignored them to reach upward to the pigeons and the clouds. The attaché dips the pen in the ink again and for no reason he gives the boy a third name. The closest he can get to Parvaneh is a name that means "heartbroken," but it will do.

Name: Reza Pejman Khourdi

And now again he is created, this time in thirds: a third homage to a false king; a third memory of another's delight; a third genesis of people erased.

And nevermore was he the boy.

Never again was he the boy that was.

What remained—the heartbeat, the smell of sutured sapling, the river's cold caught carp—all evanesced to a paradise above where these ghosts of his last life gathered to look down and watch the orphan boy pass his first year in the company of strange men.

Eagerly Reza awaits his first summons. He has yet to hear his name called and is careful to listen for it in the constant shouts and screams of the barracks.

Reza Pejman Khourdi! To the photograph station!

Reza (heretofore and hereafter) runs to the call. He climbs the same stool as the rest of the cadets, looks ahead like the rest, slumps first and is instructed to sit still like the rest, to suffer a moment of flash blindness—a darkness with neither inside nor outside, yesterday nor tomorrow, an obscurity complete where Reza waits, collared like a wild animal, stunned and captured— like the rest.

SAMESKINS

He is ordered to a barracks already full of boys of a similar age, each with his own cot and trunk and, like him, tucked neatly into a uniform, identical but for eye color, boot size and heart's desire. For the first days Reza moves through their company and wonders if they are all as he is, if they too are orphans who stood beside their baba's death silently shouting, or have slept behind the captain's whore and sucked the dry teat, or even if they are happy, like him, to find a barracks full of sameskins, brethren, as good as cousins he cannot remember and brothers he never had.

There are few conversations as the boys in the barracks are re-familied and re-clanned, instructed to gather every morning, noon and night as soldiers for the shah. They wake to the same pistol fire, eat the same long fold of lavash, piss into the same stinking trough. Together they mingle their blood, pus, semen and spit together in a soldier sauce that melds the many into the one body and the one mind and one memory until origin is of no consequence. They are boys, conscripts, vassals of the not-yet-nation, and at night they amass in the dank barracks and sit supplicant before a framed portrait of the shah to chant the six-minute paean to the painted likeness.

God praise the Persian nation, and *God protect His Most Honorable Majesty, the King of Kings, Shahenshah Pahlavi. The first.*

And the young citizens tuck themselves into cots that loll like cradles and sleep beneath the watchful eyes of their gladsome sovereign. Before he dreams Reza imagines himself walking from bed to bed to hug and kiss each boy of his new family, as they are equals to him, motherless and bound.

In the mornings they take military duty lessons from a captain with a body that spreads like a circle from his shoulder to his knees. He explains the march. *It must be a strong file, organized and straight. All following the same orders from the masterful shah.* The sun rises behind the captain as he walks beside the boys with a crop as they start their clumsy ramble across the courtyard. The captain shouts. *Keep step! Ya Ali! You want the toe of your boot in the asshole in front of you. Yes! Higher! Faster! You look as foolish as a flock of geese!* The captain goes on, all morning long, with comparisons that keep him laughing his hearty, tearful laugh. The cadets too would laugh if it were not for the constant snap of the hard leather stick for every foot too low or shout too soft. They move from one exercise—climbing the stone walls at the end of the valley, fending off attackers while on horseback, proper salutes for the shah—to the next, and the captain keeps a jolly rhythm with his heavy wand and a small silver piece he blows with his mouth that screams louder than any bird Reza has ever heard.

They spend the afternoons with a silent, immaculately attired colonel. He arranges them in a straight line and paces back and forth to gently inspect their uniforms, the lace and polish of their boots, and, for some, the trim of their new moustaches. He takes his time with certain boys, slowly caressing the line of their jaw—*No hair yet?*—or running his fingers up the inseam of their pants: *You still have to fill these trousers out . . . we cannot have skinny soldiers marching about for the shah.* At Reza the colonel stops to inspect his collar and runs a gentle finger inside and outside the topmost buttons of his jacket and shirt, tracing the line of his Adam's apple. Reza can feel the colonel's breath on his neck and hear his deep inhale in his ears as the old man buries his face in his shoulder. *Very nice fold, Khourdi. Very nice.*

In the early evenings they gather in an airless room to take history lessons from a sergeant with impatient hands.

First, of course, there was nothing: the Persian plateau, a few shrubs, maybe a bird or two. The Persian and Mede tribes migrated, as they were nomads, as they were lawless and took of a land that belonged to whoever stood on its stones and laid the groundwork for 559 when Cyrus the Great established the empire of Persia, known for compassion and love of law. Ahead now. Five twenty-nine b.c., the heathen of Babylonia surrender peacefully to Cyrus and Cyrus dies a victor and a hero. Ahead again. Darius the Great rises in his wake to build the Royal Road that makes possible significant and continuous contact between East and West, a contact that is our blessing and our curse.

He goes on, rapidly, blithely, shaking his hands as if to dry them. Underneath their desks the boys mimic him by flapping their hands and everyone is red in the face from stifled laughter.

Ahead now. Two forty-eight B.C. Parthians defeat the Greek Seleucid Empire. Sassanids follow them with some paintings of flowers and the abacus and astrology, etc., etc. Five seventy-four, the Prophet Mohammed is born.

He stops for a moment. The cadets straighten their faces into serious masks.

Let us pause and note that our great empire, enormous and victorious against the Romans and the Byzantine conquerors, succumbs like a village whore to Arab tribesmen armed with little more than asinine faith. Let us pause and note.

The cadets take no notes, as they have no pencils or paper.

But it is not the worst of times. We live relatively well under one caliphate or another and remain notorious in our advances in poetry, letters, astronomy, mathematics, theology and calligraphy, on and on, until the great Genghis Khan sacks the caliphate in 1226 and Marco Polo himself bemoans our ill fortune at the hands of the Mongol beasts. Ahead now; 1501, and we are Persia again, to stand against the encroaching Ottomans, Russians and Indians who see us as the key, the nexus, the crossroads, and we have more poetry, algebra, la, la, la, and relative peace.

He gestures his hands in a flurry as if to whip the air into a cream. A boy sitting next to Reza pulls his penis from the buttons of his pants and begins to stroke it in a mocking flurry and Reza's eyes spill with sweet tears of amusement.

Ahead again, on and on, until 1795, the Qajars come to power, a dynasty weak and irresponsible that empties the treasury for their luxury-loving endeavors and our once mighty and proud Persia is forced to offer concessions all around: our tobacco to Russia, our coal to England, our gold all over, wherever, to whomever. And we are a raped whore, sniveling on the outside and torn apart on the inside by barbaric tribes.

The boy next to Reza feigns ecstasy, and Reza clutches the back of a chair and the sweat pours as he stifles his laughs.

Yes, boys. We were so weak. So weak! Our proud Persia was a broken butterfly. From outside the hungry pillaging of English and French and from inside the lawless brigands of Kurd, Baluch, Azerbaijani and Turkoman maraud the countryside and steal from the wealthy cities, taking women and girls as they desire, whatever gold, whatever flocks, and they are bestial heathens, the whole lot of them, given to blood and greed. Not a knife or fork among the bunch and nothing of the civilized decorum or sophistication that characterize our old Persian cities of Shiraz, Tehran, Esfahan and Mashhad.

The sergeant pauses, exhausted. The word *Kurd* passes over Reza like a dark cloud and leaves him long unsettled in its shadow, and all the laughter is drained from him. The joking among the boys ceases as they listen, city boys curious at this turn in the story that makes them heroes, the tribal conscripts happy to suddenly hear a familiar word.

Ahead now; 1921 comes upon us like a miracle.

He pants.

Our glorious king, Reza Shah Pahlavi, rose out from the Cossack ranks to oust the imbecile Qajars from their ruinous throne and determine our Persia be an independent thing, a solid thing, belonging to no one aside from herself. Not the British or the Russians or the Austro-Hungarians, not the dirty tribes or their imbecile aghas. For his foresight and determination we are most blessed and grateful.

The pacing has resumed and the crimson drains from the sergeant's face. Some of the cadets stand and clap in a mock celebration that pleases the sergeant, who twists his moustache in delight. The bad feeling churns in Reza, though now he cannot remember the cause. Has he broken a rule? Did he properly make his bed? Are his trunk items in order? Are the buttons of his suit jacket rightly lined? He thinks and checks but knows that the illness in him churns at one word: *Kurd*. A shadow leans up against Reza's back and whispers. *Yes, Kurd.*

The sergeant finishes his lesson.

That's it . . . ahead now. To you boys. We are a young nation. The shah says we must build an army to stand strong as a column and keep this country together. Now you all stand in history . . .

The air is stifling and warm. On the wall, a map labeled PER-SIA, heavily marked with lines and circles, curls in at the corners from the heavy condensation of boy breaths that fills the room. Reza himself is breathless. He perspires from underneath his collar and the nausea stays with him until mealtime, when the boys are in the dining hall to devour the sour stew and onions and easily erase the entire lecture. Reza tries to eat and joke but folds under the weight of a bad feeling he cannot isolate. That night as the cadets gather to wrestle in the stone circle, he takes opponent after opponent and easily crushes them to the ground, in an effort to shake off the black sensation that covers him from within. His fervor does not go unnoticed. A captain who regularly wagers on the matches between boys calls out to Reza, pipe dangling from his lips.

Aufareen, Khourdi. Now that's a good conscript. Imagine putting that anger to work against the dirty tribes! The shah himself would be proud.

Often, there are inspections. The boys are displayed for visiting statesmen, generals, and on a particularly hot day, the shah him-self. The cadets take it as fun and games and stand atop cots and trunks and one another's shoulders to look out the high barracks windows and laugh as their dignified commanders bustle about with the scrambling gestures and hoarse whispers of children.

The shah. The shah. Look sharp! The shah.

A whistle blows. Cadets wash and dress and stand clean and straight before their beds. Names are called: Jahan Tavainshir, Keyvan Omidi, Darius Khalegi, Fereydoun Jamshidi, and the boys take positions as a young lieutenant points.

Here and here and here.

Reza stands between the Baluch twins. Both have rough faces and large hands but one is thick bodied and the other is thin with a sick coloring in his face. The thin brother sleeps on Reza's right and in the night he holds one hand to the top edge of his ear, where a large red scab heals, and another hand to his mouth, where his lips suck feverishly on his thumb. Both have skin stained a dark brown and black, marble eyes. The sick one keeps to himself and holds to his wound all day and all night, while the thick twin speaks incessantly in a clacking tongue no one, aside from his wounded brother, can understand.

The whistle blows again. Reza, who stands taller than the two boys by at least a head, keeps a strong posture: hands clasped behind his back and shoulders pushed forward to fill his uniform. The brothers take great care to imitate him but they are weedy in their jackets and crooked through their spines. Across the divide the city boys stand, clean boys, favorite boys, in an immaculate line of square shoulders and stiff lips, each chest pressed out, each heart pledged to serve the new father.

The shah is a tall man. Thick like a trunk through his every part—finger, wrist, neck—and but for epaulets of gold, his uniform is identical to Reza's. He walks slowly among the silent columns of barracks boys, with his nose held high as if in a perfumed garden. Three generals trail him in a sycophantic symphony of spurs. The shah stops to ask the cadets one by one:

And you, my son, you are a child of which province?

Reza listens to the responses.

Tabriz; Khorramabad; Tehran, Agha Shah; Mashhad; Schomal; Rasht, like yourself, Agha Shah . . .

Very good. A willing conscript, I see, a smart city boy. Here to make your father proud, I am sure.

The shah and his aides stand before the Baluch twin whose ear is missing a large top piece. He approaches the boy and fingers the wound with a gentle touch of his gloved hand.

Conscription?

The boy nods.

And you are a child of which devious province, my son?

Baluchistan.

And your father thought he was more powerful than me?

—

And he tried to resist your conscription and now you've been branded a miscreant?

Reza shifts his eyes off the floor. The shah is a rock of a man, enormous and uncut. His nose is smashed to his face and a heavy moustache grows out from underneath the uneven, stony rubble. He sweats a white sweat, thick and visible.

Some things must be done by force, my son, and now you know that, but lest you forget . . .

The shah pinches the injured ear until blood drips onto the

cadet's shoulder. On one side of Reza the thin twin flinches and screams out and on the other side the thick twin shifts in place like a child full of piss.

The shah stops and hands his crop to an attendant commander, who hands him a handkerchief in return. The barracks are still while there is a general collecting and a composing and cleaning of fingers and gloves and the shah takes a step sideways to stand before Reza.

And you, my boy? A child of which province?
Kurdistan.
A Kurd, then?
—

Reza pushes his chest out until its heart beats like a bullet between them.

You are a troubled people. Troublesome . . .
With a shake of his head he moves on to the thick Baluch twin.

And you, my boy, you are a child of which province?
Hastily, easily, the brotherhood disbands. Coagulates of new boys, formed in the sticky classroom and formed in the sweaty bunks and formed in their own happy imaginations, dissolve and the fraternity gives way to an easy enmity made of pointed finger and ha ha ha. What were before boys, simple of mind and manner, are now complications of ascendancy and memory: city boys revel in the sudden recognition of their maman's clean hands and their baba's fancy shoes and their cobbled streets and labyrinthine bazaars, while tribal conscripts keep a silent shame for their maman's ever dusty hair and their baba's disdain for the shah and the childhood friendships they kept

with stars and rain and sparrow's nests. So starts the segregation: them and us; the other and the I; the sophisticate and the savage; civilized and ingrate; the good and the undesired. At night the barracks come alive with taunts.

Hey, Baluch boy! Go back to your dead dry desert so we can defeat you and make Persia a proud place again.

Peff. I smell a smelly Lur. Does anyone else smell a smelly Lur?

Turkoman, they say your eyes are slits because that barbarian Ghengis Khan fucked all your mothers at once.

And on and on until even commanders join the fun and assign their own subnames. The Shahsevans become the *dirt-brains*, and the Turkomans *rice-eyes*, and the Baluchs *black skins* or, even worse: *Arabs*. There is identification humiliation enough for all. Some of the conscripts are glad not to understand the Farsi and keep their backs to the sagging cots and their eyes on the barracks' rusted tin roof. Few, however, are sad as Reza is sad, his sleepy heart broken by the loss of the brother love born so easily between them all on those first days, free of history and the gun-strong determinations of this new state.

THE PAINTED KING

SEE THEM SLEEP, these sons of mine.

    See them, nestled like loved ones, row after row, barrack after barrack, heads awash in the last brine of boyhood.

See them sleep, my army of sons, each suckled off a different teat and their tongues still wet with prayers to me.

See them sleep, these sons of mine, and though I am now shah, most majestic and supreme, I too was once a boy, sleeping and divine. A boy like them, beaten and bruised by the thick angry hands of a brutish baba, forced to run and hide in the folds of Maman's belly until found again.

At the turn of the western century I was the punished boy, then the runaway boy, lost to the cold hills of the Caucasus, until finally I was the eager orphan boy who tagged after the Cossack brigades that aimlessly crisscrossed the northern provinces. Yes, I, most indomitable and noble, was once the orphan tagalong who begged of the clear-eyed men: *Agha, a jacket, please? Agha, a gun?* I am the boy who Commander Sidipovko sticks in the stables to tend the horses and sleep in the hay and wait for him each night. In this time I am a good stable boy; I am a better knifeman; I am the best shot in the garrison and finally the commander's sergeant, lieutenant and then his topmost captain. One day I am the commander himself and the next day I am minister of war of the Cossack Persian brigades with four thousand men at my call. I am a man partial to spilt blood. I administer war regularly and with great panache, leading armies against the belligerent Qashqai and Lur tribes in the name of a greater notion: nation. My brigades and divisions are successful against Simko, the Bahkriyari in deserts and mountains north and west. My men and I are welcomed in cities with cries of thanks and praise, cheers and claps on the back, for we do the dirty work and in doing so make our glorious Persian past a modern thing, a proper thing, a thing to belong in the world of tanks and war and one-faced fear. Now I am the notorious Commander Reza Khan, boorish and proud, a buxom beast, a king over all I see, and I let loose my two forked hooves to prance over the hearts and heads of whomever I desire. Now I am a figure, face and father. All of it once hidden in the skin of a sleeping boy who was once woken and once loved, now cast out and forever cold.

THE SELECTION

IN THESE YEARS Reza is often chosen. They tell him to stand at the front of the class and hold the rifle in a series of poses and postures: over the shoulder, along the length of the leg, the base at the ribs, barrel out, pointed here and there, always away from the captain and toward the class of boys. He follows instructions and turns the gun at the fifty cadets, who stand stock still and stare at Reza, with his one eye shut and his one eye wide and the infinite one eye of the rifle open at them. The captain lectures alongside and explains the most efficient ways to aim, take shot, aim and take shot again. Reza is told to relax and he ends with the rifle stretched upright, from his feet to his hips, in one obedient line. He has been chosen to brandish the weapon in a mute picturesque way in front of, and at, the other boys and Reza stands, an armed and able example, to cock and load and point and almost shoot, to raise the green of envy up from under the tight collars of the empty-handed cadets.

At night, in the barracks, Reza suffers these selections. With naked backs made of sharp shoulders the cadets keep him out of their circles of conversation and games. In the shower the city boys look down at him and laugh a loud donkey laugh.

Your mother was an ass and your father must have been a heavy horse, you've got the parts of an animal, you dirty Kurd, hehehe haw haw haw.

Turkoman and Rashti and Lur and thin Baluch twin say nothing. Of the tribal conscripts only the twins' thick brother, with both ears intact, tries on the teasing and laughs.

Hehehe hawhawhaw, dirty Kurd, Khourdi is a dirty Kurd.

The viciousness fits him but Reza is unaffected, for he is chosen and favored and taller in height and firmer in muscle. For the sake of the gun he will succumb to the segregation; for the sake of the hold and the cock, the fire and the bang, the hurt or maybe the kill, Reza keeps his fist unclenched and cultivates a thick skin.

The gun has been long kept from him. His baba's gun was an accidental thing, useless like a toy, covered in dirt, bulletless and painted in rust. But Reza has seen the barracks guns and they are an army unto themselves, to stand upright against the classroom walls, erect when untouched, erect even as the cadets sleep, then still erect as they are held by the eager novice hands. In their lessons the captain manipulates the guns like he would an injured bird, with gestures gentle and small. In his hands they are suddenly shiny, slick with oil, disassembled and reassembled to make obvious the inside and the out. Reza watches the captain work, to see the way his fingers fit and flit about the metal pieces with a rhythm regular and confident, as if the weapon itself was part of his own skeleton, its assured projections part of the captain's very soul.

In the mornings Reza runs and raises his knees in exercises and in the hot day he sits in the instructional and recites the names of the cities on the map markered IRAN. In the afternoon he wrestles to the shouts and bets of the superiors and holds a boy by the neck until the knuckles of his own hands are white and the boy's eyes bulge and the face is just a glazed sheen of mud mixed with tears, dirt and sweat. All day long Reza hopes; with every bowed head and dutiful nod he hopes a gun will be given and he will have his own and that it will aim (at them) and fire (in them) and scream (he will) and shout (*hehawhehaw-hehaw*).

In exchange for a bit of news from the barracks, you may select one.

The captain points to the five guns that spread out like a hand over the colonel's empty desk. The cylinders of the four rifles reach like fingers and their butts join together in a brown-black-tan palm with the squat and potent handgun arranged to look somewhat like a thumb. Reza is tempted and hungry for the shot, but resists. The colonel and captain reassure him.

It's only a bit of information.

Just a little news of the barracks, a bit of what words are going around among the boys.

They are at ease in their asking. The captain, with his long face and sunken eyes that forever peer past the boys, and the childlike colonel, who leans up against the wall in his chair, his heavy body delicately balanced in a lackadaisical pose that makes Reza nervous. They take turns in their talking.

I am sure there is something, just a little gossip . . .

I've heard from another source there is slander against the shah . . .

That could be dangerous talk . . .

Go ahead, pick one up. They are just tested.

They fire like cannons.

The guns are German Mausers, Russian Mossines, British Lee-Enfields and the slick French Lebels, all traded with foreign armies in exchange for oil and niceties. None new, already rust covered and witness to what fear, hate, blindness and death the three men in the room cannot say. Reza's eyes grow wet at the blossomed metal flower before him, the skeleton-still hand that waits to be held. The colonel continues, as if to himself.

Now what could these boys say about the shah? After months of the highest-quality military training, who is to complain?

Still balanced in his precarious tilt he looks down his nose at Reza.

Go ahead, pick it up, they tell me you're well trained. Choose one.

Reza chooses a rifle, the longest and darkest of the lot, and raises it up to his shoulder, where it fits into a socket just below the clavicle. It is more comfortable than any handshake or embrace. The colonel continues.

Now, who could speak such treasonous words, after all we have done for them?

I wonder . . .

Ahhh, ingrates, the lot of them . . .

The voice echoes in Reza's head and the gun is solid in his hands and he tries to recall the boys, the cold and hollow barracks, the nightly banter, but the gun distracts him. It is warm, like he wanted. It is hard, like he wanted. It is almost his, like he wanted. For this gun he has turned a deaf ear to the harangues of the jackal-tongued city boys, held his hands stiffly to his sides, memorized cities and safely separated himself. Now a silence fills his memory and the colonel's questions hang in the air like laundry out to dry; Reza is close to failing, near losing the one thing he is certain will never break, disobey him or die.

This talk of dissent among them is unexpected . . . a shock, really.

Reza strains to remember a conversation but all that comes is the evening talk of mother's food and brother's game and neighbor girl's smile, sentimentalities foreign to the Kurdish cadet.

Nothing?

The colonel asks.

Come now, Khourdi, you remember nothing?

The captain asks.

Such a shame, you are first selected for the gun, first in your class, they say you are a tribe boy transformed. There has been much talk in your favor. Here, try the handgun.

The captain takes the rifle from him and puts the .45 caliber in his palm and says, in a haughty voice:

A Russian thing.

Instantly, as if he himself has just been shot, Reza remembers the faces of the city boys jeering at the everywhere-hanging photos of the bald, moustachioed and medallioned shah. They are brazen in the raillery and proud to recount overheard conversations between their fathers and city men in dens and hyatts. With the pistol in his hand Reza remembers: *My father could do it, and better; this shah is a fake thing. This old man is a fool, hungry for power with no plan . . . Our Iran is run now by the brute child of a peasant, a puppet king on British strings. They say he can't read. They say he can't write.*

Reza holds the gun and he is happy and thinks carefully:

Where will I keep it? In my trunk. No. Beneath my cot. No. Under my pillow would be best. Yes, beneath my head, in case, because . . . he clears his throat.

Aghas—

He must clear his throat again.

I have heard some of the city boys speak of their fathers' opinions of the shah. They say he cannot read. They say he is a peasant's son. They say . . . about a puppet . . .

There is a loud clap in the room and the guns on the table jump. The colonel has landed all four legs of his chair fully on the floor. The sound reverberates and the captain shifts his weight from one leg to another.

Pffft. It's not the city boys we're interested in. What do the conscripts say? You are a tribe boy just like them. They must say something in your presence?

The other conscripts are quiet (the Farsi far from their lips) and sad in their stares, pulled apart as if they have been cut from their organism of origin and something inside of them waits to die. They do not bother to slander, much less to speak, and from those boys Reza has only heard the whine of the thin Baluch brother and the jovial sleep talk of his thick twin. He places the pistol down on the table and shakes his head; it is a prize he cannot win.

No, I've heard nothing from the conscripts, they say nothing and nothing against the shah.

The colonel sighs and tells the captain to pick a gun, and turns to Reza.

Come, let's go outside.

The courtyard is empty of students and officials. Aside from the low hoot of a few owls in the nearby pines and the dribble of the fountain, it is silent. Though it is not yet night, the valley is almost dark. There is luminescence enough for Reza to see the outlines of the two figures before him, the round colonel, who smokes with a jaunty gesture, and the captain, who swings a rifle in front of him like a weighted pendulum. They are at a distance, in the dusk, and Reza can't make out the features of their faces, just their shapes, the cigarette and the ticking gun, and instantly he is nervous. Nervous to remember that here at the darkening of days just like this one, deep in the crevice of rock, deeper still in an anonymous desert, deep without witness, the courtyard has once or twice filled with cries. Locked in the blind barracks, the cadets have all heard them: shouts and screams of conscripts and disobedient city boys, taken from their bunks and brought by bored sergeants and lieutenants out into the near night and returned to the cots with bruises and burns on their arms and backs, sometimes gashes on the soles of their feet, sometimes no visible marks at all. The colonel and captain continue their conversation and Reza, suspicious of his selection, steps to a far corner to count the owls by their hoots (two? ten? twenty?). He focuses on the night's oncoming cold, the inevitability of the stars in the sliver of sky above him, and wonders who among the boys and commanders, sky and stars, will come to save a bleeding orphan, just shot. Reza distances himself from the dream of the gun. The captain walks toward him with a French rifle extended.

Come test the gun, Khourdi. You want to test the gun, now don't you? It's for you to try.

Reza leaps and the colonel laughs.

Into the air, boy, fire into the air. Pretend you are shooting one of those fine birds we serve for your dinner.

Reza fits the gun into his chest and aims up and a surge of relief and exasperation washes through him as he points into the night. He will only remember the first shot and the heavy flap of owls' wings through the air. He fires the gun again, which fires into him, again (a ram into his chest that will leave a bruise), and he fires again and the shot echoes through the valley, up through the mountains into the sky as if to shatter the already shattered stars, and leaves behind a wake of solid sound. He is all the while deaf and distracted from the colonel and the captain and their questions and he loads and fires and loads and fires and forgets everything he has remembered: his father, the barracks boys (who are now awake and wondering), the land and the shah, the cries and carp, the hoots of the owls, now silent, maybe now shot. When Reza is emptied and there are no night noises, just the sharp erasing ring in his ears, and he is positive that life cannot be without this jolting limb, they ask him again. *And now?* And it is suddenly simple; a lie grows from his gut, a fabrication so fertile that it stems through him with an urgent haste.

The Baluch twin, sir, not the one with the cut ear—the colonel nods gravely—*the other brother. I have heard him speak of his father's arsenal and his tribe's recent defeat of the shah's forces in the south. He said it was an easy victory and that the British will assist them in their fight for independence. He talks of rebellion against this Iran, he says it is the Baluch who are more powerful, who will last on the land.*

Reza is surprised how quickly it comes from his mouth, like a bullet from the barrel; the lie is a sure thing. They take him to the munitions room, where guns and artillery are kept, and they open and close boxes of bronze and steel bullets and give him permission to linger and look as long as he likes. Then they are gone and he is in a room full of destiny, full of the tools to upset the cycles of nature and the hearts of men, full of weapons to have and hold and hurt and harm. He runs his fingers along and through the lot of them and rearranges them in piles by color and length and make, touches and touches again until his fingers are numb and he is tired, drained of whatever hero's hope he had kept close.

THE CITY CADET

Mahdar, Aziz-eh-man:

Mahdar dearest, my support for eternity, first angel of my eyes, first warm breath in my lungs, first soft kiss to my new-born face, I see the beauty of the whole world through you. In the name of Allah the most merciful and compassionate, I hope that countless blessings fall on you and Baba and Shireen and Aava and (may God bless her departed soul) Maman Bozorg.

I am well, Maman-joun, healthy and arrived at the training encampment in the desert where everything is as it should be and in its place.

I beg a million apologies for not writing earlier, but here we are very busy. Just yesterday the commanders kept us awake until dawn piling stones and then unpiling them and piling them again and we sweated in the dark night like animals but the commanders tell us again and again the work of making a great Persia will demand thick arms all around. We spend some afternoons in class, where the sergeant tells us of Persia and uses maps to show us what Persia looks like. It is a big green thing and every day there are new lines around it and he says this is our proud empire, and then tomorrow it is another shape and he corrects himself and says, *No, this is our proud empire.* One day a cadet from Shiraz asked what the blue parts were at the top and the bottom of the map. The sergeant said they were the Caspian Sea and the Persian Sea and the cadet asked what is a sea? The sergeant said that the sea is the sea and he could not say more. When I come home, Maman, and we take our chai underneath the chandelier in the living room, I will listen carefully as you explain to me the sea, as I am sure you know it.

Mostly we study the magnificence of our great shah. Agha Reza Pahlavi. The king of kings. He is great enough to be God himself (but you should pray for him anyway when you go to the mosque this Friday, after all your regular prayers and after the prayers for my arms to get thicker). He is the son of a million kings before him, did you know that?

The barracks are full of boys like me, city boys with fathers who took us to the military recruitment centers and passed us along for this great duty. We are the good, clean boys. There are dirty boys too—tribe boys, Maman, and they are all as different from each other as they are from us. Some of them have dark skin like Mustaffa the Egyptian ice seller (the one who scares you with his big black-and-white eyes), some of them have thin eyes like slits and there are even some tribe boys with yellow hair and blue eyes or green eyes like Aava's English dolls. You would not like them, they cannot read or write and are all the time naughty and sad. The commanders must beat them often and we are ordered to beat them too (and I hit the black-skinned one extra hard for you, Mahdar-eh-man).

There is one tribe boy, a Kurd, who sleeps two cots away from me who speaks our Farsi well enough. Maybe that is why the commanders favor him the most, because they gave him his own gun already. The boys here say he is a traitor for it. They say he told the captain and colonel that the Baluch boy who slept under his bunk was against our great shah and that his dirty tribe family plotted against our king all day and all night. The Baluch boy was taken out into the courtyard in the middle of the night. We all listened for the sound of screams (sometimes they take boys who have been disobedient from their bunks at night, they punish them in the courtyard with hits and slaps just like you punish Ava and I in the hyatt after we fight too much) but there were none. Just the sound of the camion motor. The next morning the boy was gone. Now all the tribe boys are even quieter and the Kurd takes tea in the tent with the colonel and we city boys are mad. He lied for a gun, Maman! And now the commanders like him best. You told me lying was a bad thing, but for the Qurd boy, it is like a prize. When I return and we have our chai let us discuss this too, Mahdar-eh-man, this and the sea.

I am well and fine so do not stretch your heart to worry for me. Even if there is only a little sunlight, it is beautiful here. Hawks and ravens and white-feathered birds fly everywhere.

At night there are owls and bats. Since we only have the pigeon in Tehran, I have drawn pictures of the valley birds for you to see, Mahdar-eh-man, because the Tehran pigeon is a dreary bird.

Your devoted son, the light of your eyes,
Jamsheed Ehaladan

ORPHAN AGE

SPRING COMES QUIETLY to the valley; the season is warm winded and the mountain walls blush with small blossoms. The garrison graduates on a clear day, in a ceremony of rifle fire and empty-eyed pledges. On the afternoon of that same day they leave for their first assignment and march away from the barracks shoulder to shoulder in lines of three, out of the deep Nehavand valley into the wide flats. They walk for a night and a day along the Gaveh and Uzam rivers, toward the base of the Zagros. They walk and pass scattered outcroppings of life, clans and tribes hobbling around pasture and stream and vadose well. Boy sentries rush to catch sight of the columns and run back to their baba, uncle and brother to describe the indescribable sight.

They come like a herd of the gypsy, but no women, children . . .

Their animals make this noise: gjeeee! And this noise: bruuuueee!

They have wagons, yes, yes, like ours, but with no horses! Everything is smoke and sound!

The men listen to the fantastic gibberish and follow the boys to watch the spectacle. The garrison is a sight to behold, neither natural nor ordinary, and what the village men know of fear they sense in that moment's view. Before them, an unending intimation of force: soldiers on horseback, in the beds of sputtering trucks or tucked in the hot iron enclosures of the tanks that roll, heavy and dismal, along the desert floor. They watch as the army of stiff caps affixed with chevrons of bronze and carved with the insignia of the new state, a lion wrestling the sharp rays of the sun, slowly passes them by. The village men mutter to their wild-eyed sons.

It's nothing. Turn away. Go inside.

See him, in the file, one amid many and together with the rest. He wears an olive-green uniform of wool under which the sweat is constant and ever seeping. The stiff shako sits obediently on his head as he himself sits obediently on the leather-saddled horse. See how he rides in their line of beast and man, machine and rank, all linked by the invisible ideations of conquer (*we will*) and country (*Iran*) and king (*the most noble and high shahenshah!*), and other sundry details mastered day after dark day in the shadowed valley barracks.

Now he is fifteen. Though they are not his fifteen years (not the number of years from his mother's desiccated womb when the cord was cut and cherished and hung to dry, oiled with lard, wrapped around her wrist for good luck, the best of luck), not the years of the moon's rotation, the earth's spin around the sun or even the count of seasons where the land is fecund and then fallow. They are pen-and-ink years, years of formal assessments—size, shape and skill—years of inventory and identification. It is an orphan age, as declared by the spurious newlyweds Baba Shah and Maman Iran. It is *their* fifteen years. For this specious upbringing he should loathe and fear them, these false forefathers and artificial brethren, but it is too late; the fontanel is nearly formed, ossified into a solid, stiff knot at the base of the neck, where boys are soft with memory and possibility and men are hard with hate and fear. Here, Reza melds into a man for them, a named and aged member of the impartial, clangorous congregation. Look, how high his head. Look, how stiff his neck. See him proud and straight amidst them, brother to brother as horse is to horse. See him move, young and dead, in a slow amble beneath the morning sun, easy with the trust of the blind, trust of the duteous, trust of the nervous new soldier. See the broad horizon open before him, ivory clouds dotted and spread.

And so the mass moves. Through the night and into the dawn of the second day and not a cadet grows tired and not a cadet complains. The desert holds them, warm and windless, as they march from one end of the horizon to the other. On the afternoon of the second day mountains rise up out of the land like a gesture of God and the garrison is instructed to dismount the horses, trucks and tanks and set up camp. Some, like Reza, enjoy the vista run through with clean wind and circled about by enormous stone statues, open and real like a forgotten home. When given the order to halt, these cadets are sad to stop the march; so tranquil is the perambulatory pull of the land.

The garrison bivouacs on the flats at the base of the mountain town Saqqez. The city spreads above them, a mass of white-washed houses and cyan minarets, angles and arcs that goad up the hoary vertical rise. On the low slopes there are fields, irrigated orchards of indistinguishable trees and a pasture speckled with small, still flocks.

The sight of the town captivates Reza for reasons he cannot discern and he makes his way up the slope for a closer look. The fields are steeped in a familiar manner, long and thin, sown with rice and eggplants, zucchini and tomatoes. He comes close to the orchards and without looking carefully knows their arrangement: plum, apricot, pomegranate and mulberry. Water-hungry trees closest to the stream. Even closer he knows, without touching, the soft wool of the sheep and the curved smooth horn of the ram under his hands. He knows how they are penned and paired in numbers to spawn in the spring and he cannot explain how he knows all this, *senses* it through his bones, and so he walks back to the men, the lopsided smile of fascination and wonder spread unevenly across his face.

The cadets are jovial in their preparations. They are ordered about to build and assemble and collect. By dusk they are settled and the encampment is a stationary mass, a small city unto itself, where cadets sit by fires to shine their boots and guns and tinker with the British brass instruments they are to play upon their entry into town. They talk to rile in themselves bravery enough to carry out the shah's unexplained desires, which they have now memorized and made their own. Captains and lieutenants walk from fire to fire and question the gathered groups.

Sarbaz!

Yes, Agha!

We have come to Saqqez.

Yes, Agha!

Why have we come to Saqqez?

*To infiltrate the renowned hideout of infamous and renegade Kur-
dish commanders Simko and Dizli, who are aligned with the blasphemous Kurdish quest for independence that weakens our great nation!
Leaves us humiliated! Susceptible to invasion and attack!*

Aufareen, Sarbaz. Tomorrow we will march.

Reza is a good man in his garrison. He claps loud and laughs
hard and the captain's approvals warm him and the fires warm
him and the shouts in his head warm him most. He sits in a circle of cadets who keep a wary distance from him, unsure of his
loyalties, but make no mention of the Kurd donkey or the donkey Kurd as their hearts are swollen and restless with the fear
common in boys. Night deepens and the young untested cadets
work to believe that all is well in the battalion, all is well under
the pointed new moon and clever winking stars. And all *is* in
fact the most well in the houses of Saqqez, where women with
bunches of smoking sage bless the backs of their men and boys
as they disappear, packed and prepared, into the dark mountains. Calm wives and daughters walk from room to room, house
to house, stable to pen, mosque to granary, and consecrate their
tall town, to bless every pebble, egg, living daughter and disappeared son for the night being and the morning to come, to
seek out the protection of the mountain gods against this close
new threat.

On this first night a sharp wind blows down the slopes of the
Zagros in a furious gust that sparks the cadet fires, takes hats from
heads and cigarettes from lips. The wind carries the smell of
sage and the scent burns through Reza's nose, up each nostril

like a charge of flame, and explodes in his head, and everything that has been solidified in the orphan months, the barracks months, dissolves into a dust that fills his head and throat, heart and lungs with a sudden sickness. In a panic, Reza runs to the ditches he just dug to cough and spit, to vomit and vomit again until his mouth froths and stomach empties. He stumbles through the darkness but cannot escape the smell of burnt sage—the smell of a mother calling her children home. The cadets and commanders laugh at what they think is his naked fear and laugh harder to hide theirs, and Reza wipes his watery eyes and coughs to excise the smell and the sudden memories of his mother's soft hand on his crying face. He remembers now.

Burnt sage to stave off the evil eye.

Burnt sage passed over the slick body of the new foal for a long life.

Burnt sage to make the bird-boy sneeze.

He is fifteen, perhaps. His name is Reza Pejman Khourdi, perhaps. The soldier's spine is sealed and assured. Perhaps, perhaps not. At the smell of sage Reza can feel a pained pulse make its way up his back to the base of the brain. What was tight is now a tunnel through which the long-clogged past eagerly travels as if scent was a laxative, a calling. He spews from his mouth and eyes, asshole and nose, and in that one evening throws up his name and age and fake family and breathes in the forgotten language and familiar pattern of stars. The fontanel is fluid now. Tomorrow in Saqqez he will recognize faces and eyes that say to him, as clear as speech that screams: *We know that you know that you are what we are.* In his tent that first night Reza dreams of a horse with the head, neck and naked chest of his mother, a shadow to prance through his sleep. The she–Pegasus trots around their garrison to raise dust and call to him, *Jounam, jouñam, jounam. My boy* (though he is sworn: nevermore). She stomps and laughs, her loose breasts jostle up and down and swing side to side with each of her prancing steps, delighted that a little perfume can bring her boy back.

FIRST FACE

For seventeen days now the shah's soldiers have camped outside our village.

At first sight of them the men of our village quickly disappeared into the mountains. They kissed us on the heads and told our mamans not to worry. *Khoda is with us and we will watch over you.*

On the second day the shah soldiers came to town. We hid in the grain cellar of my uncle's house and I stayed on the top step to keep watch. They rode on horses and some sat in big moving machines and some walked. They stood in the meiydan and shouted for the men to come out. No men came. Then they shouted that any Kurd who was not a follower of the shahenshah of Iran, the king of kings, would be shot and killed. I nearly raised my voice to say *I am not! We are Kurds of these Zagros and that is all!* But my maman gave me a slap just as I was opening my mouth and my sister Halva laughed and was slapped too. The soldiers shouted again for the men and the silence that followed was soon filled with fire shots from the cracks in the mountains where the men of the village had gone to hide. First the horses, scared by the sounds, ran, and then shah soldiers, boys no older than me, scattered out of the meiydan and tried to hide behind the fountain and the mosque but were pushed out by the older soldiers with knife edges and curses until the square was filled with scared boys ducking the hail of fire shots coming from up high. Some tried to shoot back. They cocked their rifles and held them up to their shoulders, and I laughed to see them aim at the nothing all around. Our fathers were deep in the mountains, covered by stones, invisible. Then the soldiers began to fall, one by one, clutching their shoulders and legs and bellies, screaming. A few feet from me a shah soldier fell and spilled blood on the ground in front of our house. The still-standing boys ran about to drag the fallen, like I have seen ants drag their prey. We watched them collect their brothers, gather their guns and what was left of their horses and disappear. When the fire shots stopped my maman ordered us out of the grain cellar and told me to shovel the dirt in front of our door, where the soldier's blood was already drying and brown. *Take it to the stream, throw it in, wash the shovel and your hands.*

Every day now the soldiers ride or walk from their camp to our town.

And every day he comes and walks slowly through our small streets. They walk with purpose; some say they walk slowly for us to hear the clink of their sharp spurs and know them as military men, modern men, men of metal. Others say: *Hide your daughters, they are hungry, ravenous like mountain wolves.* He walks harder and looks more carefully upon everything and we think maybe he looks at us and knows us. Once he bent to Halva, my smallest sister, and touched her hair with his hands and I am sure she smiled. But we keep far from him, cautious and irresolute, for though he seems familiar the uniform is his only skin.

Nonetheless, they tell me I have his face. The women say it because the men, hidden in the mountains all around, are gone for saying. Still, the women talk. When they lift my chin up to see the resemblance all I can see are their hairy lips and chin bottoms.

Bale, bale, bale.

Yes, yes, yes, here and here, for certain . . .

And:

For sure.

Their puckered fingers carve lines in my jaw, around the sockets beneath my brow.

Yes, yes, yes.

They mutter in hushed assessment and agreement.

It is all I can do to gaze down and pretend not to know. I have seen my reflection in the still puddles of water after the rain and I have seen where the nose and eyelids and lips hang heavy with gravity's drag. I look too in the wavering water of the fountain and I am just a boy's head and a boy's neck and I look like I look, like the other boys and as myself.

Such similarities.

The women chant.

Such a resemblance. Ay Khoda.

For the first few days they came again and again; we hid, but this time they destroyed everything. They fired a big ball into the building where our bazaar is. They tore all the photographs of our hero Simko and gathered all of our Kurdish pamphlets and flags in the square and declared us traitors to Iran. When Halva asked me what Iran was I did not know, so I said it was a monster that hated Kurds. They tried for some violence on the old blind woman, who refused to hide, but she folded to the ground easily and so they left her alone. Then they left.

Now it is nineteen days and the garrison at the bottom of the hill is dirty; we can see it from here. Their machines have not moved and their tents are growing tattered. We can smell their shit in the breezes that blow up the mountains. But the soldiers still come and go among and between us as they like, kind or coarse, as they like. They are bored and use us mostly for games; they scream:

Where are your men? Where is your baba?!
Where is Simko?!

And when we don't answer they tear down our lines of laundry and wear our socks over their hands and our sisters' skirts like scarves around their necks; they smell our mothers' stained monthly cloths and let their eyelids flutter in pretend delight. They kick over the pans of crushed tomatoes we have peeled and seeded and cooked for the winter to come, hours of work that leave our hands gummy and raw, and they make a contest of kicks—who kicks the farthest—and the pans fly through the air and splash our winter's tomato sauce all over the street like blood. The one with my face is the best kicker among them and the loudest laugher and the heaviest hand, and once, when he kicked a pan farther than the rest, I had to stop myself from cheering, it was such a good kick. His face is strong, with a chin like a solid brick and smooth skin and two eyes like half moons, even and equal on his head. There is an expression too, just below the skin, a flesh mask, veined and muscled, of some great capacity.

A few days after, when my similarity is so popular I cannot walk without an old woman touching my face, my own maman takes me aside and holds my head in her two hands.

Jounam, Arash, let the familiar one catch you and go along.

My maman is not a crazy woman, at least not all the time.

Go to their camp, the tents below, and ask him in our tongue why they are here. Why have they come to harass us? What do they want? Arash, jounam, go ask him for Maman, please, light of my heart, ask him.

She begs with the brown in her eyes and I am a good boy with his face and I know that the worry is not just hers but the worry of all the women in Saqqez who gave their men to the mountains and sleep alone and lightly because of the garrison's night noise and gunfire.

Go for a quick moment and then run right back and I will have the zulbia waiting.

For two days I follow him around like one of the village's desperate dogs. First, nothing. Then he yells at me in their language and I do my best not to blink or fall back in fear. I persist and when he shouts I take a rock from my pocket and throw it at his feet. I give very little chase and without any effort on his part he drags me by the neck to the edge of the fountain, where the whole village comes to watch as he takes my shoulders in his hands and screams at me in the foreign tongue that makes the soldiers around us laugh and he thrusts my neck and head into the water such that all I can see is his jovial face, my jovial face, and the bubbles of my escaped breath as they explode on the surface. The soldiers gather closer and pound their rifle butts into the marble base of the fountain. I am lifted to hear their happy chant and immersed again, this time his face, my face, is all joy and I am deaf from the rifle pounds that reverberate through the stone and water; heavy drums that rip apart my ears, one and one. I am raised again to the silence. When my eyes clear of water and I can breathe I look into him and say in my language, without coughs or chokes, which is a miracle because I am blue already:

They say you have my face.

The mask in front of me warms and melts like a child near sleep and, in just as many seconds, hardens into stiff steel. Maman was right! I struggle out of his arms to run to her. *He speaks our language! He is one of us! My face, my brother . . .* And from where we are wet, our hands, arms and shoulders, I quickly slip through. Another soldier catches me and throws me down while our brother and son strikes blows on my head with his boot, once and then again, and then again, head and face, until I am covered in blood and the dirt of the ground, until my face is a mask of the earth and nothing more. When satisfied and tired, when the sky is gone and the courtyard is gone and the fountain is the fountain of paradise, the soldier leans down and whispers in our language. *Thank God I don't have your face.*

A swift, arced kick to the middle of me and the blood breaks its walls and tunnels and flows free and I am the first face of our dead, his dead; a molten face, cracked and filled through with dust and dirt that looks up at the women and children from the puddles and pools of Saqqez on their walks to and from our beautiful fountain.

THE PENUMBRA

A MONTH AFTER the rout the battalion still camps, shamed and idle, on the low plains beneath the indomitable city of Saqqez. The commanders are without command. Obstinate in a humiliation bred of mulishness, fastened to a mulishness bred of humiliation, they keep the garrison posted and useless as there are no instructions from Tehran or otherwise. In the weeks that pass captains and lieutenants absolve themselves of post and hierarchy and keep to their square tents and triangular fires and take to hobbies afforded by years of battle boredom—stone carving, backgammon, hour after hour of silent smoking—careful to ignore the cadets that rove about them, restive and keen for action of any sort.

It is an unanticipated tedium, an empty wait, and the cadets fill it how they like. The tribal conscripts spend the days hunting, to return each evening with the limp bodies of grouse or hare strung to the ends of their rifles. City boys, Reza the only conscript among them, quietly spurn their commander's silence to lurch into Saqqez each day, in search of food, entertainment and harassments general and satisfying to burden the people of

Saqqez. At night the cadets come together again to sit around fires of kerosene and scrub and eat whatever canned or caught food is available, to smoke from pipes of opium and drink the watered-down vodka they trade bullets for from passing gypsy caravans. In each other's lit eyes the boys find a safety to protect them against the anonymous wild dark.

In this time two moons have passed: the first, an orange harbinger of harvest, the second of veiled alabaster, dim and irregular. In their ragged euphoria of smoke and drink the cadets regard the dark moon as an unpropitious omen. To ease their suspicions the captain comes to the fire with an astrolabe. Reza stares at the bronze item, meticulous and precisely punctured, and listens to the captain explain the sequences of the stars: the horse, the ladles big and small, the giant and his square belt and all manner of resemblances the cadets can neither make out nor imagine. The moon above them grows darker, as if to collapse into night, and the cadets press the captain for cause. He holds the astrolabe in his lap and looks into the universe of the fire and tells softly and sadly of the rotations of the planets and the spherical shapes of celestial beings and the relationship of the sun to the earth and the moon to the universe, explaining that tonight they all sit witness to the sun's gentle slip behind the earth to cast its shadow on the surface of the moon's fair face.

It is but our own silhouette.

Unbelieving, the cadets return to their pipes and dice. Reza keeps focus on the apparition above him as a thing once white and sure, now darkened and covered, also comes to pass within him. A shadow grows, expands each day gaseous and swollen, to eclipse over all that was positive and bright. He re-minds himself: He *is* Reza Pejman Khourdi and he *has* x or y years and he *is* a dutiful soldier/son of the king of kings, the king of kings *is* correct in everything he does and that Reza does for him, and he *has* kicked and killed his first Kurd and that is right as it *was* the Kurd boy in himself that he kicked and killed to die and be dead and now *that* is clean and in order and erased. All of it, like the moon, becomes a shifting certainty under the wink of tonight's singular darkened eye.

In the morning he walks with a burlap sack, his rifle and three other cadets up the steep green slope in search of food to feed their many hungers. They stop in the orchards at the edge of Saqqez. It is the center of fall and the trees are laden with cherries and mulberries and the soldiers stand on the warm earth and eat their fill. Reza hoards and gobbles the red fruits until the juice stains his teeth and spills from his mouth in lines of crimson and violet. The cadets tease him.

A fan of the cherries, eh, Khourdi?

Mulberries are a child's fruit, didn't you know?

Reza cannot hear them through the churn of his rapacious appetite, as he must now feed his soldier self and the insoluble shadow self and all he hears is: *I am a child, a hungry bird boy a shadow that feasts on these favorites, favorites for the famished bird boy, and I am today a bird and a boy, ravenous for fruit and seed.* They walk on, into the diagonals of orange light that cut in from the tops of the mountains and slant down in black bars across the hills.

Every morning in the town is like every other. The fountain continues its endless trickle; the women and children walk about muted, their motions part of some eternal pantomime with only sound effects: the *slap! sizzle* of dough as thrown by old hands onto fires of hot rocks and the *splash!* of boys who wash their faces in the fountain, the *squawk!* of errant, determined hens. All of it the same as it was. The soldiers enter into a smooth current of time that does not stop or slow or scream for them or at them and they drag their burlap sacks from street to street, unable to penetrate with fear or threat or back-strapped gun the life rhythm of a morning repeated dawn after dawn for as long as the mountains have held themselves high in the sky.

In his foul humor Reza comes to stand above an old woman tending a smoky, struggling fire. At his feet she is bent into a small ball that is everything: his old stone village, his maman's dead garden, the tenacity of the Kurds. With her iron prod she stirs the ashes of his baba's body and the bodies of all the useless and defeated Kurds who left him orphaned all those years ago. The woman wears a black robe and her head is covered in a fabric of many colors. She raises her face to look at him and it is clenched, like the stone, every moment of time that she has spent sitting at this meager fire like her mother before her and all the Kurd mothers before them stuck in the doomed visage. With her dirty hair and dirty feet and dirty hands, she is seen by Reza as the shah must see her: a being just above the line of animal. A people wholly without the grace afforded by shined buttons and boots and a nation to call their own; a population low to the ground, of the ground, stuck to lose, again and again, the very stones that spawned them, useless and forgotten by history itself.

He reaches into the crotch of his pants and grips for himself, pulls out and pisses on her flameless pit. The cadets laugh and clap at this gesture, take it as the first volley, a point of permission, and lark about senselessly from alley to alley cutting into skins full of cool water, turning over the bowls of goat milk left to curdle into yogurt and trampling from one house to the next to raid the pantries of women who watch without concern, having long ago buried their food elsewhere.

So the morning goes.

The cadets: three frenzied city boys and a Kurd who harbors a dancing shadow run about the silent city, gauche and insatiable, in search of food, of grains and cheese and tea to fill their bellies, and terror and alarm to fill their hearts. Steady in its century-old self, the city gently hides its children and grows calm in the haphazard chaos. At a house at the edge of town Reza pushes down a door to find a young mother, cross-legged on a motaq, feeding a child from breasts sodden and ripe and red at the tips. The babe opens his eyes wide at the intruders but does not move his mouth from the stream, and the soldiers are quick to empty her cupboards of rice and tea leaves and fresh butter; she has taken no precautions and hidden nothing. Since her husband left the mother has thought not forward in time, but in a circle without a yesterday or tomorrow, where she is the food and her baby is her husband and the shah soldiers are angry apparitions to taunt her, waking nightmares. Reza stands in the doorway, immobile, caught hosting not one but two selves: the shadow self that craves to suckle at this all-mother's teat and the soldier self that determines this to be dirty loot, for the taking but not at all valuable. Nevertheless, the two demons are this morning bosom buddies who take each other by the hand to dance in joy at the sight of a mother and her milk. He approaches the woman.

Do you not rise for the soldiers of the shah? Where is your respect, woman?

Reza opens his gloved palm and takes a flat hand to the woman's face in a slap sturdy enough to dislodge the babe, who lets go a cry, crystalline and pure, which sears the silence of the town.

The shadow in Reza stands still.

The cadets turn from their raid to find Reza with his mouth wrapped around one breast and his hands clutching at the other and the woman lying on her back, empty eyed, as the soldier drinks and drinks. Reza cannot help himself. The cadets cannot help themselves, famished as boys are famished, and they are upon her, tossing the infant aside to squirm and howl in outrage at the brazen theft. In Reza the shadow self and soldier self dance in delight as the desire to love oneself and hate oneself is now well fed and Reza is allowed to punish and caress all at once. He sucks and slaps and thinks with certainty that he *is* Reza Pejman Khourdi, and he *is* the son of a yet undefined nation of Iran, and the babe's scream *is* music and he *does* today and *will* tomorrow seek out its sound.

THE SEVENTEEN OF US

WHEN WE HEARD Ahang scream we sent away the youngest, girls and boys, to the hiding places as planned because we feared such, as Commander Simko and Commander Dizli warned: the shah's men are beasts and they will eat even your tiniest child.

I was not chosen, thank God.

I have a blind eye and it has brought me nothing but misery my whole life. It spews pus and tears all the time and when the shah soldier took one look at it he spat in my face and then moved me to the side with the tip of his gun, and I could see, with my one good eye, all the imperfects around the square relax. And I heard them sigh too. I did. Lailya with her wooden leg; Arnick, whose mouth is always open and drooling after the horse kick; and Haleh, whose face still holds the mark from the hot coals she tripped on as a girl. The old ladies relaxed too, though a few of them were still taken.

Cursed our whole lives as imperfects, undesired, who would have thought there would be a morning of good fortune for us? But it is true and fated, and I heard the small sighs and whispers of *Ay Khoda* in gratitude as we were cast aside, spared.

That day we prayed for the perfect girls—the ones for whom life's bounty opened readily: choice cuts of meat, the most heroic husbands, the smiles every day as they walked down the street—we prayed for them as they have never prayed for us.

Ay Khoda, how you turn the face of fate . . .

In the end there were four of them and seventeen of us. They left behind the old or broken women and shouted at us in their shah soldier language to walk. And we walked to the end of the village where the streets and houses stop and the mountains start. There the rocks open in small passageways that we used to hide in as girls to kiss one another or to kiss boys and laugh at the feeling of a tongue in a mouth. We go there now as women to hammer the orange rock and crush its stone to make the fine powders for our red and yellow dye. The crevasses are sharp and narrow and the shah soldiers did not know their way and ordered us to squeeze in the narrowest space with the sharpest walls, and there were four of them and seventeen of us and our husbands had long since disappeared, yet I felt no fear. They grabbed our breasts and squeezed them like I squeeze the tits of ninnies and lifted our skirts to look and laugh at what they found beneath. They touched our hair and lips with the gestures of little boys. One followed the actions of the other, copying whatever the other did, as none had been with a woman before, I am sure.

And I was first. I am the prettiest girl too. My eyes are a deep blue and my skin is clear and white. Black hair runs down my back like ink. I have taken care to keep my lips soft with oil and my hands scrubbed with the pumice stone so when my promised returns from hiding I am clean for him.

The soldiers looked at me and one of them sat on top of me and made a big show of lifting my skirt while the others shouted, *Boro baba, boro baba, beebenem.* I turned my head and my mouth dried like the dust all around. He unbuttoned his pants and pulled out his part, the same part as my father and the same part as my brother and the same part my bastard son will have; and he pushed it in me. It was soft at first and I felt nothing and did not scream. When it turned hard and tore open my insides I did not scream. The women around me watched also and did not scream but I could feel their prayers like a dozen little hands holding my soul up and out of my body, where she would be safe. The first soldier slapped me when he pushed and pushed and I became his receptacle.

Agha, come now, let me show you how it is done.

And the short soldier with hair on his lip took his turn and tried to stuff himself in my mouth and at the sour softness of it I threw up all the nune and paneer I had eaten for breakfast. I took a hit for the disrespect but I did not scream.

The third soldier did the same as the first and then he did it again and turned me on my stomach to do it again with a force that broke open the back of me and here I let out a small cry (and my soul, ya Ali, she rose a bit higher), and all the soldiers clapped for my shout as if it was their first victory.

The last soldier threw me on my back so that I could see his face; I knew his face; he has a familiar face, our Kurd face. He sat on top of me and tried to push his soft self in and stayed soft and pushed again and again, as if to pretend, and the other boys yelled and clapped and I said to his face: *I know.* Still he stayed soft; I felt him folded up against me in the mix of blood and seed that made a mess there. Then he reached for his rifle and with one smooth move pushed it far up inside of me.

And my soul rose.

And the women prayed but this time their hands pulled me down, for my soul had risen too far. They prayed their quiet prayers and dragged my soul back into me and I screamed loud enough to shake the talus from the cliffs, loud enough to crush the orange color out from the rock, and the soldier on top of me clapped and yelled *Hurrah* and *Aufareen!* like a village boy with his first kite in the sky.

MOTHERS AND GUNS

REZA IS ATOP the young Kurdish girl who makes no noise. He is not fucking her as he should and the boys behind him know it and laugh.

A little harder. The Kurd in you has to come o-u-t.

He is clumsy with the zip of his pants and his knees bruise against the hard ground as he rocks back and forth as he has seen the other soldiers do. Reza even churns his face into a grimace and pants like a dog. He feels nothing but the hot sun on his back.

It is his first woman.

It is his first woman and he cannot stiffen or thrust and Reza tries to tuck his failure away and perform like the rest but he is soft and knows nothing of women and has no desire for any part of them that is not breast or lap or soft song. He cannot fuck his first Kurd, who smells like his maman and gazes far and away with blue eyes that belonged to his baba. But the cadets rile him to *take her take her take her* and no matter how he tries, with slaps and curses, to elicit a sound from her that proves he's inside her, fucking and marking, staking and claiming, she is silent. *Come on, Khourdi! Take her like only a Kurd can!* The shame is hot on his back and though he tries, he cannot turn his body into a weapon of any effect and so takes his rifle and pushes the long iron barrel into the space he cannot fill. In a spasm the Kurd woman arches her back and chest to the sky and opens her mouth, first to silence and finally to the scream, and it is a noise free of despair, anger or pain; a clean sound, sharp as a blade that cuts the air of the orange canyon into shards.

And the soldiers laugh and cheer at the sound.

Aufareen, Khourdi!

A rifle! That will show them to send their men away!

Imagine that, fucking a Kurd girl, as if his own mother birthed him with the parts of a gun. Imagine!

They clap and whistle and Reza is far from his moment of pride, a smile, a bow, a salute to take the credit that is his due, and can only clutch at his head with both hands. Of all the familiarities in Saqqez—the faces, arbors full of mulberries, the mother tongue and smell of sage—nothing suffocates his heart like the blanket of her scream. The cadets smack him on the back and gather their rifles and walk out of the mountain crevice. They leave the women behind, the afternoon and its actions, to echo like a memory deep in the heart of the Zagros.

The village is empty. All life—fire, hens, bazaar sounds and mangy dogs—has disappeared, and Reza walks foolishly door to door to find the mother and her newborn, desperate for the milk, the comfort after the crime. But they are gone and Reza has no recourse, no way to straighten himself in the aftermath; his legs are made of liquid and his vision is blurred with sweat and his ears bleed and bleed.

Every glance at the bloody barrel of the gun is a scream.

The sight of the empty coffeehouse: ten screams.

The madrassa: a hundred screams.

The blue tile fountain in the center of the meiydan: a thousand clean screams.

The shadow of his Kurdish self is no longer silent. It screams the song of sirens, sung by women that he left behind—his maman, aunts and girl cousins, the woman from the afternoon, the girl herself—who rush forth now in deafening daggers of sound to punish and scold their miscreant son with their fanatical wails. The cadets walk down to the garrison but he cannot follow. His ears bleed and his heart hurts and he tries to hide himself in the pen, bury himself under the hay and pray for silence. The merry cadets call.

Hurry, Khourdi! Come quick. We have to tell the captains about your victory with the Kurd women . . . and we all wagered that you'd break in the face of your people. But no! You are stronger! What a story . . . come on, Khourdi, get out of that pen, today's hero doesn't hide!

TELEGRAM DISPATCH

From:

Captain Gholam Ali Ansari

Owraman Mountain Range

Northern Zagros Division

City of Saqqez

Fall 1935

Sincerely,

It will reach the servants of His Majesty, the Royal Saturn-like King of Kings, may our souls be sacrificed for him, and it will have the honor of being presented to the sun-exalted threshold of the court of Pahlavi that we, the Fourteenth Battalion of the Royal Army of King Reza Shah, Most Beneficent, are successful in our pursuits of Kurdish rebels Simko and Dizli as they are escaped from the town of Saqqez and thus unfortunate and unable to enjoy the warm breezes of His Imperial Kindness. The town is now much pacified as its men have fled permanently, across the mountains into Iraq, and left behind their women and children, who now possess endless gratitude for Your Kingly Favor and are every moment more eager to enter among the security-revering and tranquility-worshipping citizens of our burgeoning nation, Iran (as I have heard we are officially named now, per the suggestion of the German Chancellor to His Most Imperial Majesty). Let it be known that the city of Saqqez exhibits only appreciation at our efforts and they hold countless ceremonies in our honor and swear loyalty to Your Royal Presence as they look forward to our continued presence with the corresponding possibilities of a school of the Persian language, a road connecting their small hamlet to the Great Capital Tehran and other such amenities. They are full blooded in their enthusiasm to renounce all Kurdish identities and belong exclusively, as servants of course, to Your Majesty's Imperial Pahlavi Court. For now and all the glorious centuries to follow, may Allah bless Him and the Kingly Sons to follow.

The garrison now takes leave of the city

of Saqqez (cleaned of Kurdish khan and baygzadehs) to return to the barracks of Nevabad and await Your Majesty's further instructions and directives.

As one final note, mentioned in the utmost humility, I would like to distinguish before His Majesty a singular cadet of our division who shows particular promise in his service to the ends of Your Majesty's usufruct of the Kurdish regions. His name is Reza Pejman Khourdi (a son of your own) and he takes to disciplining the most deviant elements with good judgment and proper use of force as it is in keeping with His Majesty's most Noble Intentions to subdue clans, khans and tribes.

Let me offer His Majesty but two examples of cadet Khourdi's dexterity. One afternoon a boy from the town, innocent to all of us, caught the cadet's harsh attentions. After some investigation, Cadet Khourdi maintained that the boy was known to carry messages from Saqqez to the men hidden in the mountains. He promptly dealt with the delinquent and set a valuable example to any other enterprising young lads. At a later date, Khourdi *sensed* a transgression among certain women in the village and ensured that they too received punishment. He claimed they harbored secret plans left behind by commanders Simko and Dizli that pertained to future insurgent actions against Your Royal Highness. Though there is no evidence of these plans, after Cadet Khourdi delivered said punishments, the residents of Saqqez maintained an attitude increasingly generous and open, regularly offering us their grains, fruits, breads, tea and cheese.

The cadet I mention is himself a Kurd, an early tribal conscript orphaned on the battlefields of Kermanshah. He makes no claim to comprehend his previous language or culture but clearly possesses a keen understanding of the specific sensibilities unique to the Kurds and thus was able to identify transgressions and resistances invisible to us (the civilized and high-ranking resident commanders from Tehran, Shiraz, Esfahan and Mashhad, who have no nose for such things). I believe that these particular sensitivities will prove useful in Your Most Imperial Majesty's Campaign to Tame the Tribes and thus Create Modern Iran. Therefore I recommend Reza Pejman Khourdi for temporary stationing in Tehran; further military indoctrination; possible marriage with a Tehrani woman of some education and

modernity; an eventual assignment in the
Kurdish region near his home of Kermanshah, where he will understand and discipline his own. In this way we become our
nation bringing those from the outside in.

I hope this letter most gently pene-
trates the Kingly Mind and is joined with
satisfaction and contentment at the state
of our young, yet mighty, nation, as your
heritage befits us centuries of magnitude
and wealth.

With utmost Loyalty,
Deference and Devotion,
Captain G. A. A.

Book III

TEHRAN, IRAN—1938

THE MORNING MAZE

ALLAHU AKBAR . . . the brash muezzin call pierces like the morning's light through ears and into the dreams of heads still tossed in sleep . . . *I praise the perfection of God, the Forever Existing* . . . the camion drops the soldiers in the city streets like rabbits in a warren, and so they scatter . . . without possessions Reza moves easily through the maze, wrapped tightly in his soldier suit and soldier boots . . . the looks are at him . . . *Sarbaz! Over here! We've got the finest quarters in the city! A samovar in every room* . . . and past him . . . covered women keep their heads cast down, uncovered women do the same . . . *The Desired. The Existing. The Single and the Supreme* . . . everywhere the dynamite demise of an ancient city . . . for the sake of the new, old homes explode into crumbles of rubble and boys play in the mess as if in castles, fortresses, dens and caves . . . they tie cuts of cloth to a stick to be stuck in the highest point to mean a flag, to mean theirs, to mean a child's country . . . Reza has never seen so many doors, doorway after doorway hiding a puppetry beyond . . . a rice vendor moves heavy sacks with the stretch and bend of his crooked back . . . a girl of authority and suspicion holds to the iron latticework to stare out and down . . . three men sit around a table with a pipe, two toss dice, one stares and smokes . . . *Allahu akbar* . . . last night's garbage piles on the curb: chicken bones, burnt rice, sodden tea leaves, clumps of tobacco, bloodied rags . . . refuse conquered by street urchins who search, then flies, then ants, then heat itself . . . the city devours itself, all beneath the sullen orange haze that coats Reza . . . *Sarbaz! Here we have the finest rooms, thickest motaqs, a girl to bring you chai, the sweetest sherbet to quench your desert thirst* . . . Reza moves past . . . *Go then, has the shah taught you arrogance as well? You won't find a better room in all of Tehran* . . . a coin of spit lands at Reza's feet and first the meniscus shines and then catches dust, to brown like everything else . . . a beggar, legless . . . *Agha, please. I've never had two feet or even two ankles, God cursed me to live like this* . . . Reza glances down into the lines on the beggar's open palm to see the maps of some foregone misfortune . . . *The Perfect. The Exultant. Allahu akbar!* . . . in an alley coppersmiths hammer their wares loudly, deaf to one another and to the world . . . the city is for him, to him, yet he can only see it in fragments . . . *The Most Merciful, the Most Glorious* . . . a dead body floats down the street, wrapped in white gauze, the faces of the pallbearers as somber as moneylenders who deal in daemons . . . horse shoes clop about the stone, their sorry eyes buried under the weight of concrete, copper, iron and brick . . . here and there a lamppost stands idle, the gray cresset dull and empty . . . *Sarbaz! Are you a Kurd? My grandfather, God bless his soul, was a Kurd too. Please, come into my home, brother, your pleasure is my highest order. We have taraq, kebabs, the softest dancing girls* . . . somewhere a window open . . . an eye opened then closed . . . mouths open and close . . . fish, street dog, unctuous old man alike . . . legs and assholes and cunts opened . . . the wound opens . . . a knocking . . . entering . . . entered . . . taking and taken . . . a city of history in and history out . . . time forward and forever past and *until then* and *we'll see* . . . *Allahu akbar. Let Him be the one God. The only God with none like Him, nor any disobedient, nor any deputy or equal or offspring. His Perfection be extolled* . . . odor emanates, not of the city, but of Reza himself, from deep in the damp enclosure of the wool Cossack uniform his pores open and spill forth . . . he is only a day arrived and permeable . . . he is the garbage . . . the dust . . . the child's cry and the mother's sacred slap . . . the city wraps around him and he is: transparent, diaphanous, nameless and new and so: free . . . *Here! Sarbaz! The loveliest ladies await you here, in here* . . . Reza moves through an opening . . . between two large wooden doors . . . there is a hyatt with a fountain, the emblem of a cross atop the arched door frame . . . Reza takes of the sweetened tea and the honey pastry . . . *Just in from the desert?* . . . a sweaty palm encloses his and the scent of rosewater floods over him . . . *In that case let me arrange for Marjam* . . . the damp and musty room . . . the madam's cough as she closes the door . . . street din amplified through a window high in the wall . . . she: not a face but a mask with crushed-petal-stained lips and charcoal-covered eyes . . . not a face, he takes her hand and pushes it down into his pants . . . a grip not fierce or gentle . . . holds him and does not . . . not a face but a mouth warm, a tongue warmer . . . wet . . . not a motaq but an elevated bed . . . *Allahu akbar* . . . he feels himself stiffen as there are no mountains or canyons or Kurd eyes to watch over and into him . . . the first thrust, not an embrace but an angry thrust . . . the texture of himself: desirous, durable, unabashed as she is not a face . . . a mask . . . the texture of her enclave: silken smooth, not the warren of streets or the haze of morning or the rapid fire of rifles . . . up and into, again, up and into . . . the thrust, the laugh . . . the sweat pours forth . . . her haunches in his hand . . . her laugh, not resistant but supple in the face of it and laughing . . . *Agha, why are all the soldier boys so mad? Doesn't the shah take care of your little things?* . . . his fist on her face . . . the crush of himself into the soft pillow inside her . . . and it is done: she of the no face lies naked and faceless and he of the shah dresses for the shah in heavy wool and straps and spurs . . . places coins into the old lady's hand . . . one and one and one and is chided . . . *You say, "Thank you, madam," is what you say* . . . the city sweeps around him . . . a window closes . . . the sun arcs across the alley . . . the sky present only in cracks between rooftops, and then present only as a covering, a wash of haze over the shine of a cosmos muted and erased . . . sweat covers him all over in a thick mucus of rebirth . . . Reza walks clean and without history . . . his first sexed self, a city self: a good man, the modern man of nation and king, landless and lost, complete with deeds done and forgotten . . . *Allahu akbar. The Exultant. The Supreme.*

PALIMPSEST

A s if he has never known the mountains, the boundless winds or the calm of countless stars, Reza dissolves into the maculate city. Now accustomed to the heat and incessant motion of cockroaches and buggies and street sweeps, he sleeps peacefully in the filthy boardinghouse on Jamsheedi Street where the beds are stacked and full with cadets. For meals he eats charred tripe sold by the street vendors, who give it to him two for one and pour and pour his douge without solicitation. In the afternoons he makes his way to the rooftop tea houses on Abadaan Street, where he smokes the short cigarettes and listens to the men's easy talk of war that rages among the Europeans, rising oil prices, the latest Egyptian belly dancer in town for a three-week stint at Hamedi Palace.

Another chai for our brave sarbaz!

The old men order tea for him until evening, when it is time for the long pipes that Reza and the men smoke down to the dottle and all conversation stops as they sprawl about the rooftop on cushions and rugs, lost in thoughts and afterthoughts, absorbing the dusk into their skin. At dark they smoke the short cigarettes again, fast and harsh now, and take tiny glasses of arak and sherbet and the talk turns to the shah's latest window smashing, the best bathhouse boys or the effects of French cologne on lovemaking when applied *just there*. Reza waits until the night is black enough and then walks to the Armenian whorehouse where the door opens just a crack and soldiers slide in and out, one after the next. He sits patiently in the hyatt with the other cadets, all with shined shoes and shellacked hair, to make polite conversation about the madam's tasty tea and the madam's salty nuts and the madam's lovely garden until the old lady blushes at their compliments and summons them to the back.

The hallway is an anticipation all its own. Reza has come to understand the city as sex and the bodies of these unclaimed women as his new landscapes: enigmas of flesh both powerful and barren. He slowly walks the eight-door distance between the hyatt and his bedroom and leans in without guile to spy at the rooms, peek after peek, and catch sight of the random pairs of men and women, in couplings at once animalistic and contrite, where the disheveled manflesh devours womanflesh that is already bored and resigned. Door after door he stands witness to the lure of the city and its sex: a system in constant equilibrium, the same parts give and take, deposits and withdrawals from the bank of secrets, ego, shame, pride, joy and crave. By the time Reza arrives at his own door he is eager for the exchange, eager to play the zero-sum game of fucking in rooms cavernous and dim where his soldier and shadow, cadet and orphan come to settle all accounts of fury and fear at their most naked, heavy and blank.

And so he delights in the whores, these sister orphans who meet and match him in this theater of desire and lies.

The girls are different each time and Reza proceeds like a well-trained actor, mechanical yet fluid, to perform each role in an order that arouses.

First the boy performs. He pushes them onto their backs to straddle them just above the stomach, where he grabs a breast in each hand and squeezes them like they belong to his milky maman, and shoves his stiff self between them again and again. After a series of strokes their faces reflect his own grimace and churn and the boy, the same baba's son who feigned his bravery, grows frightened and runs offstage to make room for the soldier, gallant and furious, who turns them roughly onto their stomachs and enters from behind with aggression. When the friction slacks the soldier exits left to make clear the stage for the infant, Reza as a fresh babe, the third and final act, where he inserts himself, sink after sink, into cunts connected to wombs, trying desperately to climb back into the tunnel from which he was long ago born. It is here he finally drains himself of the half truths and secrets he carries, unrepentant, through the streets of the soiled city; here he finds friction enough; here home; here fucked, jolly and erased.

But on this palimpsest a little must be writ.

Some nights he tells the girls he is a colonel of the first degree. Some nights, a lieutenant. Some nights, a battle-weary captain.

The girls, of various bodies and one face, sigh and nod.

Spent and eager to invent himself, Reza tells them he is the master of the new nation and Iran will stand determined and tall in the face of barbarians on the fringe. The heathen Lur. The black-skinned Baluchs. The tight-eyed Turkomans. The dirty Kurds. The women suck and hold and cover him in ways he believes in and he gives long speeches in honor of himself: Reza the Great, Reza the Inheritor, Reza the Conqueror, Reza definitely-not-the-bird-boy-orphan-Kurd. Definitely-not.

They clean their bellies and backs of the creamy leftovers and he walks the room gesturing with his hand like an orating king.

I am the new man of this new nation!

Yes, sarbaz, whatever you say.

I have no history, no family, and could be king. Loyal as I am to Iran!

Oh yes, sarbaz. Mmmhmm.

I have never been frightened or sad or needlessly ashamed. What greatness is beyond my reach?

The whores turn over in bed and give him extra time without charge. They know he is an orphan boy (the scent of unlove has always passed easily between the orphan and whore) and are generous with their ears and bodies.

Mmmhmm. Boshee, sarbaz. There is no greatness beyond your reach . . .

Wrapped tightly in this new skin, convinced of his creation, Reza returns to the teahouse to tell the men of the campaigns he's led and of his epic wile against the barbaric marauders, of how the fate of the whole new nation hangs from the thick thread of his heroism. He is a serious storyteller and takes the time to craft a new man, extravagant and heroic, from the assurance just conjured in the whorehouse bed.

The long beards of the teahouse clap for him and their prayer beads slap together like marbles. They pass their young son the ceramic pipe and rosewater sweets and are happy to have the oversexed nineteen-year-old in their midst. Reza smokes and smokes and sinks back into the deep cushions and lets the opium have him and, for the first time all night, lets his mind alone. An old man pulls a santir from a creaky wooden case and begins to play, and between Reza and the song there is no membrane. Its tune, intricate and lush, seeps into him and drips beyond all thought and all lies, beyond being itself; each singular note becomes a flagstone for Reza to follow on a path into memory opened by the smoke and sound.

He and his cousin are alone in a small forest at the foot of the Zagros. They are surrounded by all manner of life—butterflies, snakes, peacocks and foxes—but focus instead on a pile of bird bones and feathers. The two spend an afternoon assembling and reassembling the body of the bird. The santir plays. The grove is cool and quiet and they take their time, placing a bone here and a feather there to make wings, tail, little round ribs. They scour the forest floor for extra sticks and their bird grows until it is larger than intended and the boys must climb the first few branches of a tree to look down and admire their work. The santir plays. As they descend a flock of sparrows alights in the tree, hundreds of the little birds taking to branches and leaves with wind enough to scatter the body of the bird they just created, to upset the afternoon's art. The boys return home, laughing and joking on the walk, their fossil already a memory in their minds.

The santir plays. Up and around and out, the notes take Reza to places he has never seen, riversides and plateaus and mountain tops. He is with his cousin and then alone and sometimes with his dog. He is high with imagination and pleasure and reaches out for the pipe that is passed again. The old men, who have caught a second wind, are tricksters now who joke with the sleepy soldier.

Tell us, sarbaz, how thorny was it to capture a whole caravan of no-mads?

Did their women smell like their sheep? We are city men . . . we do not know . . . our women smell like flowers all the time . . . heh heh heh.

You're a bit young for a soldier . . . Did you single-handedly kill the khans or did your maman help?

Surely with all these glories soon you yourself will be more powerful than the shah?

Reza looks about. The santir is quiet and the room is noisy now with the laughter and coughs. In his delirium the walls are covered with enormous eyes, the faces of the old men are gone and all that is left in the room are eyes, wide and wet, that peer at him for answers. Whatever fresh self he created in the aftermath of fucking is sullied now and Reza panics as he thinks: When was he brave? Has he ever killed a khan or won a battle or done any act not instigated by fear? Is the army of the shah a powerful thing in fact? Powerful enough to give an orphan a pair of boots to kick in the face of a child and powerful enough to give an orphan a gun he can use to take the scream from an unmarried girl. *Yes,* he wants to say. *I have cried at the smell of sage and walked about craving that last suckle from my maman's teat, but yes, of course, I am powerful enough to be your king.* The opium swirls in his head, to mix the true and the false and to open the eyes of the old men until they are as white and sad as the moon. He stands and salutes them, just as he has been taught: with the sharp hand and the pop of the elbow. The room is silent now and all the eyes, pasted to the wall, faceless and enormous, blink back at him and cry.

It is dawn when he stumbles from the teahouse into the streets. He makes his way back to the filthy boardinghouse on Jamsheedi Street where the soldiers snore loudly in perfect rhythm. Reza paces the space between bunks until the walls stop shaking and the ceiling no longer spins and flips; only then can he sit at the edge of his bunk and begin to polish his boots, harshly and without break, until sunrise, when they shine back at him, a blinding black.

THE WILLING

*R**EZA PEJMAN KHOURDI?*
—

Be seated.
—

Have you found quarters?
Yes, Agha, on Abadaan Street.
It says here that you are most recently arrived from the division sta-
tioned in Saqqez?
Yes, Agha.
How old are you?
Nineteen. I am told.
Stationed at Nevabad barracks since the age of seven, it says.
Yes, Agha.
Where were you born?
In the Zagros, Agha, outside of Kermanshah. I think.
—

—

I will assume, then, that you are a properly trained and properly

loyal servant of the shahenshah, the most honored Reza Pahlavi, de-
spite your Kurdish origins?

Yes, Agha.

As a child did you ever fight on behalf of your tribe against the
shah or any of his divisions?

No, Agha. I was conscripted early on.

Are you aware that your own blood is responsible for our past weak-
ness?

Yes, Agha.

They are in fact the very brigands who irritate and resist our great
government in the name of heathen gods, those who pursue a felonious
notion of sovereignty. It is their insurgence that is a direct insult to the
respect and power your uniform affords you.

—

Are you repentant?

—

In his chair, the lieutenant swivels lazily in a hypnotizing
back-and-forth. They sit in a room of sharp edges: the sharp
edges of the desk; the edges of the map lining the wall, tan and
green, labeled IRAN; the edges of three gilt frames that surround
portraits of the shah, an angry man in each. Reza and the
lieutenant sit under the three gazes—six eyes of manifest
authority—that cut across the small room to overlap one another in a tight web in which the two subordinates are caught
and held.

I understand that you were among the most zealous in the Saqqez
campaign. Is this true?

I am in service to His Majesty.

And that they were Kurds, your own, of a tribe farther north, but still your own, yes?

—

How is it that a son can kill his own?

—

When they informed me of your prowess, degenerate and haphazard as it might have been, I was intrigued. How better, I thought, to pay repentances for your blood than with a lifelong commitment to a station in Kermanshah. Am I wrong to think this, Sarbaz Khourdi?

No, Agha, you are not wrong.

Am I wrong to think that you might have some delicate and steadfast abilities in combating your own people that could serve our purposes in the western region?

I am most willing in service to His Majesty.

Your time in Tehran is another nine months and then you shall be restationed to Kermanshah as a captain.

Yes, Agha.

That is all . . . eh, Khourdi, how are you finding our women in Tehran?

—

They are among the most sophisticated. French educated, uncovered, lovely, wouldn't you agree?

Yes, Agha.

Think to take one for a wife. She will make for a good partner for you in the west, an example to the women of the town. I hear the Kurdish girls have the heavy hands and feet of men. Is that true, Sarbaz?

Yes, Agha.

Very well. Your badges and long coat can be retrieved from the commissary post and the tailor.

Merci, Agha. Thank you very, very much.

The promotion leaves Reza in a fine mood and he walks, with the folio of order forms under his arm, the roundabout way to the bazaar, moving through the neighborhood where the French and English and rich Tehranis live. The streets are busy with early afternoon traffic and he lets his gaze wander from storefront to storefront as women with uncovered hair shop for Western clothes. He sits on a stone slab outside of a hosiery store and watches them move in and out of the glass doors. He has never thought of them before—his eyes always trained on the crack in the whorehouse door—never considered their species of woman: closed mouthed, wide eyed, stilted off the ground with heeled shoes, hair curled tight and stiff like a helmet. They are clean and cold, not familiar to his sense of desire, and he knows not how and what to want of them. Reza recognizes them as replicas of his new self: the modern woman to match his modern man, with similar uniforms of pressed wool and sharp lines, clean necks and faces held up to the sun. The captain's words come back to him. *Think to take one for a wife.* He leaves his seat in front of the hosiery store and makes his way to the tailor, who sews on his new captain badges and remarks:

Such a young man for such a high post—with a needle in his shoulder—*these days . . . where did you say you are from again? . . .*

A MATCHMAKER'S DAUGHTER

M AMAN SAYS THE soldiers are bad for business.
Bastard sons, all of them. Ack-toph.

She spits like they are dirty dog shit stuck to the bottom of her slipper.

Rotten inside through and through, with only their guns and high boots and belts to mask what they really are: dirty boys, stolen from filthy tribes without even a coin to their dead family's name. Ack-toph.

I let her go on.

Daughter of mine, do you want me to ruin our faultless reputation and mix them with the clean blood of our Tehrani girls, doktaher-eh-man? What rubbish the shah drags in for us to sweep up.

I let her talk, but I know better and I know more; that is our job: to know everything unknown and see all that is unseen. Abadaan Street is our street as it belonged to my maman bo-zorg and her maman before and will one day be the street my daughter knows. For such a long sure reign one must be gifted with sharp eyes and ears, for love hides in the tiniest crook and only talented matchmakers like us can dig it out. While my maman is in fact her mother's daughter and has the steady charm to run a house known for its successful unions, blood-lines run thick and thin through time and everyone knows that I can see more than she. Where she makes note only of the furtive glances, the scent of puberty and desire, I can see into the buildings, above the high hyatt walls, through chests and ribs, behind eyes and inside ears. To me all of Abadaan Street is exposed. And though she is a proud woman, Maman occasionally allows my insights, as they are fine for us and better for our future khanavadeh and fortune.

I see that the soldiers are good for business and I tell her quietly, as I peel cucumbers and salt their fresh flesh.

Ahh, Maman, this new Iran will be a mixed thing and soon all of the children will have blood in them from here and there and these soldiers have fortunes to spare.

Ack-toph.

She spits invisibly into the cauldron of green osh in front of her.

Mongrels. The girls of Abadaan Street have always wed the boys of Abadaan Street and this is how things have been because this is how we have made them. All the blood joined in good, clean matches.

She is a stubborn old maman and not until the day we saw the dead bookseller's daughters and made the season's most profitable match did she agree with me and stop spitting at the worth of soldier boys.

It was a regular day and my sense was set high as Maman and I went to stand on our upper veranda, to watch the street and chew on our salted pumpkin seeds. As usual I saw easily into everything beneath my gaze, behind all solid or secreted; a full view. I watched neighborhood women pull stools up to windowsills in preparation for something. They licked salt sweat off their lips, adjusted scarves around heads, massaged arthritic hands and waited as their girls gathered around them, giggling, pulling hair, anticipating for the sake of it. Men and boys loitered outside, on driveways in front of gates with cigarettes and stones. Ivy, bougainvillea and jasmine draped the weights of their flesh dully from the high marble walls blocking neighbor from neighbor, street from home. All comings and goings stopped and only used water, running down descending stone ditches on either side of the street, moved. Just before noon, just before prayer, before lunch and nap, Abadaan Street quivered deliriously in the gaseous heat of midday but was otherwise still. The residents stood at the ends of their properties, pulled like magnets of audacious curiosity: the attraction of positive to negative. Here a curtain swept aside to reveal a face or two; there a servant's eyeball pushed up against the hole in the concrete washroom wall; everywhere the child's toothless mouth gumming a peeling windowsill. But for the rivulets draining off to some unknown stream, the street came to pause, captive and eager, to watch the parade death made. They waited and did not complain, reassured that while all else goes into the wrought iron gates and high walls of the houses on Abadaan Street—love, deceit, comfort, beatings, caresses, disgust, devotion—only death comes out.

For a week now everyone has anticipated.

The young boys, who played on top of the cobblestones every afternoon with beaten-up balls or kites, knew first. Slowly fathers and old men heard the news at smoky teahouses, and before eating the cheese and honey at the evening's sofre, they told their wives, and the listening daughters heard: Iraj Ebadi, the old man down the street, is dead. *So what?* thought the daughters (for the lives of young girls existed only within the walls of the house and what lived and died on the street was irrelevant to them, insofar as it was not the neighbor boy they flirted with on the rooftop). *Interesting . . .* thought the mothers and grandmothers chewing on the news like the food in their mouths, wondering about the Ebadi widow. *Will I be next?* sighed the fathers and grandfathers as they thought of death's inescapability. *Pass it to me! Here! Here!* the boys shouted in the street, the information sliding over their slick careless youth like grease on a wheel.

Iraj Ebadi: the old man with the family, neighbor of many years with the limp and occasionally the cane; owner of the only bookstore that sold foreign books in Tehran's bazaar; a respectable bookseller (everyone assumed from the stiff felt hat he donned every morning and carried home each afternoon). The man with the wave and the smile, the man down the way, across the street, next door; the man with the light-eyed sons and fabled daughters, the oldest of whom attended school and harbored a beauty only whispered about. A man so rarely associated with calamity that even death made it impossible to fatten his gaunt, lifeless frame with suspicion or suspense. If nits were to be picked off the body of the corpse, as the residents of Abadaan Street were eager to do, the education of his oldest daughter at the Armenian school in the Christian sector would serve to raise a few scrutinizing brows. *Send a girl to school? With*

Armenians? For what? All their girls turn out to be whores, nah? But the daughter was young and without mark and left the house five days a week, escorted by her father or older brother, in a black chador that covered even the front of her face with thick, heavy gauze. Of course rumor (which cannot see more than a fraction of what I can, as it is speculation without charm) had it that she was beautiful as well.

All week long I stood on the balcony to look and listen to the curiosity of the women of Abadaan Street. For if what they say is true, and she is a beauty of rare sorts, then a bounty is to be made for Maman and I.

In the days after Iraj Ebadi's death and before his funeral I focused intently, looking in on breakfasts and naps and even the evening washings, when, with a slathered hand across a bony shoulder or a supple slippery haunch, mothers and older sisters probed their naked boys for more information from the street. *So how old is she? What color are her eyes? Is it true that she goes to school with the daughters of Armenians?* The boys, wet with bubbles that float off them, held back, pretending to know more than they did, and remembered the offhand words of Iraj Ebadi's sons, fourteen and twelve, who played football with them in the street. *She's got men calling already. We can't wait until she's gone, she doesn't do anything around the house, thinks she's too good. Baba spoils her.* The games would continue, the boys quickly forgetting the brotherly complaints. Only at home, with a piece of honey candy dangled in front of them by the fingers of their tired mothers and sisters, did they associate a value with the seemingly irrelevant information. *She's fifteen.* Eyes glazed. *She doesn't do any work.* Mouth watering. *Her eyes are blue.* Snatch. Unwrap. Suck. *Ywess* (mouth full). *Zzthey are bluuu.*

And so we gathered on the morning of the burial, not to wish old Iraj Ebadi a happy time in paradise, but for a clearer view: of the tragedy of death, the moving feast of sadness that belongs to someone else, and, of course, for a glimpse of that older daughter, the menace of beauty like a drop of liquid gossip to replenish the well of whispers long since dry.

For some time now I have kept an eye on the shah soldier who spends every afternoon on the rooftop of Agha Hajii's teashop. Many soldiers have come and gone from Agha Hajii, as he is a kind old man with a reputation for being generous with the smoke and the arak, but few are as sour as this young sarbaz, none so handsome or brooding. I have watched the street boys follow him in the afternoons when he makes his way to the agha's door. They like the look of him, stern and impenetrable. They like his long gun and high shined boots and tug on the straps and try to twirl the spurs and yell at him, *Eh, sarbaz! Let me play with your gun!* And even though he whisks them away with his hand and says, *Na na na,* there is always a smile curled under his lips. Otherwise the street ignores him as just another soldier, but I know better. I know more.

The afternoon of the burial I spotted him, six rooftops away, crouched over one of the round copper tables, drinking tea and cleaning out his fingernails with the blade of a knife. Today, like most days, he was in a foul mood, concentrating on the task at hand and impervious to the hushed activity of the street. I could even hear him mumble, *You can never leave the whorehouse clean, a little bit of the whore always comes with you . . .* , while below us the street began to buzz as the gates of Iraj Ebadi's house opened with loud metal cries. When the widow's scream rose from the end of the street he was digging deep at a stubborn clump beneath his thumbnail and the sound startled him. I watched him flinch, pierce himself and curse. *Mother of a dog!* Only then did he look up to see the circus of grief gathered below.

The wife of the dead bookseller pounded her chest with a rhythm the soldier found appealing. With each step she fired out a fist, retracted it and released a wail. The soldier moved to the edge of the balcony to watch, pulled to the procession like all the other residents of Abadaan Street and leaned his pelvis against the bar of the balcony to inadvertently rub himself on the metal banister. He could not resist the sensation that washed over him in a heady mix: curiosity, desire, calm, desire, arousal, desire, serenity, promise.

For what? I could not tell. It was not the coffin, not the pallbearers, not the widow, with her screeching sobs and one drum rhythm of grief (though her sharp blue eyes did call to something in him). Not the still street or the body covered in white cloth. The soldier pushed and pushed his pelvis up against the bar, arousing not so much a feeling but assuring himself that *something* was coming, entranced by the possibilities. I must admit I stared at him with some degree of excitement; for once I could not see everything happening in the human heart and had to watch and wait with the rest.

At the end of the formal procession, last to leave the gates of Iraj Ebadi's house, the girls emerged, covered but for their clasped hands. *Ah ha.* The soldier swayed his hips back and forth, never once losing contact with the bar. *Ah ha.*

A taller and a shorter. This much everyone expected. A young and an old. The veils, the same ones they wore to school, were not as much a surprise as a disappointment. Old women relied on the experience of age to gauge weight through the black draperies falling around round heads, across one set of sharp shoulders and one set of curved shoulders, down one chest formidable and round and the other still lean and girlish. On the street, the men left scrutiny aside and imagined the breasts beneath, the faces, the plump cheeks and red lips, so expertly had they spent their lives weaving their imaginations around and through the dark chadors.

And I saw that the soldier who knew nothing of Iraj Ebadi, his death or his daughters, wanted to take the taller girl for himself, swallow her like a black nugget of licorice and walk out into the empty western desert with a belly full of dead bookseller's daughter. *Why?* my maman asked, and I could not say until the girl reached the center of the street, pulled loose the chador off her head and glowed like a ground-bound star.

The scarf fell off her hair to her shoulders and for a moment the street froze. Quickly the youngest sister pulled it back up. Quickly she tugged it down and shook her hair out from its confines, pushing it away from her eyes, getting a clear view of a street she had never seen.

I looked to Agha Hajii's rooftop to find the soldier and in that moment it became as clear to me as the sky after the storm. I tugged on my maman's sleeve, and though she is normally reluctant to deal with my particulars, this time she listened carefully as I whispered.

See that soldier on the rooftop over there? The one who leans against the banister? When he was young, just a small Kurd boy, he loved his maman very much—she was once a girl with a basket of onions on her hip—and they spent many mornings together in her dead garden, he at her breast and she tangled in nightmares and dreams, sighs and songs. Now and again she would place him in between her legs and show him the center of her, the scar from which he was born, and the boy would touch it, and when he did a whole history would come over him, the history of pain as caused by strange men, his baba and even his own slick oblong body. The history of the land and of his people was buried in there too, the battles and losses and dry, empty spaces. All of these sensations flashed through his young head like a flood, a drowning, and the boy would pull his finger out, upset his own maman was so corrupted through and through. At night he goes to the Armenian whorehouses to clean himself off on the women and moves from whore to whore to stick a finger in here and there and probe for some sensation to calm him, to clear out the racket that plays in his head, so he can invent himself anew. And every night he pulls out annoyed as they are all finished girls, full of the same chaos of overuse and unlove that plagues his own orphan soul. Yes, yes, Maman, he is an orphan, more a son of the shah than anything else, but look, can you see him now? He is all craven bones and heart and head for this girl, Ebadi's oldest daughter, who won't cover herself at any cost, whose beauty promises the soldier some clean truth. A new start.

I see how weak he is with desire for her set family and good life and city blood and how desperately he wants to costume himself in her, in them, to pass himself off as the man he's invented and not the boy in which he was born.

You know as well as I do, Maman, that matchmaking is just as simple as balancing accounts. For her own reasons this girl is brave enough to take a life with a broken soldier and this soldier is broken enough to take a life with this brazen girl. Yes, yes, I know her loveliness blankets the street like fog and there will be other suitors, but he will be the best match. Trust me.

My maman nods as the girls pass beneath us. We gaze down at the dead man's oldest daughter as she, unsheathed, fair, defiant, illuminates the street.

How much will he pay us?

I tell her what I know. A soldier seeking out the privilege of a blank canvas, a place to make an original carve in a lifetime's shape of pain . . .

Any price you ask, Maman-joun, the sarbaz will pay any price.

A PROPOSAL

T HE MATCHMAKER AND her daughter specified: *You are to take Agha Hajii and his wife as if they were your parents, as if you belong to someone and are not some un-loved orphan that comes from nothing . . . your chances are better this way . . .* At first Reza turned away from the idea, embarrassed that the mother and daughter knew he was an orphan. But tonight, with the memory of the girl still fresh in his mind, he walks to the Ebadis' gate in the company of Agha Hajii, owner of the teahouse, and his one-eyed wife. He has filled their arms with gifts for the widow and his bride-to-be and the elderly couple walk weighed down like mules alongside the strong soldier. With little else to do the neighbors of Abadaan Street crane their necks to watch the theatrical trio make their way to the dead bookseller's door, where the gates open and close and leave nothing to be seen.

The introductions: men embracing men, discreet nods between women, the tedium of standing greetings that lead immediately to condolences—*God rest his soul. God rest his dear and departed soul*—prayers and calls to Allah and finally the seating. The divan has been cleaned of all character to serve as a flat

172

stage, where Reza is placed like a peg between his mother and father on a couch too small. In his boredom at the ceremony of passed fruit and nuts, he searches the room for any sign of her, a scent, a fallen unswept thread of hair, anything. From what was witnessed on the street, Reza has extrapolated much. She is fair skinned and petite with the wide-set eyes of a doe. Because that is all he knows for sure (and that was enough to make him seek out the matchmaker and her daughter, inquire into fees and percentages and agree to adopt these clumsy temporary parents) he has imagined much more. He envisions her laid out beneath him, flat and pure as a pail of milk that he alternately drinks and dirties. When he thinks of the sound of her voice he hears the soothing coo of a warbler or thrush and excites at the possibility of this new pet and thinks not at all of her mind, the self within the skin.

With renewed interest, he turns to the mandatory conversations between men—news of the world, news of the nation, news of the neighborhood, all of it returning back to death. The widow cries quietly and publicly. Agha Hajii's old woman pours tears forth too, madly, from her one eye, though she never met the dead bookseller and cannot read. Reza clears his throat to express regret and the muscles of his neck strain as he bows his head to shake it from side to side. *God show mercy on his soul. Abadaan Street's one true thinking man, and so young . . .* The air in the room grows dismal and he cannot bring himself to say the words the matchmaker, for her 15 percent, instructed him to say: *Khanoum Ebadi, I come with the best of intentions to ask your daughter's hand in marriage.* But it is not time yet and the youngest daughter is paraded out as if to distract him. The khanoum wipes her nose.

This is Haleh, the youngest. She is a good girl, not as smart as her sister. Meena can speak French. You know her baba, God bless his departed soul, was determined they both become "modern" Iranian women. But I said nah, nah, nah. One at a time. Who knows how long this modernity is going to last. Best be safe.

Reza nods once at the sister but does not see her. He looks around the room. They are all sitting on chairs, high off the floor. The table is stocked with sweets he has never seen, cream-filled dough and tiny colorful candies and small dark squares that have little smell. Their divan is crowded with color and light and Reza gets nervous and impatient as he waits for the tea ceremony (of which he was warned by the matchmaker and her daughter) where the oldest daughter, the bride in question, the hand he's after, will serve him from a silver tray.

And she does. With her head bowed and her hand shaking not at all, Meena leans before Agha Hajii with the tea and sugar and before his one-eyed wife with the tea and sugar and finally before Reza. She lowers herself slowly and tilts her head to face the tray, and in the space left by the taken demitasses, he clearly sees the reflection of her face. Reza reaches for the tea and lets his sleeve graze her hand. The reflection smiles and bites her lip. He reaches again for the sugar and brushes against the last finger of her hand. The reflection smiles and stays completely still. The banter is extinguished and the room feels empty. Her presence is not light, as he anticipated. An air of defiance emanates off the girl, some ungainly strength of self Reza had not expected. He senses the daring that lives deep within her and as the reflection smiles and lifts its head up and away, a challenge cuts out from her beauty like a knife. And though the matchmaker told the truth—her hair is straight and her eyes are blue and her virginity is everywhere evident—she is by no means a hollow body in which he can climb into and belong.

The girl unbends and Reza looks once more into the silver tray for the reflection and is instead blinded by a glint of light where her eyes just were. He clears his throat. It is too late; he cannot change his mind now. He has come this far, paid the matchmaker and sat upon this unwelcoming stage. He clears his throat.

Ahem.

The widow tightens the black shawl around her face.

Khanoum Ebadi, I come as a soldier of the shah to ask for your daughter's hand in marriage. I am well paid and soon to be promoted and I can provide for your daughter in the manner in which she is accustomed.

The widow looks down and nods.

And your offer?

Reza replies with an amount sufficient to keep the household running for nearly a year.

The widow comes to kiss Reza on the forehead, tears streaming down her face. Though not his own, he relaxes in the embrace of this maman, tight and soft, careful not to melt into it and disappear.

Inshallah, yours will be a fortunate marriage, my son. Inshallah.

Hands are shaken and doors are opened and closed, and Reza and the Hajiis make it only a few steps down the street before one-eyed old lady Hajii clutches him to her chest, which is sodden from the nonstop flow of her tears.

A blessed union for the two of you, my son! Ay Khoda! May your years be long and full of sons!

Reza pulls violently out of the hold and catches a look at her—the one eye full of tears and joy and wrinkled at the edges, the other dead, turbid and wandering—and for hours afterward he cannot shake the sight of fate itself, as it churned atop that age-old face.

MEENA GIRL

A S THE STREET told it, it was. My own baba, washed and powdered and shrouded, was carried before me on wooden slats. The midday heat was enough to cook a corpse and the hollow thud of Maman's chest rang out beneath the glare of Abadaan Street, a glare irreverent and wolfish, scavenging for some morsel of tittle-tattle to flavor their evening meal. And as always, I felt the uncanny eyes of the matchmaker's daughter rove easily and with pure instinct from one heart to the next, seeking out the match of dark to light, empty to full, living to dead, and land once on me—a virgin midstride, unveiled and radiant in the center of the street—and once on him: a soldier, a boy in the suit of the shah, long severed from family and blood and hungry for a new flesh to claim and plague with his handful of untidy secrets.

As it happened in our den, it was done. The soldier of no family and no origin approached my own maman with a tower of banknotes so high, a military certificate so new and a smile of such guile the old woman blushed behind her chador and then wept openly. A month later we were wed on a night made of hasty ceremonies: the candles and cloth held above our heads, the green sharbot taken into our mouths, the mirrors and prayers and even hastier celebrations: the scent of rosewater, cooked stews and lamps lit. My brothers took to the dombak and santir and the air filled with music and mixed with the laughter of girls and the incessant buzz of my sister's taunts in my ear.

You will have to open yourself up to him until you bleed; let's hope you don't break, sister of mine. You know Maman is happy to see you go, imagine how upset she will be when you are returned . . . It is such a shame Baba isn't here to protect you.

She points at the man I have just wed. He sits in a circle of men, shoeless, crossed-legged on a densely patterned rug. His face is blank as he raises and lets fall a cigarette from his lips. The other men laugh and pass around a bottle of Russian vodka that is tilted into tiny painted glasses as delicate as flowers. Their revelry is boisterous and inclusive but he does not change face, or position, or attitude, and the air around him is thick with a dark consternation. He is handsome. I say it to myself and I say it to my sister, who scowls and walks away.

The evening withers into deep night, empty of guest and music, and I burgeon with a curiosity far from fear. My hands are eager to divest the man of his uniform, his stiff cap, his spurs and boots. I cannot lie. I am hungry to touch the flesh beneath that will pour into and fill me, the flesh responsible for my escape from this nest of chattering woman talk and girl gossip; the flesh that will let grow in me the seed my own baba planted, the promise of what is possible: a life of books and schools to teach my boys and girls, roads for cars and parades for the shah, a watch for my wrist and my own modern country to be proud of in this modern world.

I am rushed to the room by a mass of screaming, happy women from my family. They sing and clap and spread me across the motaq carefully arranged on the floor, sheeted in white and clean. I burn through the center of my stomach as I hear the sound of spurs approach the door and then he is with me and the doors are closed and the women's high wails and clacking tongues are drowned out.

(In the hammam the old women explained to the little girls, to scare us:

You will take the hard part of him; the same part that dangles soft and small between your brother's little legs—they point to a little boy running through the tiled rooms—*will be solid and filled with seed and he will push it inside of you*—here the women open the opening between their legs and point to the pink just beyond the withered brown—*in and out, in and out, like to milk himself in you, and you will cry, that first time, and your blood will spread across the white sheet and then you are joined until you are dead in the ground.* At this the old women laughed and fell asleep like cats in the steam, and we were left to wonder if this was a threshold made of pleasure or pain.)

As it was on the first night, it has been since: a ghost empty-ing into a girl.

I lay still and watched as he undressed, slowly casting off everything but the green of his eyes (a color that reminded me of bottles, or the brooding waters of rivers that my baba would paint in his tiny masterpieces); without his uniform he was smaller, hairless like my brothers. I thought of my brothers' bodies, their flesh soft and generous from affection, their boy-hood figures growing into forms assured of love so far and love to come. The soldier who stood before me on that first night had no such marks; his body was empty of imprints, the stamps of embraces and caresses left behind by love. He was made of bone and skin sewn together by a thread of scars, long and un-wieldy, that looked older than the body over which they spread. Nothing of the robust soldier remained. His shoulders were broad but slim. His back, long and narrow, strained as if flattened by some steady weight. All over his body the skeleton poked out from beneath the skin as if it were hungry to show off more than the eye wanted to see.

Without clothes or glances in my direction he spread him-self next to me, flat on his back. He was hard in all senses. The breath, the flesh, even the air around him was encased in a brit-tle shell. As if stung with anticipation, everything inside me be-gan to flutter. I have always been a brave girl—my baba taught me to move forward without questions or fear—and on that first night I was brave with desire. I felt the space between my legs grow damp and yearned to touch myself, to grab hold of the excitement as it came, but kept quiet and still to see what offerings this new life had for me.

He said my name. *Meena.* Once, as if the word were a flavor he had never tasted before. He said the word again, this time with a sigh. I turned my body to him, to answer the call, and he caught me by the shoulders and pushed me back and in a sec-ond was on top, the way my sister does when we fight. He raised my nightshirt and took off the white French shorts beneath with a speed I did not understand and I was a thin stick underneath him, not a twig but a limber new branch, resilient and elastic. Careful not to imagine what came next, I closed my eyes, patient and curious and unafraid, certain whatever pain or force would be a small fee for my freedom. He was over me with his mouth and hands and I smiled to myself, and to him, in the dark, all the while imagining I was a princess from one of my baba's fairy-tale books, turning the golden knob of a door that leads far from Abadaan Street. I grabbed on to him as he pushed in and out of me, thinking all the while of the wonderful woman I would become.

But as it was on our first night, it will be.

A ghost emptying into a girl.

From the time our hips locked and he grew rigid inside me I was overwhelmed by the singular sensation, vacant and effortless, of a secret as it passed. There was little of the rip and fury the hammam women warned about, the shred and tear that would pull the girl from my skin to make room for the woman, mother and wife. He moved delicately, with a gentle touch, fluid and steady, in and out of me until I was tense with the delight, hopeful for the explosion that would break me out from the shell of this sequestered life.

But as it was on our first night, it will be.

A ghost emptying into a girl.

The soldier carried on slowly, almost sadly, his eyes fixed on mine, the gaze in them lost to a focus that had little to do with me. The slower he moved the more I craved violence, a shattering of sorts. I wanted to scream at him, like I scream at my sister when we fight. *Is that all you have? Is that it?* I wanted to pull from him the desire that will devour me. But he was lost to me, moving with an infuriating deliberateness until he finally stilled, pushed one last time and emptied the rise of semen, secrets and confessions long caught in the throat that spill in a moment of weakness or love.

He slept immediately, exhausted, from what I could not say. I climbed on him, my body still charged with expectation, and rocked atop his soft sex, traced a fingertip along the length of his clavicle and torso and moved my lips from nipple to nipple. *Shu-har* . . . I whispered, *husband of mine, where are you? Reza* . . . His thin body shook with erratic breaths and I rocked atop him more, my hands braced on his thin shoulders, my wet sex rubbing against his. He moved beneath me in tiny jerks and snaps and I could not stop my arousal, my determination or myself, and I rode atop his quivering unsuspecting body like I might one day ride a horse: to get from one place to another. The awareness of pleasure opened in me like a tempest and I collapsed atop him and kissed his sleeping face and beating heart and small sex. All over my husband's body I could smell the woman I'd become: a woman who recognizes that marriage is but a basket of desires, both handy and pathetic, from which you must pick what you want. As it was on our first night, it will be.

WHAT THE ORPHAN HOLDS

I T I S T H E first night, wedding night, and Reza sits with the
men. They feed him rich lamb stew and buttered rice and
French pastries filled with cream. Between bites they ask of
his battles and victories and he gladly tells them of the nation
emerging from the wilds and the bloody encounters with certain tribes—all of them necessary and obvious, of course—and
of the barren mountain landscapes they can be grateful they
have never seen. He goes on in exaggerated detail to distract
them from the real question that lurks about the room: *Soldier,
where are you from?* The men of the family are well deterred and
listen with jaws hung loose as the pipe is passed between them
around and around. The brothers joke with him and hold his
hand in theirs with affection for the soldier of dubious origin
who is family now, patron to their humble home. The old men
nod and smoke, cross and uncross legs and listen to the women
scream in the room down the hall as they sing and click tongues
and bless the bride.

Getting a bit anxious, eh, sarbaz?

The time comes and the men clear the room with claps on

the back, embraces and kisses to the mouth and cheek. In the emptiness, where he waits for the widow's summons, Reza wishes the room full again, with men and camaraderie and lies, and dreads this upcoming union. The widow comes for him and escorts him to a room where the girl is laid out on the mo-taq, perfect and still beneath an immaculate duvet. Her face is clean and her hair is uncovered and well combed. Her eyelids jitter with feigned sleep and Reza notices them flinch with each snap of his spurs. There is nothing of the whores' comely gaze or easy laugh. The wife is covered and clean and there is only a mattress on the floor and nothing else. Reza looks toward the one window for a breath of the cool night, to take in whatever random sounds the street has to offer—dogs, merchants' empty carts, the whistle of a lone walker—and for a moment he is composed. The girl opens her eyes and smiles at him. They are bluer in the dark, vivid and shining; under their sheen all he can do is undress.

What the orphan suffers: a life without love.

Love as it is in the nest of mother and father, where there is careful holding and crafting of the infant, toddler and child heart and great care is taken to ensure it is not dropped or dirt-ied or left aside accidentally as food for snakes and wolves. On those cast out, such love is easily lost.

What the orphan lives: a life where he must hold his own heart in one hand or two and there is no time to caress or cher-ish it as it slips and slides and all energy is spent just keeping it from falling through his fingers and onto a ground that may or may not belong to him. In his time Reza's own orphan heart grows full with lies, heavier and more slippery each day. Even each night he visits his unloved sisters in the whorehouse (where together, orphan and whore, they throw their un-kept hearts about the room in a friendly or viscous volley until exhausted and isolated, heartless and spent) but still has to leave the room with the bloody thing in his hand.

What the orphan craves: a place to put his heart, a way to love.

In the dark room where the girl lies on the bed, still beneath an immaculate lace duvet, Reza drops the red and drippy organ on the white sheet with a plop and a great gasp of relief as it stains through the fine-brushed cotton, layer after layer. Here, in the presence of this girl, product of family love, street love and nation love, is a place to put his heart, a place for him. To take, through marriage, all that does not belong to him and claim that legitimate life as his own. Under the gaze of the girl he cannot resist the promise of comfort, the thin body that re-sembles nothing of the blood and loneliness and chaos that spins through him day in and day out; the thin body that resembles nothing. He crawls on top of the nothing (ignoring the obvious fullness in the air, the air that is filled with the resolve of a dreamy girl walking into the world of women), presses himself into it and closes his eyes to worship and weaken in the face of such a docile emptiness.

What the orphan cannot help: a yearning to confess.

On that first night he comes to lose himself in her. Just as the semen leaks from him into her, so do his secrets. In words with-out sounds he tells her what he knows: that he is one of a kind, the dirty and the hidden, of rock and desert wind, the sullied blood of the shamed and unburied dead, an orphan, a Kurd. They are engaged in the hips, in the bodies and in sweat, and though he is certain she can't hear, he goes on to tell her that it is true, he has come to costume himself in her, in the Tehran flesh and shah love, to write his future history through her and the children of her womb, but really he is nothing but a boy who cannot stop looking for love. When it is done her face is blank, with a small turn at the edges of her lips. He is relieved and sleeps easily, exhausted and oblivious to the girl by his side.

He dreams of a journey. In the dream he is a boy again, ecstatic; he has finally learned how to fly from the rooftop and wants desperately to show his maman, demonstrate the sudden lightness of his body and the ease of his jump and the long soar before the landing. When he spots her, at a distance, she is perched atop a large rock. Her hair falls from her head all the way to the ground and is strung through with branches and grouse, small rabbits and flowers. *Maman!* He shouts and waves and tries to run but the earth between them is pocked with black abyss after black abyss. He walks it carefully; he is a boy again, agile and shoeless, who navigates the holes and darkness wondering all the while: what good is flight if this distance to maman cannot be drawn close?

OF SMOKE AND STEAM AND
WASH AND WIND

IT IS THE fourth and fifth week and in the house of the dead bookseller all goes unassumed and unspoken. Without request, servants wash his uniform and polish his shoes and leave them in the wooden armoire in his room. He takes his evening smoke on rugs of colored silk laid end to end across the hall. It is the third month of marriage and the whistle of the kettle rings high and sharp through the house to wake him. He walks automatically to the room of tile and water and removes the shorts and the cotton undershirt to sit here, on a short three-legged stool in the cold washroom, naked and alone, to smoke and wait for the new wife to attend her morning's chore.

She wears a loose skirt and a thin blouse and nothing covers her head as she proficiently shoulders a basin of hot water. A white cloth towel curves over her arm, stiff from yesterday's soap, and her eyes stare only at the floor, the faucet, and the pattern of blue and gray squares. Never at him. The only sound between them is the clap of her wooden bathhouse slippers as she maneuvers into and about the small, loud room. They snap judicially in Reza's ears.

Clack. Clack. Clack.

She squats somewhere about his knees and pours the hot water on his feet.

Clack. Clack. Clack.

She adjusts and adjusts around him to the side and the back, her hair a frizzy luminescent halo of black. Implicated by the incessant cannon-fire of her small feet, Reza looks away as she washes him inside and all over with scented water.

Through these ablutions Reza smokes and smokes. He cannot help but take pleasure in the steam that rises to meet the smoke and he sits subsumed in a gray cloud, folded in a nebulous blanket of delicate touch and particulate gas, and it is all he can do to stare away from her as she is unearthing him, sloughing off all the skin he has borne to cover and sheath himself, disarming an already naked man. She washes the nipples, the anus, the back, the stiff neck and the underarms with a generous soaping, and all of the places in between get a finger-full of lotion and oil.

Clack. Clack. Clack.

Reza closes his eyes and goes deaf to the gavel footsteps that march out their invisible accusation. He sits and smokes in his own dark and thinks of her face: the broad mouth, an expanse of cheek that spreads from here to there, the expression in her eyes that shines out every night in doughty confidence to let her new husband know:

You are my exit from this place.

And:

I am a determined girl.

He feels the cream she lathers on his face and listens for the high and tiny ring of the hair as it is shaved away by the edge of the blade. Every once in a while he can hear her strop the blade carelessly against her smooth forearm to clean it. They are fresh in a marriage less than three months old and the heels speak for them both.

Clack. As if to say: I know the Kurd in you. I care not.

Clack. As if to say: I cannot clean your sullied self. I care nothing for your silly sins.

Clack. This love is born of ambition, and I will keep your secrets insofar as I am allowed permissions both great and small.

With closed eyes Reza finds his lips with the cigarette, breathes the gray haze of smoke and steam and imagines the wife before, beneath and around him who washes and clacks and he knows he is naked and weak. And yet he sits to look at the back of his eyelids, where the black pandemonium shrinks and expands like a gas, like the great tides of tears that rise and fall with her every touch.

Before she takes out the towels he makes an attempt to engage his wife with a gentleness that does not come naturally to him. He smiles. He touches a finger to her chin. He thanks her with the flowery language that the madam at the whorehouse uses once the coins are in her hand, the kindest way he knows how. For her part, Meena adjusts and clacks and adjusts and clacks and keeps her eyes downward in a farce of obedience, uninterested in the face he cannot hide from her: the face that confesses, the face that begs. She washes and adjusts and clacks. She dries the limp hairy limbs and refuses him absolution or affection. She takes the empty basin and the wet cloth with today's skin and soap and leaves behind the new man, her husband, in the damp and smoke, to suffer the infliction of desire's clean ache.

It is the fourth month of marriage and little has changed. He still sits in their den with the brothers and uncles, tells stories and lies, and still comes to his wife, craven, morning, noon and night. She washes him, lies beneath as they fuck (when he can catch her smiling occasionally at some surreptitious thought), but still does not love. He has told all of his secrets and received nothing in return. Whatever softened in him in those first weeks now begins to harden. In the space left by want bitterness brews, and each night after their cold conjunctions (which are always silent and without friction and leave him craving the noisy whores that he seeks out whenever he can) he lies next to her, propped up on a bent elbow in the dark, and takes in her porcelain body, hinged elegantly at the limbs, as it rises and falls. He does not know how this came to be, this woman, himself, the empty night. He cannot remember the proposal, the polite asking, *Your daughter . . . I am a soldier for the shah . . . yes, ranked . . .* , and he cannot recall the motivations that drove him to knock on their lattice gate. Extended, here beside her body, Reza can only remember her as she was during the funeral march: unveiled and open, open to his possibilities for her. That afternoon she walked whole and he watched her, enviously, with his various halves. When the matchmaker came with her winking eye and whispering tongue he considered the union a type of purchase: one whole and true heart, head, belly and back for the price of his soldier suit, and Reza agreed, satisfied with the trade.

★   ★   ★

In the dark he can only just make out the fine features of her face and knows they are relaxed and washed over with the assuredness of mother's steady love and brother's steady love and even dead father's steady ghost love.

It is a beauty Reza dares not disturb, though it disturbs him to no end. He cannot sleep in its presence and so lies down and imagines doctoring her, opening the clean flesh encasement, prying apart the chest cavity and pulling out, one after another, the organs and slushy innards and gore-covered bones. To inspect and fondle them, as they are the proper parts of an Iranian and she is a pedigreed Tehrani girl. In his dreams he wears no gloves, licks his fingers often and throws the uninteresting bits out the window for the neighborhood dogs to fight over. Meena sleeps the sleep of the sanctified and Reza dreams and digs around to find the right chunks, lumps and wedges, the ones that will make him more right, more erect to the eye and true to the soul—the parts that he can sew into himself and so draw in the love he craves and she withholds.

It is the fifth month of marriage and spring winds blow through the city to arouse life incipient in branch, bud and bulb so that they all might bloom, reveal and run to rot. It is the fifth month of marriage and Reza sits in the bathing room, with the bloody dream still fresh in his head. He holds in his smoke and pinches his nose so as not to smell the stench of his wife's vomit, which has filled up the bathroom as of late. She cleans him and vomits and cleans and clacks and he objects not at all to the mess and stench, preoccupied instead with thoughts of the budding half of himself that grows inside her, unborn and already ill at ease.

THE DEAD BOOKSELLER'S
SECOND SON

H E CANNOT READ.
I know because our house is full with books and I have watched him walk from room to room touching their spines with an empty look. Never once has he pulled one from the shelves, never once has he turned their pages. He doesn't tell anyone and nods yes yes yes when we are discussing the latest translations. He doesn't make mention and so neither do I, but if Baba knew that Meena married an unreading man he would smack his cane about in his grave loud enough to disturb the dead. Baba told us that only idiots can't read, and that is why we are all reading people—me, Meena, Maman, Shireen, Arash and Kashiar—so that we will not be idiots. I am only ten and I have already read a library full. Science books, mostly.

Because I do not want my new brother to be an idiot I have asked him to meet me every afternoon, in secret, to teach him how letters make words and words make stories and stories make smarts. He sits beside me, smokes and looks out the window and never at the book, unless there are pictures, like in the Shahnameh or the book of Hafez. Even then he looks down with just his eyes, careful not to turn his head. He is a difficult student.

I am a determined teacher and I bring him more books with pictures, science books, since I am a science boy: the planets, the oceans, the weather, the animals, the human body, everything that lives and moves. When we start the British encyclopedia of animals he stops smoking and stares without distractions at the photographs of giraffes, zebras, snakes and rabbits. I read for him. *The Himalayan Gazelle. Move in male-led herds. Distinguished by a large hump between the shoulder blades, a black stripe down the middle of the belly and lyre-shaped horns. The females have black skin, though white fur surrounds the teats of the udder. This is helpful for the young to locate the source of milk. Herbivores.* He sits beside me as still as a good schoolboy.

Now we make good progress; though I do all the reading, he is interested every day and every day we meet in the hyatt after nahar when the rest of the house is napping, and every day he is less of an idiot (and I am doing a great service to the family, and Meena especially, because she has little patience, especially for the stupid). Every day he asks me to start with the hawk. It is his favorite. *The Levant Sparrowhawk. Kingdom: animalia.* To tease him I take my time getting to the part he likes best. *Phylum: Cordata. Class: Aves. Their flight is distinguished by "flap-flap-glide" movements. Females are smaller with reddish undersides. The sparrowhawk reaches sexual maturity at three years of age.* Here he folds his hands and closes his eyes. *Their ritual mating techniques consist of high-flying circles between male and female. The ornate flying patterns and caws draw the two closer and closer until they collide, midair, and conjoin to spiral downward in a locked free fall during*

which the male inseminates the female, the two splitting apart just
before a sure death crash in the sharp treetops. Here, my new brother
listens without inhale or exhale. I try to imagine what he is
imagining.

MEENA WIFE

IN THE HAMMAM they whisper.

Look! She is rounding now. Beabeen! You can see it already.

Na, na. It's too early. That's just the newlywed cushioning, though now that you mention it . . .

On our own street! And now in our clean hammam? A bastard grows in that girl. I don't know how you two can stand the sight of her.

They are indelicate women, yet they whisper anyway. And because the walls are marble and the floors are tile and the ceilings are covered with stained and thick glass, each murmur, however slight and offhand, explodes like a smack, loud enough for the whole bathhouse to hear, myself most included.

Her baba must be turning in his grave. Such a good man, an educated man, and now grandfather to a half Kurd! Imagine!

I cannot see them through the steam but I know their faces well enough. In the white light I can just make out their eyebrows as they curl disapprovingly in the mist.

The hags continue on, throwing a breast over a shoulder and washing the sweat-stained skin beneath and running their hands through their mud- and dye-soaked hair. The water streaks along their stomachs and shins and down the drain in rainbows of gold, burgundy and black. I watch the outline of their limbs as they wash the soles of their feet and reach down in between their thighs. Through the loud chambers of the hammam sighs echo all around in a hushed and desperate chorus of whispers.

They are old women, naked and heavy, but they are not wrong. The child grows inside me, half the blood of this old street and old city, half the blood of my husband, scion of stones and mountains that God himself forgot. A new babe for this new Iran. I am determined not to allow them the righteousness of their judgment and walk toward their octagonal inlet, my bath shoes clapping heavily against the tiles, just as they do when I give Reza his morning wash.

Excuse me, khanoums . . . do you have a bit of soap? I've left all of mine at home.

With mouths shut and eyes wide open they fumble and I stand before them, my body exposed and smooth-lined and not yet trespassed by baby after baby and so: perfect. They look through their bath baskets and buckets for the soap and I gently rub a hand across my breasts, across my rounding belly, and sigh for dramatic effect.

These shah soldiers, khanoums, let me tell you, enough energy to tire any girl . . . but such pleasure. Some nights I can barely see anything but desire in the dark . . . their bodies are made for the love union.

The search for the soap stops and now they stare at me, three faces of worn wonder.

Well, no one suffered too much love. The gifts are nice (I lie) *and his monthly check is enough to take care of Maman and the boys for a year* (I lie) *and after his posting to Kermanshah we will have a house with*

French chandeliers in every room and two cars with drivers and a khol-
fat to do all the cooking. I can't really complain about a few exhausting
nights, now can I?

A sliver of soap lands at my feet. I bend down to pick it up, slowly, to give them a long look at my smooth, unburdened back.

Yes, pregnancy is a difficult thing, as you know, but alas, for our new
Iran a woman must make her sacrifices—so she is not forgotten like the
women of the old time who just disappeared into history, like your own
mamans, I imagine . . . I have even heard of city girls mixing their
blood with the old tribes for the sake of the country, so that all the blood
may one day bleed together harmoniously and we can be as great as
France or England. It is for sure those women will keep a place in his-
tory for themselves.

I clap the soap between my hands.

Merci, khanoums, for the soap. I will return what's left.

I walk to the arched entryway and throw a toothy smile over my shoulder. Behind me the women sit in shock, naked, heavy and long unloved, and smile back at me, for they may be meddlesome and mean in their afternoon gossip, but they are not wrong.

I take my sliver of soap to the hammam maid, who lays my body down across the warm marble slab and takes to it with her coarse burlap gloves, rough like a mother of many. Under her touch I can feel the babe in me move, make its way around my belly, avoiding her harsh hands. The bathhouse women are quiet, tired, maybe gone to their homes and hot kitchens to wash the greens, brew the tea and bustle about in their scrubbed skin, calm and convinced of my curse.

A SUCCULENT WRIST

THE MANDARIN SUMMONS applies only to soldiers recently married, and so Reza goes to the central barracks to receive a certificate valid in any of the small shops on Jomhuri Street, where international fashions for women are sold. The shined glass windows display hangers of suits and lines of shoes. In the same proud and precise manner with which he dresses himself he selects for his wife what he thinks she will like. A pair of laceless black shoes of shined leather with heels that push up from the ground. Two dresses: one of cotton with a delicate pattern of bunched flowers, and another a suit, like his own, of dark olive gabardine, thick wool, both cuffed at the elbow and hemmed at the knee. He knows the handsome costumes will please her; they always do.

The wrists are a great show these days, eh, sarbaz?

From behind the wooden counter a sparsely toothed shopkeeper grins at Reza.

Some talk of the ankles and others of the calf and the knees, but I myself, I am a man of the tasty wrists. Heh, heh, heh.

Reza picks a white hat with a wide stiff brim and gloves to

match and walks back to Abadaan Street with smells of France and Germany and Italy under his arm. The weather is warm and he smokes one cigarette after another until he and the clothes reek of tobacco.

The dead bookseller's widow stands all day long at the door. When she sees the packages she holds her dirty white handkerchief to her lips and wails.

Khodahr-eh-shokr, Meena! Daughter of mine, you are the most fortunate.

What generosity from your husband, what beautiful fabrics!

European! Modern!

Ay Khoda, what can we do to thank such a man?

He pretends not to watch Meena as she lifts the fine fabrics to her nose.

They smell like smoke.

She chides. He sees her face flush pink. She unwraps and lifts and lingers about the cut shapes before gathering the dresses and their tissue-paper wrapping in her arms to stand before him, a girl clutching the woman to her chest. She curtsies briefly and runs from the room, the awkward bundle slowing her escape.

They are regulars in the Noruz procession: a soldier and his wife indistinguishable from the others. Here their union works best. She is tautly uniformed in the short-sleeved suit and gloves and squared heels, and he is beside her with buttons affixed and gleaming, epaulets straight across the shoulders and a collar that cinches tightly about his ever-stiffening neck. They are striking and strict and forward looking: the captain and the wife of the captain. At the behest of the lieutenant they ride in the open-air automobile that leads the cavalcade to the Meiydan of the Marble Throne, where the shah gives his annual New Year's speech. Behind them march lines of cadets, followed by the slow-rolling tanks and then by horses and finally by boys who shout and cheer at the passing and the passed. The narrow streets and new avenues are full of people celebrating spring, indifferent to the blandishments of nation and king. Vendors sell roasted nuts and tea from tall and cumbersome samovars; burnt and salted corn; prayer beads; sweets and wooden toys cloyed by children whose parents watch the procession with the same intrigue they allot a passing storm.

The Meiydan is square and perfectly manicured. Clean water washes through fountains of cut and gilded marble and everywhere green grass grows. In the bright white light of spring the assembly makes its formation: cadets in standing lines; tanks surrounding, on display; officers seated with their wives in the first rows of wooden chairs. There is a small orchestra of European instruments just below the lip of a stage that holds politicians from the new Majlis, foreign statesmen and an enormous marble chair, ill fit for any human or giant, of a size compatible for an imaginary king alone. The shah sits on the chair in a brocaded sash, a jewel-encrusted crown and a moustache that covers the entirety of his mouth.

Eh, Khourdi—

A voice sounds from behind where he stands and Reza remembers a pug-faced boy from the Nevabad barracks; a city boy; a loud-laugher; an arrogant cadet. Reza turns to find him, nameless and familiar, in a suit exactly like Reza's, with a wife on his arm. The woman wears a thin cotton dress and greasy paint is smeared far outside the lines of her lips and eyes. She peers at Reza with a squint. He cannot decide if she is meek or monstrous.

Khourdi! So long since Saqqez!

Reza nods and stands tall in his stiff suit.

Still the serious Kurd, eh?

The city cadet laughs and takes Reza's hand to kiss him once on each cheek in the manner of friends.

They made you a captain, I hear? Complete with a transfer to Kermanshah. Bah, bah, bah. Very nice.

Reza nods and takes his wife by the arm. She is not listening, Reza is convinced. She is warm and round with child and hoisted on heels and she cannot hear. The soldier talks on and on about their cadet days, his *Kurdish habits,* and for the first time in Tehran Reza must listen to his secrets spoken aloud. He looks at his wife and thinks: *She is round and warm and full with child and cannot hear. I am a proper man who paid for her proper marriage and we are well with child. The sun rises and sets on Tehran and her and the baby within and she cannot hear. She is warm and well and full with child and knows nothing and cannot hear that I have been a dirty Kurd, an abandoned orphan and an imposter in this very moment and for all the moments until she is dead. No. She cannot hear. It is warm and she is well with a child of mixed blood that she will come to consider a stain, but today she is warm and happy in her international suit and hat and claps and does not one bit care.*

Remembering not to remember, as it was another lifetime ago and as shame is a thing to stuff into a corner or a small box or a lantern that needs to be lit, Reza takes Meena's arm to walk away from the soldier and the wife with her skewed smile, garish and ignoble. The city boy shouts to Reza's back.

It is a rare move, no? To put you back so close to the nest? A rare move, don't you think?

Though the spring air is cool and the mulberries bloom pleasant and juicy, blackness spreads through Reza like spilled ink. He loses vision of the neat garden plots around him and holds his hat in a clutched grasp. He escorts his wife to a chair, where she sits, round in the belly and straight through the spine, and squints up at him from beneath the white rim of her new hat. He cannot see her because she has disappeared into the blackness, as the time before has come up to meet the time now and the time to come in a suffocating triangulation of fate.

The band begins to play a lopsided, brash tune. Now Reza recognizes himself as he is seen: a demon made; responsible and held aloft by rank and pay, woman and stature. He sits beside the rounding girl, who is satisfied in her high dress and enraptured by the shah's speech and clapping: a wife of the new state, brazen and, to her mind, free. She claps and claps and claps. In the instant he cannot fathom the Farsi spoken by the shah, cannot clap when they all clap and does not jolt as the rifle shots slap the air. He works to restrain a sudden and exuberant violence—an urge to kick a boy in the face, smack used girls in damp rooms, grasp the snarling city soldier by the hair until the bloodline stretches across his gallant forehead. He reaches for Meena's hand, which she gives to him once the clapping is done, and Reza holds it and keeps shut his eyes and ears to everything but the birds that perch in the trees above, joyfully chirping their songs of spring.

Book IV

KERMANSHAH, IRAN—1940 TO 1969

THE BAROMETER

L AND SPREADS OUT in all directions, scorched and cratered and held back by the plate-glass windows of the train. The heat, however, pervades, and for the first days Reza takes the window seat to suck from a vein of air that blows in through a slim opening. The cabin is full and quiet. An infantry of soldiers takes up most of the seats, their faces blank, their hands busy fanning themselves with caps and newspapers. They nod courteously to the captain when they pass his seat. In the front of the car a statesman from the Majlis converses with a trio of dour-faced Europeans whose crisp white chins and cheeks are beaded in sweat. In the back corner an old woman holds a wire cage filled with parakeets on her lap. The birds, restless, move about in silence, threads strung tight through their brittle beaks. For days this is how they move and Reza sits quietly next to his wife, who knits without abate, the clink of the metal needles in counter-rhythm to the snap of the wheels on the tracks. The sound aggravates him but the train ride is even and the scenery flat and unassuming, and so he remains calm as the soldiers smoke, the

Europeans sweat and the parakeets flit and dart against the smooth motion of the train.

In time the earth changes shape and shade. Cimarron and orange ground, deep blue and violet skies give way to a constant, monochromatic gray. They travel over an expanse of colorless boulders held down by an undifferentiated sky. No gradations separate night from day and no villages show human life. The air chills and creeps through Reza and he moves Meena to the window seat, where she then shivers and knits. He cannot bring himself to look at the new land that passes outside the window; the very sight of it makes him nervous and he takes to his corner to nurse the sudden disquiet that oscillates through him as if he were a barometer, an elevated sphere of soul, so sensitive to shifts in atmosphere and panorama that what forces were once stable and primary in Reza (his suit, his boots, the title of his rank) fall now, volatile and subordinate, and he can't remember for what reasons he took the train in the first place.

Meena adds another line to the blanket and changes hands, lost in her own thoughts. The needles click happily, out of syncopation with the click of the train on the tracks below. Rocked by this new nausea, Reza grows aggravated at the disjointed sound and slaps the insidious metal wands, and the small blue blanket they birth, from his wife's hands. Oblivious to such outbursts Meena hoists her girth, now formidable and awkward, out of the compartment and leaves Reza alone to sit, shiver and smoke.

Days pass and the conductor stands on the last step of the boxcar and yells.

Bistoun!

Mashhad!

Shiraz!

The train empties and moves on, empties and moves on. The sky pushes down in fists and folds of clouds and the earth reaches high in hillocks and mounts to meet it until just the narrow black band of the train separates earth from heaven, paradise from the dead. Reza feels the pressure from above and below as distinctly as a dreamer feels held up and down by the floors and ceiling of sleep.

Kermanshah!

The captain and his wife are the only ones who disembark. The platform smells of new wood and the train falls silent beside them as they await the military consort that will take them to their new house.

KERMANSHAH. The sign swings in the wind.

Ker-man-shah, Meena reads aloud.

The rain starts, gentle at first, then steady, then adamant and hard. The vista of the town, the mountains, their new home, is dimmed by pendulous drops that fall rapidly around the captain and his wife. After some minutes two cars and a large camion arrive and soldiers, cadets, sergeants—high and low ranks alike stationed to await his arrival and build his house and prepare the city for his imminent command—spill out to pay respect to their captain, who is wet and getting wetter. Reza points his crop in the direction of their luggage and uses all his energy to order the loading of all trunks and supplies as the rain falls, downward on the captain's hat and hands, downward on his wife's globe stomach, down on their valises and everywhere. They ride in the car: Reza, his wife, the driver and the unborn child. They see nothing of the land through windows obscured with steam. The driver, a young lieutenant, focuses his eyes on the rearview mirror and addresses his captain.

Agha Captain, I trust your train journey went well.

Yes.

And that the khanoum was comfortable?

Yes.

I am sure they informed you in Tehran that we are dealing with the reverberations of the Kurd revolt and uprising of Kurds in Mahabad.

Yes, I am informed.

To have a state of their own, can you believe it, Agha Captain? They are but Kurds; what would they do with a nation?

—

These are interesting times, Agha Captain, very interesting . . . I am told you are to be responsible for the introduction of schools and programs and technology?

Yes, those are some of my assignments.

We are glad to have you. We are a small division but we will do for you what we can.

Merci, sarhang.

They drive through the rainy town, a tangle of twenty or thirty streets woven together with stones and old brick, and Reza wipes the steam from the window with his sleeve. The roads are made of dirt that is now mud and everywhere animals are tied to posts, women stoke fires with long flat pieces of tin and boys flap about, their heavy pant legs muddy and wet. They are dirty, these Kurds, and Reza makes no association between himself—the shine of his boots and the gleam of his belt—and these unfortunates who cannot even find shelter in the rain. The barometer evens out as he cannot recognize the land, the town or the people and he is glad to dismiss them, to feel no love in the face of their familiar faces, and tells the lieutenant the streets must be paved, at once.

When they reach the house the rain has stopped.

There is a kitchen with clay floors and a porcelain sink whose faucets only run cold. There is a divan and one electric light. Two rooms for sleeping, one with a door and one without. A veranda wraps around the house on all sides and an outhouse stands in the back. Reza's house is made of concrete blocks and raised off the ground by concrete blocks and reached by five steps. The rain has turned all the builder's dust and unmixed concrete powder to an ashen mud, and Reza leads Meena from the car by the crook of her elbow and watches her shoes sully quickly with the gray paste. She shields her eyes from the mist, as if dryness would afford her a better view of the bare house, the empty shed, the half-finished stable, the mountains and sagebrush. Meena turns to him after a quick moment, her eyes wide and watery with offense.

Where is the glass for the windows? Why is there no marble on the floor?

Reza leaves her and her remarks and what are soon to be tears of disbelief on the veranda and walks about with his crop, shouting to the men to place their things here and there. The men's boots echo loudly on the dusty wood floors of the hollow home. He commands and orders and Meena paces the wet veranda with her hands on her head. When the men are done they stand before him to shake hands and welcome him with the cheek kisses more customary to father and son than captain and cadet. They congratulate their captain on his new home and apologize that it is not yet complete—*The supplies were late in coming* and *Soon we will be finished*—and then they leave. Their camion splashes off with the car behind it and Meena follows, dazed and indomitable. Reza watches her pregnant shape stumble pointlessly in the mud of the road that leads back to the train station. Not once does she look back to his calls, not once does she respond, and moves steadily away, like a pilgrim unconvinced of her new home.

After the rain, the mountain air turns dry and brisk. Reza sits on the step and smokes a sodden cigarette and stares at the bend where Meena disappeared. After a time the clouds crack and indigo light pours through, sunless and clean, to illuminate the slate peaks around him, one after another, until he is sitting in the center of their steel glow. They are the same Zagros of his youth, the hiding place of his barracks, the peaks that shadowed over Saqqez; the spine of the Kurds. After the months in Tehran, a congested time made of doors and hallways and high tiny windows, Reza has forgotten how a horizon could be so consumed by such stone majesty, forgotten the manner in which these rocks, risen and ageless and labyrinthine, easily own the souls of all the men and children, birds and beasts that move before them.

Reza smokes and thinks: if the rocks own all that is around, what then does he own?

He sits up straight to take stock of what he, Agha Captain, can claim.

There is the house, which does not belong to him but to his

rank and his ability to do deeds both unwholesome and mind-less. The trunks that are strewn about belong to his wife and his wife's family. Not the ground, not the cement on it, not the cigarettes or his wet matches. Not his name or the money in his wallet. Even the clothes on his back and the boots on his feet are assigned by the shah and not for his purchase or keep.

He is a man of nineteen or twenty or twenty-one, with a slim build. A man returned. A man without.

He would like to claim Meena, and most especially the child in her belly, but they are gone. After his last cigarette Reza stands and spits out the bits of tobacco in his mouth and approaches the mud road, to set out and find his wife and hold something to him that will stay, if not in spirit at least in flesh. After a few steps in the direction of the mountains he stops. Their enor-mity presses forward to taunt him, to stop him. The endeavor is too much and he turns and walks back to his perch on the ve-randa, tired from the short effort and the heavy concern. He leans against the trunks and cases and night sets in, dark but for a half moon whose light outlines the highest peaks in bold traces of silver and white like heaven's own fence.

The throttle of the camion wakes him and before Reza re-members where he is, the engine stops and the air fills with the sound of laughter. For a moment Reza smiles too, mistaking it for a happy dream he might have had. He clears the sleep from his eyes to watch as the lieutenant, a tall man with clean boots, jumps out to open the door and offer his arm to Meena. The are joking and still laughing and she holds the crook of his elbow with two hands as the mud churns beneath her feet. The lieu-tenant calls to Reza, slumped against the luggage on the porch.

Look what I found for you, Agha Captain! A pretty Tehrani girl. How did you manage to lose a gem like this?

Meena looks down and says nothing as the lieutenant speaks.

She was on the road into town, by herself, and I took her in for tea and some warming up in the barracks. You shouldn't let this one out of your sight. The mountains are too high for a lady like this.

On the steps she releases the lieutenant's arm and thanks him with a shy smile Reza has never seen. She walks past him, into the house, where he can hear her heels thud and the sound of a faucet. Without a glance up at him, Reza thanks the soldier.

You are a lucky man to have such a lovely wife. What I would give for a Tehrani woman in this place . . . the women here are bitter and already old at fifteen. But what can you do? This is our sacrifice to the shah, mageh-nah?

The lieutenant stands a moment too long before leaving the porch and walking back to the camion, which he starts with a noisy acceleration. When he is gone the night quiets again and Meena comes out to the veranda and stands beside him, her shoes dripping, wet and clean. Reza notices her face is wet too, moist and flush from the walking and crying. Whatever astonishment and anger she carried from the train station is gone and the softness is entirely sad.

Our house, you promised . . . the chandeliers and marble . . .

She shakes her head and walks into the house, leaving him on the veranda, where he cannot find reason or energy to follow after her, the landscape around him so incapacitating, so calming. Reza digs his hands deep into his pockets, slides closer to the cement of the floor and closes his eyes for an easy sleep.

★   ★   ★

They come when it is darkest, in the nadir of the night. From land and sky, branch and burrow, to watch the flesh in slumber. The host of truth tellers gathers: the owl and javelina, the silent basilisk and lurking coyote, the living and the dead, sent forth by the land herself to carefully circle the sleeping form and keep their gaze fixed with their black-eyed, blue-eyed, red-eyed stares. He is not their captain or cadet or incapable husband, but a long-lost son, and they come to gently welcome their boy back.

GLASSES FOR THE GLARE

H E   W E A R S   T H E glasses all the time, so much, in fact, that the cadets and officers at the barracks mimic their new captain's shaded look, thinking it the most recent trend from Tehran. For the first month the military office in Kermanshah is filled with soldiers in sunglasses, even on the cloudy late summer days, bumping into desks, each other and the occasional old man, each in his individual dark.

Reza does not explain himself and keeps busy with paperwork and patrols of Kermanshah and the surrounding lands. No one questions the young captain's ways as he walks through the streets and alleys ordering the instant removal of posters that claim KURDISH INDEPENDENCE! and A CALL FOR UNITY! and JOIN TO SUPPORT THE REPUBLIC OF MAHABAD! A HOME FOR THE KURDS OF IRAN! Now and again he will tear the poster off himself, with the tip of his rifle or even his hands, in such a controlled fury that all the Kurds and cadets watching quickly understand how a man so young came to hold such an important post. They follow him without further question and his first days and weeks are flamboyant ones, everyone certain a worthy flame burns behind those dark glasses.

The cadets and officers are happy to oblige Reza and drive him from house to house, farm to farm, where he stands in the doorways and at the edges of fences and claps his hands once or twice and calls for the men. The Kurd men come and stand without fear at the instant interrogation. They answer all his questions (*Have you made contact with Barzani's men? Do you have weapons? How many sons do you have?*) with shakes (*No, no, none*) of their head and the captain believes none of it. He orders the houses searched, the animals let out of pens and sheds, the women and daughters disturbed in the kitchens. The captain makes a great show of his disgust at their meager homes and smelly flocks, and the cadets, who toss about hay and rugs and grain and chickens and small children in search of guns, hold their noses alongside. The scene of guns and boots and unnecessary humiliation follow the captain wherever he goes and the word spreads among the Kurds, who begin to dread the rumble of motor engines and the sound of his shout.

In the barracks his popularity grows as he encourages the men to smoke and sit through the hot afternoons, telling them stories of his time as a cadet, his first gun, the now infamous battle for Saqqez and how beautiful the shah's wife is up close. *Sarbaze, you will not believe the loveliness, so delicate, just the opposite of all these rocks. She alone is a force worth fighting for.* Though he is only their captain they are just as easily his sons, and they sit and stare at their handsome commander only to see rounded versions of themselves reflected in his black lenses. In the evenings they take him to the whorehouse, where each disappears as rank declares, the higher the post the prettier the whore, and reconvene to smoke and drink in the green hyatt thick with the scents of hibiscus and jasmine. In the first days and weeks the captain is a quick fit and begins to walk the town alone in the evenings, relaxed and without weaponry, like a man of leisure, to stop in the bazaar stalls and sample the tea and nuts, pet the sleeping cat and lose himself in the afternoon street games with neighborhood boys. So tranquil is the captain that the mothers, aunts, cousins and old men of Kermanshah come forth cautiously to watch the young man with the familiar face, the new man who seems old to them, play like a child at silly games. It is here, under the bright glare of their curiosity and recognition, that Reza finds the dark glasses most useful.

THE WAY THE FRENCH DO IT

H E CANNOT LOOK and he cannot turn away.
For hours now the house has rung with screams. Reza
stands back, unaffected by their pierce, to watch Meena uncoil
into a beast before him. Uninterested in his fixation, the midwife moves briskly about the room with pails and damp rags,
bumping into Reza as if he were the bed or nightstand. For his
part he takes no notice of the woman, a short Kurd who yelled
and cursed at him as he ordered the soldiers to take her from
her home. In the truck she sat between him and the driver soldier and muttered to herself the whole time. When they arrived at the house the midwife spat on the ground and kept up
her angry rants as Reza escorted her to the bedroom, where
Meena lay covered in sweat and bleeding, and the old woman
took a quick look, quieted completely and busied herself with
the task at hand.

He cannot look and he cannot turn away.

Hours have passed and the blood has stopped leaking. Meena
sleeps and wakes to grab and curse at the midwife because she
is an *idiot Kurd* and at Reza for *bringing her to these forsaken*

mountains, only to fall back again into tormented sleep. Reza keeps his distance and stands in the far corner of the room, where he is unavailable for the grabbing and screaming and has a perfectly clear view of the wound, the opening he has penetrated—flesh gates that lead into the dark tunnel he has wanted so badly to enter and the babe wants so badly exit—now spread out before him, pulsing slightly in pain as if taking in and letting out tiny breaths.

When the time nears Meena lets out one long howl, half shout, half screech, and Reza no longer recognizes the place between her legs—it has pushed out so much liquid and blood and now the top of a head; the midwife takes her at the neck and back and lifts her out of the bed and motions that she should stand and then squat. The old woman does this with a gentleness Reza finds surprising and Meena resists, thrashing her arms about this way and that, and growls at the woman in Farsi.

In Tehran they deliver on their backs! That is how the French and the British do it! I want to deliver on my back, not squatting like a filthy animal.

The midwife cannot understand the language and smoothes down Meena's hair and tries to rub her shoulders and temples. She stands in front of Meena and squats herself, showing her the way to bend the legs, stick out the back and force the child out in a manner that reminds Reza of shitting. Meena slaps the woman but screams herself as a spasm of pain jolts through her. She takes to the bed, where she lies again on her back and spreads her legs and gives Reza a view of the half head of a child, glossy with mucus and the size of a large orange. And here is the first happiness: this bloody ball with the matted hair is his orange and does not belong to the shah or to the mountains but to him alone, Reza Khourdi, and his surly yet beautiful wife, who, for some reason, is suddenly capable of producing such fruits. He wants to pluck it, as if from a tree, and walk about the town to tell everyone, *Look at this! This orange belongs to me!* Meena screams again and pushes down on her own stomach and the midwife, resigned to this new posture, grabs at the shoulders and chest as they emerge, only to have them slip through her fingers and sink back in.

The room goes silent and the old woman shakes her head and motions to Reza to help her lift Meena, who is suddenly pale and quiet, off the bed. He holds her limp, wet body up by the armpits as the midwife crouches beneath her and shoves her arms in, elbow deep. For a moment she is stiff and then alive and shaking with seizures that keep her unsteady in Reza's arms. The old woman, who has disappeared between the legs of the young girl, laughs and sings an encouraging song until Meena lets out a long sigh, and all her weight falls into Reza's arms and their bedroom fills with determined, choking cries.

He cannot look and he cannot turn away.

The babe is ugly. Covered in liquid and blood with a face that looks like nothing Reza has ever seen, compacted, grimacing, more nightmare than dream. The midwife slaps a few chunks from his throat and cuts the cord with a small blade she finds on Reza's dresser and hands the child to him, and he is immediately astonished by the weight, neither light nor heavy, but formidable and entirely his. He brings the babe close, near his heart, near the brass on the breast of his uniform, and feels his own organs relax, his muscles give way, the roil in his head dissipate. The child screams and Reza holds him closer, certain the sound is echoing on the slate of the mountains all around. He walks to Meena, who sleeps soundly on the bed, and leans down with the babe to wake her. With soft eyes she stares first at Reza and then at the babe.

A boy?

Reza nods.

Jounam, Reza, a soldier just like his baba . . .

A smile spreads across her face like a cloud expanding across a blue sky and she is asleep again. He searches the babe for a sign, some mark of the child's fate, and the baby writhes in his arms as if to escape. Reza clutches at the new body, forcing himself to find a guarantee that this half self will not suffer his father's secrets or sins. The babe begins to whine and then squeal and then cry and Reza holds him tightly: it is not easy to look at the pained face; it is impossible to turn away. Impatient, the midwife grabs the babe from his hands and starts to wash and swaddle the child with the efficiency of a cook preparing a hen for the midday meal.

HE AND SHE

WITH THE BABE at her breast she asks him in her sweetest voice, *Where does your love lie?* He says, *There*, and points to the trinity of babe, maman and teat. *Then tell me of your deeds, Agha Captain. How have you been a hero today?* She wants to know of the latest uprisings, the schoolhouse he's building, the status of her order of fine lace from Tehran. He clears his throat to explain that just yesterday there were three boys, the sons of farmers from Taq-e-Bustan, gathered in the meiydan and shouting to draw a crowd. *What were they shouting, my love?* He tells her of their pleas for Kurdish independence, how they asked the group: If Iran can suddenly have its own country then why not the Kurds? Are they not the oldest people of these mountains, is this not the era of country making? Who is to stop us? With the baby at her breast and her eyes sparkling she asks, *So what did you do, Reza, jounam?* And because the babe is at her breast he tells her proudly, *I locked them in a room without water or food and when the families came to bribe me with their goats and copper I locked them inside too. Three days should be humiliation enough.* Intent and listening, her full lips part just a bit as the baby sucks noisily at her. He goes on. *Soon I will make Kermanshah as lovely and peaceful as your own Tehran.* She pulls the baby from her breast and lays it on a woolen blanket and whispers, *Aufareen, my captain,* and brings his head close to cradle in her arms and let him take of the milk, the tender teat and the ecstatic stream that ties him to his own beginning.

THE MIDWIFE

IN THESE TEN years I have delivered them all.
From the first boy to this last girl just a few months ago, I
have delivered all six, reached my hand into that Tehrani bitch
and pulled loose the babes one by one. They all come out full
of breath and alive and so every time she is ready a truck comes
to get me and my family rejoices because they know the captain, who is normally cruel with the Kurds but holds us in
his favor, will send me home with a goat or a few tins of sweet
milk.

Mind you, not once has the Tehrani woman uttered her appreciation.

Still, I go when I am called.

For the first babe, the captain was forceful, cramming me into
the car with another soldier; neither of them explained anything
so I was sure they were taking me to their building in Kermanshah where the Kurds are kept and punished. The woman was
there, still more girl to her body than mother, and I did what I
could.

After the boy was born they took me back and the captain

signaled the driver to stop next to the slopes of the three sister mountains. He left us, me, the driver and the babe, and walked to the mountains like they were a stream and he was a thirsty man. When he returned he had a different look to him. All of the seriousness that kept his face stiff and empty was gone and suddenly he looked Kurd, with the high bones and the green eyes. I remember how my eyes watered to see the Kurd in him, the Kurd he is. He took the babe from my arms and walked to the edge of a steep slope, where he held him out to the gray inclines, and then back to the car, as if the child needed a bit of air. As we drove back the driver and I tried not to look over at the captain, as it was clear that he was taking great pains to keep his head down and hide the tears that were falling onto his son's face.

For the second child the captain came by himself and brought a leather ball for my boys and a small pistol for my husband. The woman birthed another son easily that afternoon and I heard from those in Kermanshah that the captain took his two sons to town to show the men, kept cradles in the barracks and his wife on hand for the nursing.

With the third, the driver came alone and the Tehrani woman suffered much this time. The babe was sideways and needed to be righted, and in her agony the khanoum screamed in that language that means nothing to me. Their kholfat translated what she could.

It's all the same . . . She is calling you a useless Kurd, unfit to touch her or her babies. She says that right now, as she speaks, her husband, the captain, is in town punishing your brothers and fathers for ruining this new Iran.

I listened with my hands in her, feeling for the babe, and I resisted the urge to turn it backward so that it suffocated on the way out. Instead I remembered the captain, the afternoon after his first son's birth, the softness in his face as he walked to and from the edge of the mountains, and I righted the babe as much as I could and left the rest up to God. The Tehrani bitch screamed and the first girl was born. I left without washing her. The following day the captain sent my boys two pairs of leather shoes and a fig tree for the yard.

The fourth, a girl. The fifth, a boy. The woman grows wider through the hips and when they come to call for me I whisper to my husband: *Why? They are practically falling out of her now.* My husband hushes me and says we need to stay in the captain's favor; times are changing and the Kurds are no longer content with suckling up to the mountains, no longer a quiet people in the face of the shah. He himself has heard the talk of a nation of our own and explained that we too should live as the captain and his family do: under the protection of a nation, with leather shoes, guns and kitchens with running water. I laugh and tell him I am but a midwife, a guardian for the crossing, and our sweet well water is just fine for me.

When the last girl came my husband was gone, off to the mountains, or to Mahabad, or to fight with Barzani's men—I knew better than to ask; I knew better than to know. I rode in the truck next to the captain, who had no gifts and whose face was layered again, thick and brooding and masked. In the ten years I had known him not once had he come to fetch me in such a mood as this; usually the news of a coming child turns him into a grinning boy.

At the house there were soldiers everywhere. I kept my eyes to the ground as I walk up the veranda steps into the bedroom, where the khanoum was squatting over a pallet of cushions—I have taught her well. I checked her and it was not yet time and so turned to the window where I could see the men gathered in a line to meet the trucks that come, five or six, up to the house. The kholfat whispered to me.

They caught them in the mountains. There was some fight and the Barzani men fled to Iraq and everyone from Kermanshah and around was caught. There are too many to take quietly into town, so they brought them here.

The Tehrani woman moaned and I didn't even turn to look at her. I thought of Arash and my boys. I thought: *Let that baby fall and break on the ground.*

When the trucks stopped the captain ordered them to be emptied and one by one our men spilled out, our men in soft shoes, with turbans to keep their heads from the sun and loose pants to keep them comfortable on horses. I could not see Arash, but I knew he was there, among them. The khanoum moaned again and called to me by smacking her hand violently on the nightstand. I didn't turn around. The captain walked up and down along the line of men, prisoners now, with their hands roped behind their backs, and selected a few boys, a few fathers, a few old men. Arash was chosen and he stepped forward. The khanoum shouted to the kholfat, who told me. *She says it's time.* I left them in the house and walked to the veranda and stood until the captain and all the soldiers turned to look at me. The captain pushed Arash back into the line and selected the man next to him.

The selected men were taken to the side, undressed to their pants and held by soldiers while the captain hit them with a sturdy leather crop. His hits were lazy and uninspired and each lift of his arm was a forced gesture. I could not help but cringe, not at the violence of the weak hits, but at the captain's clumsy, obvious pain. Our men didn't cry and the soldiers tried not to seem ashamed of their commander. When it was done Arash and the others were loaded back into two trucks and driven away; only then did I return to the room, where the khanoum was red in the face from the effort. Without any effort I pulled the babe from her, a girl, born with open blue eyes. I wanted to drop the messy thing into her lap, let her cut the cord herself, but the child screamed at me with the joy brought from the other side and I recognized she is half us; one half this Tehrani bitch and one half Kurd, like her baba, the kind captain. I washed her and took her to the captain, who was smoking and serious and by himself in the aftermath. He held the babe and I watched the blue eyes enchant him, pull him in, bring him back.

In these ten years I have delivered them all: six children from the womb of the Tehrani bitch, my husband from humiliation and the captain from his lost heart.

THE NEST

WHAT THE CAMERA captures: a woman with hair curled and short and six children wrapped around her, along the shoulders, on the lap, behind her smiling head. A riverbed to their left; underneath them, a rug that buckles and folds.

What the captain captures: his wife and the smile she brandishes readily that is a lie and for the sake of false memories. Six children, one happier than the next, for they are *at the river! on a picnic!* and their maman is beautiful and their baba strong and full of their same childish joy and life between these mountain walls is lovely and no heavier than the air between a butterfly's wings.

In his hands the camera is a silly thing, and after he succumbs to Meena's demands to *take a photo!* Reza tosses it aside and takes the children who can walk, who run and shout, *Baba, wait!* at his brisk step, up the slope of the river valley to the foothills of the Zagros. At the spot where the ground turns from an uphill curve to a vertiginous launch of stone and moss and then cloud, he lifts the children up, youngest to oldest, to climb a bit of the uneven rock, to feel it beneath them, supporting them. The girl squeals as he pretends to let go her hips—*Baba, no!*—while the oldest boys scuttle up and out of his lift, like spiders, across the rough rock face. Some make it as far as the first perch, where Reza yells to them.

Go on, jump, act the bird, spread your arms and try for the soar! Go on!

They leap and the ground pulls them down and they roll and laugh and let their baba lift them again to fly, to see who can keep fastened longest, to tease their baba—*Try it! Try it, Baba! How come you don't try?!*—until they are tired enough to walk back to their maman and the two youngest babies.

Meena sits on a blanket, livid at their escapade. She is quick to chastise the boys for their scraped knees and the girls for their torn dresses and their baba for his irresponsible behavior.

I am tired, the children are a mess. Enough of this. Let's go home.

Reza follows like his sons and daughters: dutifully, arms and legs loose with exhaustion and mind clear of everything but the memories he will make of this day, ingredients to mix with imagination and longing when he needs to cook himself a pot of happy dreams.

PEACOCK FEATHERS AND
STRONG SOAP

IN 1946 BEHAD Chezani, a schoolteacher, went crazy during class and threatened his students with the needled end of a compass for a whole afternoon before finally—*pop!*—piercing his own throat. That same year Kaavan Izadi, a local man with a farm, experimented with pesticides distributed by the modernizing committee and, mixing them with lye—*boom!*—exploded himself and the shed he worked in, and injured a donkey who stood nearby, unprepared. The village farmers swore off pesticides, and the hinny healed but gave birth to a lame foal the next spring. That was the fall when General Il'al Dizayee, who the Kurds sang about in their songs, was killed and we stared at newspaper pictures of his body laid out in front of a line of soldiers suited up just like our baba. Our maman took the picture to our baba and laughed in his face: *Ha ha ha. Now this is progress. You pretend to take care of state business, Mr. Captain, but these soldiers really do. Who have you killed? Too much of a Kurd to take care of your own? Ha. Ha. Ha.* Our baba had only two types of response to our maman's hahahas. One was silence and stillness and the other one was the opposite of silence and stillness.

Before he stuck the compass in his throat, Behad Chezani came to our house to ask our baba, slowly, because his voice was shaking, *W-hhy can't I speak Kku-rrd in the school?* And our baba didn't take his sunglasses off to talk to him and said it just like this: *It is the orders of the most imperial shah.* And from somewhere in the house we heard our maman make a snorting sound, and it was one of our baba's still times because Behad was there, watching him.

Without their clothes on, Kurd faces and hands didn't look that much different from those of our maman or the men in the modernizing committee who lived in the house in Kermanshah and drove a car. They had lighter eyes sometimes, and sometimes light hair, but everything else—neck, wrists, lips and ears—was pretty much the same. Only when you looked at their Kurd clothes could you tell a difference: they were dirtier, like they had all rolled around here and there, and full of color, sometimes little mirrors where you could see your blurry self.

In school it was even harder to tell because we all wore the same white shirts and black pants and sweaters with a sharp dip in the middle. Our maman said, *Now this is how the little boys and girls in England dress, you should be proud, they are very smart.* I had friends named Darius Safanejad, Afsaneh Khorshand, Mehrnaz Miraftabi, and on and on, but I also had friends named Erdelan Dermikorol, Gazin Ocalean, Kilda Teimourvian and Nivad Qourdeh. Gazin Ocalean had a peacock in his yard and we pulled its feathers from the tail to see it run and then take them home to our maman, because Gazin Ocalean's mother said, *These are always good luck.* Our maman would always burn them and make us wash our hands in detergent.

Nivad Qourdeh was the son of another Kurd soldier who worked for our baba and when I asked him who his best friend was, he said, *My gun!* And that his father let him sleep with it at night, *just in case.* When our baba heard that he just shook his head and asked, *What do children need guns for? I never wanted a gun as a child.* And Nivad Qourdeh's baba nodded his head in serious agreement. Nivad Qourdeh's baba had only one eye; the other one must have fallen out, because they put a big white marble in its place and it rolled around covered in tears. He always brought nuts for the house, and when he found out our maman didn't like nuts he brought boxes of nabots instead. Our baba stayed friends with him to the end, even after he was hung for treason against the shah and his head puffed up so much that his marble eye popped out and a street dog sniffed at it and walked away. After that our baba smoked so much of the flower that he wore sunglasses all the time and didn't take off his uniform for days.

When I was six, baba ordered that a cinema be built in our town. When they showed the film *The Great Ziegfield* a man from the modernizing committee walked up and down the aisle shouting, *Imagine those buildings, imagine those cars! Kermanshah of the future could look just like that.* As he walked he stepped on all the shells of sunflower seeds that people had spit out and the audience shouted back at him, *Choke up! Be quiet! We are watching cinema!* The frustrated state employee yelled back, *Choke up yourself! What do you need quiet for? You can't even understand English!* And he was right, and we were all looking at the pictures of gold-haired women in long dresses with shoes like nails and tall buildings that reached up to the sky and streets covered in smooth stone, and not understanding a word. This didn't stop us from throwing the sunflower seeds at him or laughing when someone on the screen slipped.

Of all the movies I liked the ones with the newsreels most. They were full of pictures of important men and women and important airplanes and ships. When they showed a picture of the shah of Iran, our king, Maman clapped and Erdelan Dermikorol's father threw sunflower seeds at her, but she ignored him and whispered to us, *Look how straight and clean he stands. Look at his Soraya. That dress!* And then she would sigh. Every time we saw a picture or a film of the shah we sighed.

For the fall our maman was asked to teach Farsi at our school in Kermanshah, since she was born and raised in the Farsi capital, Tehran. After one day of all of us repeating in song the names of great cities and foreign countries—*Dam-a-vand, Shee-raz, Amrika*—Ferydoon Moididi and Taba Kazeen and Nisar Montandahr didn't come to school the next day. But all the time Jahan Khaligizad kept on bringing peacock feathers to our house as gifts from his family and our maman kept burning them and sending Jahan home with hands rubbed raw from detergent.

And all these times there were parades on the one smooth street in Kermanshah. On the mornings of the parades, our baba would shout, *Clean the kids! Wash their hair and their faces!* while our maman was scrubbing the seven of us so hard that our skin stung and everybody cried a little bit, even Hooshang, who was almost a man. Our maman yelled back: *I can't wash the Kurd out of them! They'll never be clean!* And baba usually did not stay silent and still at this and someone always wore a little bit of blood to the parade.

Ferydoon Faroukheyzade told me he came to the parades to see army men in their suits. He called them Iran suits and I didn't tell him what our baba told us, that their suits were old Russian Cossack suits and itched all over in the winter and in the summer, but I don't think he cared. He liked the medals and the colors and the guns the soldiers carried with them. Kilda Teimourvian came to the parades to see the horses in a line because at her house, she said, the horses were wild and ran around and you couldn't get close enough to touch them. Once, at a parade, she was bitten by a horse ridden by an Iranian-suited general. The bite sounded like this, *snapglumph*, because the horse bit first with its teeth and then its lips. Kilda didn't blame the horse and still came to see them with her wide blue eyes. Our maman came to the parades with red color on her lips and cheeks in a very tight jacket and skirt, like a man's suit for a woman, but so tight that she couldn't breathe very much. She would sit under a parasol with the men from the modern-izing committee, who wore dark suits and oil in their hair, and while our baba walked around and shook hands and clapped backs and waved and rode in the cars, she would fan herself and smile and say things like: *Yes, beautiful day, this fresh mountain air is so good for the lungs*, and then she would try to take a deep breath to show how good it was, except that she couldn't be-cause of her tight man-woman suit. *Of course they speak Farsi, I'll send them to Tehran for proper schooling, oh, of course, even the girls. I was educated in Tehran, the shah encourages it, you know. We must knit this new country together somehow.* The modernizing committee men would nod their shiny oily heads.

Our maman did not talk to Nivad's mother or Kilda's mother

or Taba's mother, who let their kids run in the street and watched the parade from inside buildings or on rooftops. Our maman talked only to the men on the modernizing committee, who held her parasol and lit her cigarettes.

There were no contests at the parades, but sometimes there were prizes. We thought the Iranian modernizing committee was very generous to give out so many exciting and free things. Kilda's baba once won a free phone call from the phone house and he stood in the street thanking God for his good fortune, and our baba said, *Allah has nothing to do with it. Thank the shah!* And Kilda's baba smiled in a secret way and said, *The shah, Allah, it's all the same thing, isn't it?* You could see our baba was confused by that question; for a moment his body was in between being still and unstill. Kilda told me that when her baba went to the phone house he stood there and called our baba a *pedarsag* because he had no one to call and he felt tricked. I realized that was a big difference between being a whole Kurd and a half Kurd like us; the whole Kurds didn't know about anyone or anything outside of the mountains.

But everyone came to see the cars: Darius Safanejad, Afsaneh Khorshand, Mehrnaz Miraftabi, Erdelan Dermikorol, Gazin Ocalean and Nivad Qourdeh. People got tired of the Iran suits, and the horses and the guns, but no one ever got tired of the cars, and they would move so slowly and smoothly down the street that Erdelan thought there were a thousand snails inside the hood, pulling and sliding slowly across the ground. When our maman heard that she laughed: *Ha!* Our baba was sometimes in the car waving, sometimes alone and sometimes next to a big-framed painting of the shah. The shah had a bald head and a serious smile and he wore an Iran suit with more medals and badges and crosses than any other soldier I had ever seen. Sometimes our maman would make a wreath of flowers to hang around the frame and the cars floated down the street like that, with all of the boys and girls from school in constant contact with the feel of their slick metal sides, fascinated by our curved reflections looking back upon us. Erdelan was disappointed when they opened the hood and there were no snails, just the engine. He told me he didn't understand the engine, and that was less exciting. He died of gassing that winter, when the kerosene heater his family had won at a parade leaked and killed them all while they slept. It was winter and for the first time they were able to keep the windows closed, glad for their new smokeless heat.

APOSTATE BREED

*M*AHABAD!

Reza sits at his barracks desk. The front room is full of soldiers gathered around newspapers and radios, each announcing in a loud whisper:

They say Kermanshah is the next to go.

They speak as if Reza is not there, but he is there, perfectly there; within earshot he smokes and listens, smokes and hears the din outside. They have come from all the villages around to parade in the streets of Kermanshah with their wives and daughters and flocks. Through the thin barracks wall and the one window the cries seep in, triumphant and merry.

Mahabad!

Mahabad!

Long live the Kurd republic of Mahabad!

Reza taps his finger to the beat of their simple shouts.

Mahabad! The children will speak Kurdish at school!

Mahabad! Off with the yoke of Iran and shah! Mahabad! A home for Kurds everywhere!

Three taps for the word. Ma. Ha. Bad. Tap. Tap. Tap. Today

their dream is true. A Kurdish republic in Mahabad. A dictionary and a printing press. Leaders in suits. A constitution for Kurds and a declaration of Kurdish autonomy. A country of their own. Reza closes his eyes to imagine the scene: the square full of people, barely room enough to move, so they have to shuffle and shout while good feeling spreads and gels them together until they are an impervious mass of Kurd and flock animal and possibility. Even the old wart-faced mule smiles. Vendors toss out fruits and burnt ears of corn (. . . *no one goes hungry in the motherland* . . .). There are kites and candies and the joy is general as birds of all varieties fly above in a sky blue and inestimable. He hears the voices of young boys rise above the commotion, more sonorous and zealous than the yells of their fathers and uncles.

Mahabad!

Mahabad!

Mahabad!

Reza cannot help but smile. The captain sits at his desk, eyes closed, taps his finger, smiles. Was he not that boy just yesterday, just last year, just last lifetime? Maybe here, behind closed eyes, he can be that boy again. All around him the cadets pace, impatient for command. Their spurs clink and chink about the room, some part of them forever ticking.

Excuse me, Agha Captain?

The lieutenant approaches to interrupt Reza's imaginings (a street vendor hawks ears of burnt corn—*How tasty and salty!*—but gets no business as there is no hunger anywhere; all the stomachs are sated with pride).

Yes, Sarhang?

Agha Captain, perhaps we should dispel the gathering. They have amassed like this for three days now and the news from Mahabad is becoming more worrisome. Do you not think the situation is getting a bit dangerous? Perhaps we should just scare them a bit, fire a few shots in the air, a few at their feet, just a little something to let them know that Kermanshah is not the next city to go.

The lieutenant is a Tehrani boy, the same staunch young face that brought Meena back on their first night. He is well read and versed but a clumsy soldier, heavy and brusque. Reza finds him an annoyance on many levels: his tireless reciting of the Shahnameh; his odious habit of speaking French at any opportunity; the way his teeth crush on top of each other like badly laid tile.

Sarhang, I believe the latrines are due for another mopping?

The lieutenant looks down and turns on his heel, his spurs clicking and chinking with an even, angry beat.

Reza closes his eyes to return to the happy fantasy.

Ma. Ha. Bad. Ma. Ha. Bad. A kite of yellow in a cobalt sky.

She nurses and reads and does not look up.

Are your barbarian brothers rioting again? How were the streets today?

He doesn't respond and looks instead into the empty paper pack with tobacco flakes at the bottom.

Busy, like yesterday.

Naasi suckles gently on her mother's teat, one hand clenched in a fist and another open. Meena sits turning the pages of the newspaper with her free hand. Without looking up she speaks to the black-and-white print.

They say Mahabad is the first, and all the other Kurdish cities will fall right behind in this hysterical claim for a country. What do Kurds know about a country? They can barely tend their flea-ridden sheep. They say the ideas are already spreading through the Azerbaijan and Turkoman provinces.

Reza stares into his empty pack and aches for just one cigarette, one inhale to silence her pinprick voice and one exhale to make him deaf. Inhale. Exhale. All day he has listened carefully to the happiness and the joy and his ears are tired and hot and not interested in this worry and complaint. Did he leave the cigarettes in the jeep? His jacket pocket? Are there any in the house?

They say Kermanshah is the next to go.

The baby sucks gleefully. Meena looks up at him.

What are you going to do, Captain Khourdi? How are you going to keep us safe? They say you are letting things go . . .

The whorehouse is overflowing with cigarettes; the madam keeps a stash in each room. It is the other common passion among the patrons; some take opium, some vodka, but all of the men who frequent Madam Husili's many-roomed house at the north end of town smoke cigarettes.

Are you as weak as they say you are? Useless as the rumors claim? You are definitely useless to me and these children of yours. It would be a benefit to us all if I simply announced to them all, the soldiers, the Kurds, everyone: Your captain is a Kurd! No different from the rotten peshmergas that shit in the mountains and take goats as their wives. A coward, pitiful in this Iran.

Reza gathers his wallet and gun and Meena switches the baby from one breast to the other, leaving the first exposed and drooping. Slowly she turns the pages of the paper spread out in front of her and the babe and mutters.

Ah, Reza joon, I have always thought you to be an apostate breed, one way or another.

The Assyrian and Armenian, Christian and Coptic girls meet him at the door with squeals and hisses. The tile floor echoes loudly with the sound of their heeled shoes as they circle around to remove his coat, hand him a cigarette, free him of his hat and holster; Reza is a regular customer. With a gesture of his lit cigarette he chooses Heidieah, his medium favorite, because his favorite is pregnant again, and smokes half a pack before he lays his tobacco-stained lips on her in a fury meant for his wife. As he is fucking his sweaty arduous fuck, Reza re-minds himself that he is the shah's captain and an accomplished soldier who has taken the census, collected the tithes and harnessed all the wandering flocks and tribes (and he wants desperately for someone, the shah, this whore perhaps, the Kurd boy who brings them water, the town mongrels, anyone really, to lick and pet and smooth his shellacked head and compliment him: *good job, good job, aufareen, my boy, aufareen*). Reza thrusts into the young girl and re-minds himself that he has done his duty and started the Farsi school, hoisted the red, green and white flag, learned the proper tone of the new anthem and generally represented this invisible thing called Iran to the Kurds, who only believe what they see. The whore laughs in delight and he turns her over to see her happy face and fuck her and in the fucking remembers his own wife, that she is a soft, negligible thing and the slice of her sharp tongue is useless against his bullets and boots. Heidieah giggles in ecstasy and her flush round cheeks press up against eyes that shine like diamonds in a bed of rock. The sight of their blaze fuels the machine in Reza and he floods the girl with all his re-minding and remembering. She screams in theatrical delight, for he is a good customer and the captain, after all.

When it is over Reza smokes one cigarette after the next and lies beside the sleeping whore and thinks happily of happiness as it has manifested today in the twinkling eyes of a loose woman and in the shouts of proud Kurdish boys, and he smiles at himself for the beneficence of his command as captain of Kermanshah, a kindly captain who allows all manners of joy.

But since he has allowed—and because there is talk of the captain's excessive and incapacitating sentimentality; because the republic of Mahabad has come to a swift and sudden end; because the town's joy has flipped to its other side: upset—Reza must now disallow. The decree is drafted by the lieutenant and sung happily throughout Kermanshah by the garrison of shah soldiers until even the smallest daughter knows that to gather in the square is forbidden and all mentions of Mahabad are now illegal and that any remnants of last month's joy and good feeling concerning nation or state will be dealt with as transgressions against his majesty the shah. They announce that the republic of Mahabad is, as of yesterday, terminated, the printing presses burned and the town patrolled by tanks. Reza listens to the pronouncements through the walls of his barracks office and can hear nothing else but the occasional bray of some anonymous hoofed animal tied unwillingly to a post.

★ ★ ★

They bring them into the office strung together in a human chain made of rope and sharp twine. Reza sees that each one's fists are tied fast around the neck of the man in front of him and the line of men, ten or twelve, moves slowly and cautiously behind the cadets. The lieutenant looks to Reza proudly.

We caught them conspiring to organize. Some are men of Kermanshah. Some from Hormoz. They were found in a cave in the mountains with guns, ammunition, and literature of the Kurdish National Front, though none of them can read. Interesting, isn't it, Agha Captain?

Reza does not look at the men, not in the eye, not at their bound arms and necks, not even at their silly sandals, and stays seated behind his desk. He picks up the newspaper, opens it wide like a blanket in front of his face and pretends to read.

Very well, Sarhang. Carry on.

The barracks fill with the stench of the Kurds; they smell like a flock after the rain. The lieutenant lines them up and paces, uncertain what to do next. He tells them to stand. Then he tells them to sit. He unties their hands and then thinks twice and ties them again as a cadet holds a gun in the direction of their faces and chests. Finally he places them in hard-backed wooden chairs with their hands bound tightly behind them. Reza lowers the paper a bit and sees a middle-aged Kurd so devoid of fear that he is shaking his head and chuckling. The lieutenant looks about for a crop and, finding none, grabs at a long thin shish that the cadets use for grilling their Friday kebabs in the barracks and begins to pace and preach, his speech punctuated by the cymbals of his spurs. The lieutenant clearly enjoys the sound of his own voice.

What is this feeling of wanting a state all your own?

The Kurds keep silent.

Our Iran isn't good enough for you?

Reza hears the spurs stop and lowers the paper a bit more. The lieutenant stands in front of a man with a grizzly chin and a scowl, a man clearly unimpressed by the immaculate soldier. Reza smiles to himself and raises the paper again. The lieutenant continues.

Maybe you can tell me?

The shish lands again and again, this time leaving marks, but the man makes no sound. The lieutenant is awash in his own eroticism, a flash hot mix of high idea, poetry and violence.

You have only seen the mountains and never the sea.

The shish snaps.

How can you possibly understand our new nation when you don't understand the borders of the whole earth?

The shish snaps.

That we live on a planet with lines of water, lines of ice, lines through the middle of the hemispheres?

The shish lands and the man shouts out. Reza raises the paper higher to avoid the sight of the blood and the piercing, and the photographs are right before his eyes: pictures from the last days at Mahabad, where Gazi Mohammad, Abul Gassem Adr Gazi and Mohammad Houssein Khan Safe Gazi, leaders of the Kurdish National Front, hung from the gallows pole erected in Chwar Chera Square. Their faces are smudged but the shoes and nooses and tongues are clear and the effect is one of suspension: a graceful, almost willing, pendant of body and might, heart and hope. Reza thinks: when was he ever a man like that? Not yesterday, not last year, not a lifetime ago.

For weeks after Reza is slow with sadness. In the face of Meena's derision, in the company of his men and even before the women he cannot drink or smoke or sex and walks about, trapped in the husk of his mortal self, feeling himself sink nearer and nearer to the ground; a biped; a quadruped; a slithering snake; a man milled down like stone into dust; re-minded and remembered into the earth and whatever worlds below.

THE RETURNED BIRDS

Now the body drags. What elastic tendencies snapped readily before, this manner to the next, this loyalty to that, to toss him from one side of himself to another (shadow dance, craven city liar, baba-son, shah-son, mountain-son; etc.) are now stretched and slack. He is a heavy man lumbering behind his two oldest sons, Hameed and Hooshang, who are jaunty over grass and boulders and through the mazes of sage and rabbit brush at the mountains' base. They are off to the hunt, the three together, as prophesied in mountain caves, and though he is breathless with a body that drags—nothing about him like the warrior with the cuirass and the shield and nowhere are the horses in armor and no one sounds the victory bell—he is still their father and they are still the sons and morning passes into midday and the mountains loom. Hopefully they will hunt and hopefully they will kill. The boys amble ahead easily, occupied in their own talk.

. . . *and if I return the marbles to Ali and then score a twenty on my next dictee she said cinema . . .*

. . . *I wouldn't beg for the cinema like you, I am not a begging baby . . .*

. . . Maman doesn't think so, she told the agha at school she would be happy to help him make a trip, a school trip, to the cinema and to the train . . . and he said thank you, Khanoum Khourdi, we are so honored to have your assistance . . . and she was very smiley at that . . . and I will go if you won't. You can stay at home with the girls. Ha ha.

Time turns and the body drags. Of what was flighty and fit, there remains only a heavy mass with lungs more faulty by the day, a liver of weak proportions and a mind bloated with soft desires and misgivings. The decrepitude grows like a mold in Reza's small parts and spreads into a florid revulsion of all beauty and whimsy, belonging and love.

All things Meena cultivates with an easy hand.

She is his mirror, in opposition to him, an inverse reflection: each year he sulks closer to the ground, she cuts a sharper frame, keen to herself and her abilities. Never the sweet girl, she has not turned sour but into a shrew, unstoppable in ridicule that he has never *provided her chandeliers in the divan or gala festivities befitting a captain's wife*. He has fallen lazy, fallen fat and slow, and can no longer thrust out his chest and lust for blood and respect, while, all-power she has birthed child after child and taught them specifically: how to disregard their father, how to hate the Kurds all around, how to hunger for some invisible refinement of mind and body. In these fourteen years she blossomed into the vindictive seductress, an able sway about her hips and a glint through her eyes, and he has thickened to drag, to sweat, to cough and watch her draw over her face with black kohl around the eyes and burgundy whale wax on the lips. To make a gift of herself, masked and wrapped and given to any of the few eligible who come to Kermanshah to serve their two-year post. He has overheard their murmurs in the barracks.

Yes, with the schoolteacher.

Oh, I heard it was the lieutenant.

Either way, she's always after the Tehrani types.

If only we were stationed closer to those city hives and farther from tribal girls! I'll wait my turn for the captain's wife, if that's all right with you . . .

The body drags, and the motivation along with it. Reza cannot bring himself to shock or shame, or even the heat of humiliation. Where there was excitement in the boy and determination in the cadet and vainglory in the soldier there is sadness in the captain, a languid sorrow from which he cannot even lift one finger or two. She takes from him the energy required for pride and arrogance, gobbles it up and spits it back as seeds for the children to eat. They are a marriage separated by six children, nation and king, and he watches her grow against the land while he dissolves into it and does not care what hands have touched her, what wetness seeps through her, what unholy transgressions delight her. Now the body drags and Reza sinks within it, caring little for the reputation he leaves in its sluggish wake. Captain Reza Khourdi, the cuckold of Kermanshah.

He follows his sons up the hill to a labyrinth of stones in the mountains where they have many times spotted and shot wild turkeys, horned goats and even foxes. The day is warm and a mass of cirrus churns above them to hold the air thick and close to the earth. They come to a dale between two rising stone slopes and the sun emerges brilliant to clean the sky and sparkle in the water, and the two boys make their way down a ravine in search of rabbits or snakes. They call to their father.

Baba, here. Baba, over here.

He goes to sit against a trunk as his boys kick about the stones with their leather boots, startling a flock of starlings out of the shrubs. The small birds fly off in a thrum to re-seek their solitude. Reza takes a cigarette from his breast pocket and lights it, the fire tip the only red around. The boys sit beside him and the three listen to the air, the trickle of a distant stream, the tucking and jumping of wings, beaks, the flit and flash eyes. The man and boys are still. They are father and sons, together and vanished, for moments on end. In the silence the rest of the birds return, first a falcon and then two sparrows and then a handful of vireos and finally the starlings, an entire murmuration, reconvene in the brush again, alighting on the tiny branches with their tiny feet.

From behind an esker slides a fox, languorous and thin, and Reza motions to his boys (he is their father and so must teach them how to kill) to keep still. He hoists the rifle to his shoulder, makes a one-eyed gesture with his face and fires to break skin, flesh, bone and earthly calm. Hooshang and Hameed run to the fallen animal and Reza walks behind, drags his heavy body filled with age and fragments, until they come upon the carcass. Blood runs from a wound through the neck to mat the fur and stain the stone all around, incarnadine and hot. The boys stick their fingers in the hole, wipe the blood along the body of fur, along their stones and their own arms and legs. Hameed closes the eyes of the animal and asks:

Baba, now what?

Reza does not answer. He waits for the echo of the rifle shot to dissipate, for silence to return. The boys make a game with the body of the fox and then play with each other and finally come to sit beside their baba and fall asleep. In the time of afternoon and then dusk, insects, birds and animals surround them and Reza thinks: *Who will miss this fox?* and *What is the weight of a bag of bones?*

The boys sleep beside him and Reza wonders if they sit long enough, the three of them, to wither here and die, will their bones be left whole, intact, a testimony to their human form? Or will they be caught and dragged about, strewn in dens and nests, here and there, disappear into the life of a wild they cannot control?

It is an ending neither happy nor sad, the only ending he can offer his sons, for he has little else. Nothing of nights in caves gathered around fires where the sound and clap and song bound you to the man next to you to the man next to him through time and space. Nothing of histories in stone, the victories and massacres that connect today to yesterday to the beginning of time; nothing of the lovepride his own baba cloaked him in when he was a boy, his Kurd boy.

To his boys Reza can only give flags and state songs and portraits of a medallioned shah. He can give them streets and citizenship but never the freedom to travel the borderless land or the stable sensation of home. But none of it satisfies, not the boots or the cinema or the afternoon drives in the state car where they scream, *Baba, faster! Faster!* He would like to take them deep into these Zagros, hold them by their shoulders and give them the mountains, the flurry of birds, the age-old blue dusk, all the love buried deep in his Kurdish heart. He cannot give them the proud lesson and say: *This is your home. Let it keep you well.*

In the soft early evening air, with the shallow sleep breaths of his boys in his right and left ears and the fox bleeding before him, Reza considers his wife. He thinks of her in vivid detail: the wrapping and masking, the constant churn and query, the unsettled mind and modern, unsatisfied heart. He sees himself trapped beneath her: a run-down specimen, impotent and without history, unable to give her the love of a strong shah soldier she so craves and not brave enough to be the Kurdish baba his children deserve. A life of determinations and lies; forced to march about as a falsity; a captain in command of nothing. Would any of them love him after the truth? Once he is naked and announcing: *I am a Kurd of these mountains, an old Kurd at that, heavy and worn and heartless. You, my children, are half bloods, half Kurd, and this land will take you in as its child and so let it. And you, my wife, have married a man torn in everything but the love in his blood.*

Reza considers what he must do. He looks to the faces of his boys and gains strength at the thought that they too will live on the land and hunt it, know its shape and designs, for it is theirs, and it was once his. He thinks of their faces and how they are no different from the faces of cousins he has long forgotten, the faces of the boys in Kermanshah and in Saqqez. He thinks of how easily his six children could slip into the fold of the land if only their mother would allow it. She will not. And so they are damned to remain as homeless as he.

Reza cannot offer his children much; in fact, he knows he has one gift to give. A simple truth *he has been living a lie he's Kurdish and hasn't bothered to tell the truth living the lie in front of his boys* that will serve his children now and the boy he was once and all the Kurds that came to make him a man of these mountains. In his sunken self Reza recognizes that just as the stars align each night in the sky, century after century, it is now his duty to align the Kurds long dead with the Kurd in him and the Kurds in his sleeping sons. He looks at the dispersed life of the slim fox laid out before them as a guide, true and passed into the next dominion, and thinks of the simplicity of death. Death, Reza thinks happily, the quieting of life's insatiable storm.

The boys wake and stand beside him rubbing the sleep from their eyes as Reza skins the beast. Off comes hair, bits of head flesh, globs of animal brain. Hameed carries the sturdy tangle of muscle and meat as it drips a trail of drops, red drops, now black drops, now dried drops, behind them and Reza mutters, *Who will miss her bag of slutty bones? Not I, swimming about in my bag of shamed bones? Who will miss the bloodless fox . . .* The boys run ahead, singing an old child's rhyme.

Yeki bood, yeki nabood . . . Once there was one and once there was not one . . .

THE FARMER

THE FIRST YEAR they asked us and we told them nothing. The soldiers said: how many are in your family? I answered: enough. He asked again, this time standing a bit closer to his captain, and I answered: in my family there are enough, enough for me and for you. All those behind me in the line laughed and laughed. The line, which stretched out the barracks door and down the streets of Kermanshah, was longer than any line our town had ever known. I was told that my little joke spread the entire length of it and it was a line of laughing Kurds.

The second year they ordered us back to ask us the same question again. Inches from my face the soldier demanded: How many are in your family? I must have an accurate count of mothers, sons, daughters, uncles and cousins and aunts, even grandmothers and grandfathers. Well, I replied, let me see. Before me there were maybe twenty or thirty, our small tribe goes back a long way, you know, maybe forty grandfathers on my side and forty on Leela's side, then there are the dead to count and the un-born. Do you have the counting beads? Because I can't add. Maybe you can make the number for me? Some tidy sum of the living and the dead? The soldier looked to the captain, who dismissed me with his hand. As I walked out all the faces I passed had smiles spread across them.

The third year they called us again and we stood in that ridiculous line all morning long. When it was my turn to enter the barracks I saw that the desk in front of the captain and the soldier was covered with tools, shovels, axes and hammers. There were also seeds in small packets and bags of fertilizer and pesticide. The soldier (he was every year the same) asked me again: how many Iranians are there in your family? I tried to take my eyes off the bounty before me, a farmer's dream—the ax, the saw and the hammer, the strong new seeds from the city—and I answered in a daze. There are no Iranians in our family. We are Kurd. The soldier kept his eyes on his paper and asked again. How many Iranians in your family? Tell us and you can take home one of the shah's tools. It seemed a fair deal: a little lie in exchange for an ax that lasts for years? Why not? I cleared my throat. I am one myself, two my wife, seven my children—four girls and three boys—and one my brother, but he is missing an arm and a leg, does he count as half or whole?

Behind me I heard the line start its happy jitter. The soldier made a note of what I said and handed me a bag with a human skull on the front. *New pesticides, to kill the insects that eat your crops. Careful*—this time it was his turn to smile—*it is very strong and very dangerous.*

I left with the poison powder in my hand, though I would have rather taken the hammer. If you can't joke in such serious times then it's nice to leave a heavy mark.

★　★　★

I am a funny man and fate has a funny way of going about my life. I was born, just like all the other Kurds, in this green valley. My father is a farmer and I am a farmer to follow him. I married a girl whose brows meet in the middle of her forehead, brows more lush and verdant than the best season of my fields, and together we had seven children to follow and farm. All of this was set out for me under the sky and stars, until the sky shrank and the stars became dimmer and the shah determined everything about my life, including my name, my occupation and the language my own children speak. Now I, the most illustrious farmer in Kermanshah, harvester of life from dirt, must sell poison (a new fashion among the Kurds in the valley—*Did you see how it kept the locusts off his melons? Ya Ali, let's sprinkle the tomatoes with it too, a whole season of food untouched by bugs!*) to all the planters north and south of here in order to make enough money to pay the tithes that keep the soldiers off my land, away from my ignored plots. It's a funny fate, I must admit, but I make what I can of it and spend days in my shed, painting the little sacks of powder not with the fearsome skull but with flowers and oranges, red hibiscus and cherries. When the farmers come to buy the bags I make sure to joke, *a little murder for the pesky gadfly is a lot of life for your eggplant crop.* I get a few laughs here and there but everyone can tell I have my baba's hands—better for making life than for taking it.

That was the year the captain—who everyone knows is a Kurd though he himself tries to hide it—started to walk across my land. Those days I rarely left my shed. Once a week an army truck would make its delivery of chemicals and powders.

They would say, *So you are saving crops, eh, Kurd? Where are all those excess harvests? It's about time the shah saw the fruits of his generosity.* If I wanted I could tell them the extra, the prize vegetables and fruits, were going straight to the mountains to feed the resistance, those fled from Mahabad, but I smiled and said nothing; the money I've made so far is enough to buy my wife an iron stove and my boys a radio.

So I stay in my shed mixing and causing a stink and watching the captain, who is not old but looks it from a distance, walk from south to north across my land, in the direction of the mountains. Sometimes he is with his two oldest sons but mostly he is alone, with a rifle and a bag for hunting. On the few occasions we caught eyes he raised a hand and I raised mine, like friendly men do in passing. It was then, once, many years ago, sometime before his wife died, that he approached the shed and I invited him in to have some tea.

We stood sipping and silent in the heat of late morning. At this distance I could clearly see the Kurd in him. He reminded me a little of my uncle Abbas when he was young and I was still a boy who would run behind him and beg to use his knife, ride his horse, take a smoke of the pipe he kept in his pocket. We drank and the captain kept his face down, as if he was afraid I would recognize him. *You make the pesticides for the crops, yes?* he asked, pointing to the shed behind us. *Yes. Though I used to be a farmer of the spiciest radishes you've ever tasted,* I bragged. The captain nodded. *And the business of making poison, is it simple?* A sudden feeling of pride came over me, pride for my shed, my occupation, that here I stood, a simple Kurd, sharing tea with the captain, who was curious about my expertise. *Oh, it's a little more complicated than you think.* And I took him in and showed him my new tools. The carbon tetrachloride and benzene, the arsenic for rodents, the measuring spoons and little glass wand I use to stir. *Do you have pests on your crops? Because I could mix up a good little potion for them . . .* The captain stared at me, his teacup halfway to his mouth, his eyes empty and clear. *Yes, mix up a packet for me. I have worms in my apricots and plums, they are thick worms that burrow straight through the heart of my fruit . . . make something strong so my children will have good-tasting fruit this fall.* I am a farmer and a father and I knew just what the captain asked. So I mixed for him a delicate and potent poison, all the while telling him jokes and keeping lively, so proud I was to host such an esteemed guest in my shed. Every now and again he would take his cigarette from his mouth to laugh, but mostly he sat and stared at the mountains with his cold eyes.

THE HOLY DAY

IN THE TIME after the failed republic the town quiets. The Kurds who marched on the square have folded back into the mountains and the only ruckus comes from the occasional parade for the shah or the random rifle practices of bored cadets.

Like a shopkeeper with little to sell, Reza closes the barracks every third Friday of the month. He locks the munitions shed and tells the officers and cadets to find recreation in prayer or gambling or letters to their dear mamans. He leaves behind his jacket and cap and walks alone out from the town, in the direction of the mountains just west. He sports his hunting rifle and a game sack for the quail and pheasants he has no intention of catching and waves at the village residents, who wish him luck in his hunt. They mutter beneath their grins: *There goes the happy captain, smiling through all that sin*. There are fewer huts and houses at the edge of town; here no one calls to him. The eyes on Reza are narrow with suspicion and he keeps a fast step up the steep and sparsely populated roads until the roads themselves end and he is walking up the mountain itself. On nice days, the only glare he suffers is that of the sun.

He makes all the appropriate turns by memory and walks through the hot noon and into the afternoon, when he makes it to the top of the first peak. Here he stops, takes rest and water if he has it, turns his back on the town, the flats, even the small plot in the distance where Meena primps herself for the invisible shah and his children run about oblivious to the war in their blood. Reza turns his back and walks down into the mountains, where he is certain nothing will seek him out.

What he has made habit: the walk, the turned back, the descent into the valley, the long smoke and the swim in the always cold stream, the smoke again and then the dreamless nap from which he wakes, forgiven and composed. The mountains ask him no questions and give no guidance and he takes to them for the relief. He walks away from the derision of his crimson-lipped wife, the angry eyes of the Kurds, who accuse *But you are us . . . how could you be the captain against us?* and the aching faces of his children, who wonder why their baba, *who has his own gun!* grows each day weaker. There is little glory in these reminders and Reza takes to the walk, to the silence and the wind for an intermission. He is old and hopes one day to stumble and fall and die on these trails, undiscovered until dry and decomposed.

At the river he watches the water carve the frozen edges of ice that form along the banks. He does not understand how ice keeps solid well into the spring, or why some of the water freezes and some moves on. He forgoes his usual frigid swim and walks through the valley, up the next incline, to the second tier of mountaintops. The climb is hard and after a while he adjusts so that his steps grow light and his breath is in pace. At the peak Reza looks not back toward town but ahead into the crevasse that spreads out in an infinite series of stone folds. He takes in the possibility of walking on, one range to the next, without care for daylight or supplies, and does not hesitate moving forward and down, craving a point of no return.

IN THE END

THE CHILDREN ARE busy with their breakfast. Naasi whines and Hooshang rocks her with one hand and writes out the last of his dictee with the other. Hamid shovels the lavash and paneer into his face, following it with spoonfuls of honey. He keeps the food close to him so his younger brother can't have it. Afsaneh and Heideh sit in front of Meena as she combs their hair with rough pulls that make their eyes water. Reza keeps to himself at the end of the sofre. He takes no food and only a half glass of tea and fills his pipe with enough opium to make the scene distant and lovely like a dream. In his pocket he keeps the tiny tin container with the brown paste, a lighter and the packet of poison the farmer mixed for him just last week. Each time he reaches to refill his pipe or light his cigarette his hand brushes past the packet. Reza smokes and smokes and thinks of what is possible.

One of the girls starts to cry. Meena yanks her head back with fierce pulls, working at an obstinate tangle in the girl's hair. There is no sympathy in her stroke. *Eh, Afsaneh, do you think for one moment that I am going to let you go to school with the knotty hair of a goat? No, maman.* The girl sniffles. *And why not?* Reza watches his daughter, cheeks wet with tears, her green eyes glistening, answer without thinking. *Because then we will be mistaken for Kurds.* Meena's tone grows soft and her strokes are slower as the knot is cleared and the brush runs evenly through the girl's hair. *Aufareen, jounam. Very good.*

They eat and drink and the table is quiet again, each child lost in himself, as nothing unusual has happened. At the summons of the driver they pack for school and Reza takes their cheek kisses and good-byes with a mouth full of smoke, his head thick in a haze. The room is empty and the table before him is full; the kholfat knows not to remove any of the honey or preserves or cheese until Meena returns to take her breakfast. At the other end of the sofre her pot of tea sits, steeping with the special herbs she has sent to her from Tehran, *good for the circulation and weight loss.* Reza stands to stretch and inhales once or twice on his pipe and pushes his right hand into his pocket.

In the end he will follow the farmer's instructions—*You must dilute with water, depending on your desired potency*—and leave the room as Meena returns to drink her tea and read a magazine. Reza will think randomly of borders and how, in the end, he is glad not to belong to a people locked in by the invisible boundaries of nation or state or law. In the end all borders will fall off him that morning until he is just lightness and then emptiness and then there is nothing to the man; no lie, no boy, no Kurd, no proud captain, just dusty air through the lungs and mouth. In the very end, when the smoke clears and his children return to an empty house, Reza will leave them and their confusion and walk to the mountain's edge where he will scramble and search for the sharpest, heaviest rocks to pound and slice out the cold air that gusts through him in a never-ending gale that freezes his head and numbs his heart.

DAUGHTER

OUR MAMAN DIED when she was still young. She came to a close abruptly, in a way that made a lot of people think that death didn't come from within her, but from outside. When the doctors opened her skin and took out some of the cold congealed blood in her veins, weighed it, prodded it, tasted and tested it, they showed open surprise at the density of toxins therein. They called it an *impressive testimony to the resilience of life* that a woman as poisoned and as pregnant (eight months in with the seventh child) managed to last into the following morning. But our maman was a strong woman and pushed life through her well into her next and last morning, calling for us to sit, here and here, on her lap and legs and hold her shoulders and neck and hair as she felt the final concession approach. By noon we were so exhausted from the spectacle and the uncertainty, from the day and night of silence, that when the house filled with cries and Baba walked outside and calmly lit another cigarette we thought maybe it was a celebration, maybe the baby was born, maybe all the nervousness about death stemmed needlessly from our childish imaginings.

I was seven and Afsaneh maybe four or five. We were young. That our mother should disappear was one thing, impossible and shocking, but that she should go somewhere else, somewhere without us, was cause for great alarm. In the days after her passing we wondered not why or how she had left us (she would never leave us, our maman) but where did she go? What place existed besides our four-room house, our rocky courtyard and the high mountain walls all around it? This Kermanshah was a world and we had never left it, nor had our maman, so then where did this death take her?

Ringed in by the Zagros, we could not think of a world beyond and so we confined the relocation of our evaporated maman to the dirty white walls of our bedroom, to the wired pens that held the animals, to the life in the forest behind our house, and so we locked her neatly into our world with us. With the confidence of children we concluded that our mother did not die like so many of our useless over-loved pets (whose slow decay we watched with curious certitude), she was not killed (like her angry brothers would come from Tehran to claim, pointing a finger first at the piece of paper with the doctor's findings and then at our father's head), but that she simply, of her own volition, vanished. Vanishing, like a flash of lightning or steam from a kettle, was a forgivable, almost graceful act. In death she vanished, the air taking her and she evaporating in it, and in those first few days she became a small part of everything we saw and breathed. Believing so, we kept a wishful watch for our mother's equally instant return.

We all waited in our own ways. Hooshang, fourteen, the oldest and almost a man, was found at the river wearing Maman's

265

clothes: a silk sweater and one of her wool skirts unbuttoned around his hips. He had the cream-colored stockings pulled over his hands and forearms like long gloves and had fallen asleep with his arms wrapped around himself. We all saw him and none of us told Baba or laughed. There was a grace period between us after she died; without a mother to police our vicious love for one another both the love and the viciousness dissipated, and we lived, for a time, un-knit, in a small common space and distanced from each other, learning that mourning required a sort of privacy we had never needed or known.

I'd like to think that parts of that open benevolence still last in these adult versions of those suddenly motherless siblings. But what I feel, most regularly and honestly, is that, with time, our love for each other has faltered, as if Maman's presence was a constant reminder of how the seven of us, in belonging to her, were connected to one another. Now that we have left Kermanshah, climbed over those mountains in our own secret escapes, there is no evidence of a shared starting place, as our mother's body was the first and only home.

As we lived inside and around each other's grief during those first few days, the news of our mother's death traveled locally, and the village women, wives of low-level cadets and low-rank local conscripts, descended upon our house in determined droves, dropped their luggage of clothing, bedding, pots, pans, live and dead poultry, herbs, sewing kits, sleeping pads and children at the door and sought out Baba. They wanted to pay their respects, to kiss his hand and cry convincingly in his face to remind him of their loyalty and secure for their husbands a good standing in his fickle favor. They searched the house for us, like hens pecking in dark corners for seed, and poured forth anew, crying out our names, our mother's name, God's name, and smearing their tear-stained faces against our own dry, bewildered skin. They were foolish women, these Kurdish wives, always hunched and cloaked, and their hatred of our mother was so public and so proud that this sudden grief played out for us as comedy and we left the crying (which they had turned into a language of its own) to them and kept a steady, waiting silence for ourselves.

It was not until the arrival of our mother's body, wrapped in a thick sheet of canvas and unloaded from the trunk of Baba's car, did their crying stop and ours start. I remember the six of us stood on the porch and watched the men carry the sack of her to the shed behind the garden. We watched the sharp-chinned village wives follow, whispering and giggling to each other like schoolgirls, their hands full with buckets of water, lengths of white cloth, small brushes and soap.

All of us, even the boys, pried at the closed shed door to be let in. From inside we could hear rustling, shapes shifting positions, laughter, gasps, the sound of water splashed and cloths being wrung and snapped. My seven-year-old imagination writhed as I thought of our mother coming alive inside the dank dusty room, clean of the sickness and all that pain. Long after the others had gone Afsaneh and I sat in the tall grasses that grew up alongside the shed and picked the knots out of each other's hair, cleaned our cheeks with spit and made ourselves presentable for Maman's return. You can't say we should have known better, two young girls, but we sat for a long time, long enough for the sharp silhouettes of day to soften, long enough for the air around us to darken with evening. We waited until our hands were numb and our spines spasmed with chill and nothing could be seen or separated from anything else. We stayed there a long time, our backs up against that shed wall in the thick inky night, in a darkness that was everything, and listened as the sounds of village women's laughter and crickets' quick strums closed the space around our hope.

They started with a map of the world. It hung on the wall of the room where we slept shoulder to shoulder and head to toe. The "world" was flat, expansive, covered in a deep blue that separated small quilts of pastel patchwork that were supposed to be countries on a landmass. Aside from Parvin's defacement with crayon (Baba, once after smoking, had taken a piece of coal and circled the area where Iran, Turkey and Iraq met and scrawled *Kurdistan*) the map was without blemish, the only wall décor in the house. Every night before we fell asleep, Maman stood in front of the map, with some baby or other on her hip, swaying back and forth as she pronounced the names of oceans, seas, mountains, countries. It was our trick to avoid sleep, to sing back her pronunciations of *Amree-kah! Rusee-ia! EE-ta-lee-ah!* and her trick to have us dream outside of what we knew. Of course it made no sense to us at the time, that these words were places, but there is a lot to be said for those songs, as we have fled that home to live, scattershot, all over the world. The village women took down the maps and the area around them had tanned a slightly darker shade of blue over the years, leaving the imprint of a dark rectangle on our bedroom wall. I spent many nights staring at that stained shape and pretended it was a square of sun flooding through a high window.

They waited for night, for the twang of the sitar, the thump
of the daq and the scent of opium to slip out from the crack in
the den door, before they went into Maman's room. Afsaneh,
Parvin and I couldn't sleep and so we stood in the dark spaces
between bedrooms and watched three women walk around
our mother's room with panther steps and thieving eyes. They
emptied closet and dresser indiscriminately and occasionally
one would pause on a pair of pants, a heeled shoe, a silk stock-
ing, and try it on. At the dressing table they smelled the glass
bottles of perfume, inspected the tubes of lipstick, marked up
the backs of their hands with the imported sticks of black and
brown kohl. We tried, my sisters and I, stuck in that dark silent
space, not to laugh as they masked their faces with colors and
lines that pushed their lips forward and sank their eyes. I watched
them stare into the oval mirror at the unfamiliar painted versions of themselves, and my chest stretched tight with stifled
laughter until finally they spit insolently on the edges of their
shawls and wiped their faces clean.

Alongside the mirror our mother had tacked up three images,
two magazine cutouts and a photograph. In one, Princess Fawzia,
Reza shah's first wife, at a ball masque, stands to pose with a star-
let's smile. The other was a snapshot of Soraya, the shah's second
wife, on a ski trip; the royal couple pose at the top of an alpine
mountain, small pins of the flag of Iran tacked to both their lapels,
and smile broadly behind sunglasses. The women removed the
magazine cutouts and tucked them in hidden pockets, next to
the tubes of cosmetics and tiny bottles of perfume.

They left our photograph stuck to the wall. In it Maman sits
by the bank of a stone-bottomed stream while the seven of us

circle around her: Naasi on her lap, me at her knee, Parvin and Hooshang at her shoulder, Ali and Afsaneh behind her, Hameed a bit off to the side. The village women didn't touch the photo as theirs was an incomplete and judicious scouring, much like how I imagine the mind selects memories—leaving some up and taking some down. In the dark of that night I snuck into that abandoned bedroom and took the picture down in a sort of child's cleaning. It still floats around among the seven of us in copies and reproductions, each a bit more dim, each farther from the true feeling of her kept in that dark room.

Our uncles arrived from Tehran unannounced and we did not recognize the family in them. Hooshang, who had grown mean and defensive in those first few weeks and months, noticed them first and mistook them, with their narrow suits and timepieces and oiled hair, as traveling salesmen and rudely told them to leave. They smiled at him and asked, *Hooshang, jounam, how are you going to ask your uncles to leave? Eh, he's just like Meena described in her letters, quite the hardheaded Kurd, eh?* They singled us out with precision: *and you must be, and you must be, and you must be.* It was a strange feeling, to be touched and talked to by these foreign men, and to this day I remember how easily I bypassed fear and suspicion when they cupped my face and called my name.

I imagine the two uncles leaving Tehran on new trains, ending up on old roads, soliciting rides on the backs of mules, camels, military and cargo trucks, shouting politely at drivers and herders, *Kermanshah? Kermanshah?* They made their uncharted way across the desert and through the crevices of the Zagros, taking tea in the dirty cups and keeping our baba's stern face at the forefront of their mind. They must have taken some looks as they moved through. Two men, a doctor and a chemist, European educated, suited and softly shod. Fueled by the steam of an adamant rectitude they must not have returned the curious stares and I imagine their steps bounced jauntily at the thought of imposing justice for their sister's murder: the accusations, the trial they would demand, the somber walk to the courthouse or the jail, the magistrate's even face as he considered the severity of the claims before him. And I imagine their steps did slacken a bit, churning down through the heel, at the memory of their own willingness to marry their sister off to the unknown man at the end of Abadaan Street, the opium-smoking soldier who sat on the rooftop, on the patio, in their divan, and said very little. They were not so ready to admit how badly they wanted to empty the house of their shamefully beautiful sister, to take the money for her bride price, to be rid of her. If they had those thoughts I am sure the mountains around them doubled in height and the mules carrying their bags groaned at the weight of such human hypocrisy. But maybe they forgot the details of the past and marched proudly, like the city men they were, into mountains that would quickly make boys of them again.

They greeted us and waited for our somewhat aggrieved baba to emerge from the house. Wordlessly he took the two men in his arms, kissing both cheeks of both faces and crying. It was the first time since our maman's death that we saw any emotion on our father's face, and I can still remember how it frightened me; his stiff skin was suddenly contorted and pulsing and monstrous. He shuffled the uncles into the den, where men had sat for days with crossed legs endlessly smoking cigarettes and pipes. He made space for them, the best spaces, next to him and gave them plates of warm food, dark tea and Russian cigarettes. He asked of Tehran, of Abadaan Street, of news of the city, politics and the shah. He wanted to know if the city was a modern place yet, made of glass and steel, he wanted to know if in its center Iran existed as the place the shah's father had promised. He passed them pipe after pipe, and by nighttime it was all they could do, these two uncles from Tehran, to sit and smoke, accept condolences on their dead sister, give condolences on his dead wife and revel in the music of duduk and sitar that filled the room, their blood and bones.

They stayed for three days, sequestered in the den, sated with food and smoke and our father's breathless storytelling. Bit by bit they wandered out into the afternoon. One of them, the doctor I think, walked the house, looking for remnants of Maman. Naasi and I told him, when he asked, that they had been carried out, pocketed, burned. *Burned*, he repeated. We nodded. They walked the courtyard, into and out of the shed and around the garden. On the third day they walked to Kermanshah. *To see the town, to meet the Kurds. What fascinating people, these Kurds, we are interested in the Kurds. It is not often we get to leave Tehran to see this new Iran of ours.* And Baba let them go, insisting that Hooshang and Hameed accompany them as guides, and the four set off in the direction of town, the two nephews in front, kicking stones ahead of themselves.

We waited at the end of our drive, brothers and sisters alike, and watched for their return that afternoon. The sun had just dropped, but it was a determined day and thick orange beams filtered out from the spaces between western mountain peaks,

covering the slope behind our house in stripes of sunset and
shadow. We spotted them, figures moving toward us through
the panels of dark and light, the two city men briskly ahead and
our brothers barely keeping pace. I think we must have been
waiting for gifts, because I remember the disappointment when
they walked through the gate, past the line of us without so
much as a hello, and stomped up the drive to the house. The uncles reemerged calmly escorting our father out of his own door
into the courtyard, because some things are easier to do out-
doors. Maybe the brisk air called to their cultivated sense of justice; maybe they couldn't accuse a man of murder in his own
house, with family and friends so tightly around.

They spoke as if the coming night itself was judge and the
steel-gray mountains a somber jury. Carefully the two brothers
laid out their evidence. Baba dropped his cigarette, pushed it
into the ground with his toe and lit another. They read to him
directly from the piece of paper. Cyanide 27 percent. Arsenic 9
percent. Benzene 19 percent. Carbon tetrachloride 12 percent.
Bleach 4 percent. The contents of her blood as autopsied in
Kermanshah, as it was exhumed from the still-tidy grave. The
uncles stood proudly in the dark silence. The two men stood
sure in their stronghold of doctor's reports and dead woman's
claims that Baba's guilt was as obvious to the world as the small
fire he held in his hand. With a false humility they nodded *yes*
and *yes, of course* when Baba asked if they would be kind enough
to accompany him to the jail in town.

The jail was a new addition to the town. Criminals in Kermanshah came few and far between and justice itself was an intimate transaction with sentences dealt in dens, fields and off

the branches of trees in silent orchards. At that point the one-room cell had yet to hold a human soul (though it held mules when the rain turned to hail). He took the uncles to the cinder-block building and introduced them to the gendarme on duty, a young boy of seventeen or eighteen who, thinking these suited men were part of some tour or inspection, easily returned our father's affectionate embrace, answered dutifully, *Yes, Captain, yes, Captain, yes, sir,* locked my father in the cell and went to find the magistrate. An accusation needed recording. The magistrate laughed loudly at the sight of our baba, his longtime hunting partner and his superior, sitting on a wooden bench in the town's one jail cell, and jovially took down the uncles' statements, teasing Baba all the while. *Vayvayvay, you say she was full of poison? Reza, do you hear that, your own wife full of poison. Didn't you think to suck it out? Heheheh.*

Even though we heard this story, the story of Baba's night in jail, in many versions for many months after his return, there is no accounting for the emptiness the two uncles must have felt at the sight of Baba locked and laughing in the jail cell. They spent the night in a roominghouse where I imagine they sat nervously and waited for the sun to come up. Our father stayed up to play backgammon with the gendarme (who, I heard, was promoted to lieutenant soon after) until word came that the two brothers had left town. He released himself and drove home to recount the hilarity of his evening to the men waiting in the divan and to all of us listening at the door. We never saw our uncles again and all of their accusations of murder slipped out of the mountains as mysteriously as they did.

Our father was a man who liked to sit in the dark. That night when the room was cleared of well-fed, sleepy guests, we snuck in and sat behind him as the light disappeared from the air. In darkness he was assured and comfortable in the same way an animal might be. We watched him, lying on his side, propped up on one elbow, at an angle to the floor. He sat still far longer than we could and emitted such fearlessness and such certainty; on these evenings he became myth to us. We feared him—this man who rarely spoke, whose angled profile mimicked the barren mountain range out the window, who breathed at the steady clip of a confident animal—and there was a comfort in our fear. As children we knew, like we knew in all the moments of our abandoning and all our moments of exile, that this presence, even and imperceptible, would always hold closer to the cold elements around him—the air, the stones, the smoke, the high invisible sky—than to the flesh of any child or wife.

Book V

THE DIRGES OF OLD MAN
KHOURDI, TAQIBUSTAN—1979

THE STONE THRONE

FROM THE VANTAGE of the perch the land spreads before him, infinite and serene. He is a lonely old man, a left alone man, determined every day to make his way here to sit on a jut of granite shaped in the form of a seat, nearly in the cut of a throne. It is a good place to be. A good place to smoke. A good place to sing the dirges of old man Khourdi.

From habit, he first feels out the flesh of his face. This is it in the end, the leaden cheeks, the chin, the eye sockets filled with gelatin and tears, the macula dark and ever despairing. Today, same as yesterday, no guarantee for tomorrow. Then he surveys the land before him: beige beneath the blue with a spine of smoke that reaches across from east to west. It is a peasant fire, a Kurd fire to burn the fields so they may lay fallow, to burn the fields so they may again grow. The wind blows from east to west in a soft caress that hits the old man behind the ears and between the fingers and spreads the distant smoke along in a line to connect sky and earth, a translucent haze that mixes the two: part ash, part atmosphere, part dirt. It is an offering in Reza's honor, fire to immolate the sins of one who is neither son nor father and so un-belonging, loveless and trapped in a delirium: weightless, cordless, divine. He cannot help but inhale the air and search for birds; a falcon flies far off, then two hawks, then nothing. The old man sits on his perch, to turn to stone, to turn to dust, to turn his eyes upon the ruin-strewn land and weep, or not.

OLD MAN KHOURDI

I AM A spectacle at your gardens, shah oh shah.

Though your father, the first shah, my namesake, made a motion to regale the new in its ancient history, you are a prodigal son to make a circus of it, to plant gardens around my caves. With little else to do, and still in service to you, I come and perform. And the visitors all cry, *Look! The captain has come, with his big-beaked bird!* They smile and salute and admire the bird out of obligation before returning to their vending, corn roasting, music box grinding and humble hawking. The bird and I walk on, among your French-styled flowerbeds, the planted magnolias and rows of holly bush, their blossoms drained of color and wilted in this desert spring, and we admire their silent, mute deaths. Look how lovely the peony, the snapdragon and bent-neck hydrangea. The falcon, my devoted peregrine, my love doll with the hooded head, claws my arm in cordial agreement. *Yes, oh yes, delicious flowers, the whole withered lot.*

We are such good guests at your gardens, shah oh shah, the captain and his tethered falcon, who is aroused, of course, by the scents of sumac and cooked meats, the sounds of small children and the clack of foreign tongues. I can see it in the blunt jerks of his neck and the sharp pincers that open and close on my sleeve: he is a bird eager for flight, for an escape from these unfamiliar fairgrounds, the glory circus of these disgraced ruins. But he is a smart bird, trained in association and memory, a bird who knows from the time before and the time before that what is expected of him and what is declined. I don't assume his patience though, military man that I am; I assume nothing and keep a firm hold on the leather line attached to his neck and hooded head. Such is our suffocation, shah oh shah, such is our fear of flight.

And so we walk through your gardens hand in tenuous talon, I dressed in my military suit and the bird in his black blinding cap. They used to be my gardens, shah oh shah, before they were gardens at all. Here is where I came for my first blinding, here to these caves of father and child and hero and dead. I rode in on the back of a cart and out on my own horse. I sat in my baba's lap and took in his sweat and song and love and let myself become a man among them. In your reign the story is the same: bristled boars hang upside down and the armies of the vanquished lie still and dead under the feet of the victors and I was a boy in their presence and I am certain they know me still. Yes, here, in these very caves, I was taught to hate you, shah oh shah, and the state that you devised to harness our freedom. But do not take the insult personally, for as the stone story tells, we Kurds have always taken issue with the powers that pass by us.

Now visitors pace among the rocks and into and out of caves wearing ornaments of hats and linens, leather boots and scarves, journals and sketchbooks, sunglasses, always *ah ha!* this and *splendid!* that, and they are impressed, shah oh shah, by this false history you have so expertly excavated for them. Your storybook Persia is carved into plaques that explain and sudden signage that celebrates and they are filled with delight. But as I walk I wonder, how did you get the stones to shine so? All the moss scrubbed away and the dust cleaned off? Even dark-eyed Mithra looks polished. Are those marbles that sparkle in the eyeholes of his smashed and stolen face? History must rise for you only, shah oh shah. We walk to the lake and when I catch the reflection of myself in the waters it is for me to laugh because I am a comedy among your foreign visitors: a stern-faced army captain walking a bird like a weapon from cave to cave, carving to carving, silent as a statue.

Those are my days.

I spend my afternoons alone at the stone perch.

Remembering.

They are about her like bees, shah oh shah. Look at her—now bent over, now straight—her arms wet to the elbows with wash. My children run back and forth, to grab the dripping shirts, the flattened pants, the soiled kitchen rags, and hang them on the line, these servile children, darting to and fro in a swarm, their maman in the midst to watch with easy majesty over the eager child state. They sing back to her, *aleph, beh, ceh, al-ef, be-eh, ssse-eh,* and from here you can watch them push sound out from those sparrow lungs, right up and out of those little gendarme throats, watch as she calls to them with instructions, *Now again, aleph, beh, ceh* . . . The obedient echoes buzz in my ear, an un-swattable fly, and my gut rolls with nausea. Just a bit of tasty tar to push down the bile, soften the sharp buzz, keep the scene of them all at a blurred distance. It is for me to sit on the porch and smoke and squint at the sight of the swarm, to watch her wring and snap, wring and snap, like the state at my neck.

Yes yes yes, shah oh shah, I have followed the orders, I have taken the old men into their fields and given proper warnings all around. I have used a map, spelled out the words of edicts for their illiterate minds, explained the idea of it, this end of the Kurds, the Lurs, the Turkomans, this initiation into our Iran. They did ask, the old tribesmen with their half-toothed mouths, they wanted to know, *What is this Iran? Who is this Iran?* I say it is noth-ing. I tell them it is an idea, *made up on paper, a mark on a map, a nothing.* But they've seen the trucks and the soldiers and their guns, they've seen me in my suit with my gun and they know it's not nothing. Still they ask, *Who is this Iran? We are Quordie. You, under that suit, you are Quordie, your father was Quordie too, so who is this Iran and what can it ask from us?* The explanations exhaust me, these old men harder than the ground, born over and over again to the same mountains, the same streams and rocks, so I lie to them and say: *It's nothing, open your gates and guards to the soldiers when they ask, and there will be no harm. Send your children to the school in town, and there will be no harm. Bow obediently when you see me pass and there will be no harm.*

Listen. Can you hear them now? Buzzing just over there, do you hear it? They sing to their mother, they sing a new song with rhyme, *Ir-an, Ma-man, Ir-an, Ma-man,* my dutiful six. She wrings and snaps and they hold and hang. And here I must hang my own head, as I have lied to you, shah. I lie to you when I lie with her. She is a fine woman, one of your very own, a proper Tehrani, lover of all things foreign: perfume and books, ideas and attitudes. I lie with her every night, our ma-man Ir-an. But let me not be unduly dutiful—let us have honesty among modern men—I take her, like a good husband, proper in the eyes of God, but think only of washing her, inside out, with the white cream soap of my Kurdish seed. A pardon for my vulgarity (but come now, what is a little vulgarity among men?). Let me admit: I take this woman who is my wife from behind, where she cannot reach me with the wring and snap of her hands (she is forever wringing and snapping), and spread myself out inside her until my loyalty to you is extinguished. I scatter inside her the timeless seed of this un-named, un-nationed place and curse you. For what is a nation, shah oh shah, but a growth in the wall of a womb? I lie to you when I lie with her and her schooled mind, street walk and songs, her hate of well water and dry air and the stone gods all around us.

And I lie with my own shame, night and after night.

I could not help my blasphemous imaginings: I'll lie with her, and lie to you, and fill her full with my mountain blood and then erase her and we will see whose soldiers my children will grow to be, shah oh shah.

They are gone, have gone in, our queen and her bees, and I have filled my head with smoke and heat enough for the sting to subside into a dull throb, enough for the laundry to hang and swing before me like flags. Ah, shah oh shah, what do we care? This land will outlive us and there will be nothing but to lie beneath it atop each other: I lie on you, you on her, the lot of us on the bodies of the long dead. We lie together under the earth, first as flesh, then as rot, then as dry, sandy bone, then as sand itself. Even my children, those dutiful little sarbazes, holding and hanging the wash, will not outlive the cracks in mountain rocks, the push of a summer storm. It's all I can do, to lie and smoke and sigh and know that just as the wind blows the drops of water from the wash, we too will be dry and gone. It is a thought I sleep to, shah oh shah.

Ah, but, shah oh shah, in these years my flock has flown.

For the loss of mother and love, shah oh shah, for nothing, away my flock has flown. I have orphaned them just as I was once orphaned and now they have absconded from these stone palaces and abandoned me in the shadows of their escapes. Escapes you made possible with your modern Iran full of roads and rails to drain this long-loved land of so much blood. They have taken a flight above these Zagros, across this Iran, and traveled distances I cannot contest, farther than far. Even my Naasi, young and last and most un-mothered, folded herself into the trunk of the valet's car and disappeared. And I am left, an old man, impotent and encased in a flaccid shell, without brethren, wife or child, a eunuch of devotion beholden to you, shah oh shah. (You too will soon flee, to keep the blood in your neck and the beat in your heart, and just barely escape the revolution that will crush your father's legacy and hand over the rubble to an ayatollah wrapped in black robes and myths so old even you can't remember them.)

Maybe a map?

Maybe a map with lines that lead?

That is how I will seek my fledglings, shah oh shah. I will draw a map for myself and a map for them and that is how we will all be found.

Your father was quite the mapmaker, shah oh shah, determined on his unlined images of Iran, without borders, unconstrained, larger in the old man's imagination than whatever dimensions a page could hold. In service to your father with such faith, I too made some of the finest maps. Maps to extend borders, maps to bring troops from here to there, maps to find the clandestine tribe, maps to still the nomads and a map to punish those who would not stay still. Maps to capture the aghas, militiamen and brigands. Maps to find the weather-wizened shepherd and his frightened wife and a special map for killing them and yet another map to give directions for the placement of their bodies for all determined shepherds to find and fear. There were maps for the shoot and kill and maps to make you forget the shot and death.

I have made a dozen maps and now I must make another.

A map to lead the orphan home; a map to love.

I will begin with the crisscross of my own maman's lap, an X to start from. From there a line to the massacre and another line away from the fright of the boy who gave himself readily to an army, all for the sake of shined boots. Here is where I took my first wrong turn of many, shah oh shah. Out of fear and the slow spin of my baba's severed head I ran into your lap, from which I sucked at the sour metal milk and misery. But on this map, I make no mistakes and draw a circle to return the boy home, to take his place in the X of his maman's lap and wait for the next battle and victory, to be a hero on his land.

Then there will be instructions for how to find the love of a Kurdish girl, light-eyed and thick-legged and proud (including the scant hints on where to dig the children out from her). And finally a map for the children with clear directions for how to move through and around the mountains into the dark and joyous caves and then down again into the crisscross of their maman's lap and then away again, to the mountains for my boys and to the gardens where my girls will weave peacock feathers into fans. All the movements in a circle, from lap to lap and love to love.

Yes, shah, I must draw a map, a map to bring back the hearts that have strayed from love.

The night is mild and the moon is bright and I have pen and paper enough. So I must begin here, with this land drained of my blood, void of the cry of swaddled child, running child, fallen child; from this perch I will draw my children back to me. I will devise a clear key and mark all lines boldly so there will be no mistakes and no heart will get lost. Let us work then, shah oh shah, burn a candle through this night and hold tight for the welcoming of the father and mother and child, the imagined reunions: an oncoming cavalcade, bright eyes and shouts of *Salaam, Maman! Salaam, Baba!* sweet enough to make an old man cry.

Alas, I lie again.

I am not a mapmaker, only a man of stone.

Here I am immobile and clutched in this cunt of rock where all I can do is watch the line of smoke that stretches across the horizon. I am as frail as that silver wisp. I can sit here on my stone throne, as a boy birthed of the mountain (see, is this not a mountain in the shape of a snug chair?), and I am at once a boy and at once an old man and time cinches itself and I am re-turned, frail, to an earth strong and revolving that each day spins beneath our feet such that no matter how much we move, how far we pledge our loyalties, how long the distance to our desires, we will forever step and die in the same spot. She turns and turns below our feet each day and around the sun each year and we are always and again ourselves on top of her, on top of our history and our dead. I have marched, shah oh shah, once with the Kurds, once with you, once alone with the thrush of starlings at my fingertips, and still I am an orphan of this earth, left behind by her slow spin. Though I have left my step here and there, now I must sit, stuck on this perch, over this vista, in this tight clasp of rock, stuck to watch, to smoke, to sing and die, die into dust, loyal to the winds of an unspeakable home.

ACKNOWLEDGMENTS

I am indebted to the creative writing faculty at the University of Wisconsin, Madison, and to Carl Djerassi for his generous fellowship that allowed me the crucial nine months of snow and solitude to complete this book. I would also like to thank Emory University for awarding me the 2007–2009 Creative Writing Fiction Fellowship.

Thank you to Ellen Levine for loving the book and helping it find a home. And to that home, which turned out to be Anton Mueller, editor extraordinaire, to whom I am grateful for the encouragement and the challenges. A million thanks for believing in the work, championing it and taking it with you.

This book would not exist if not for the generous storytelling, memory, and time of my aunts, uncle and father: Kambiz, Kamran, Gashi, Minou, Mandana and Fariba. Though the characters and events of this book are fictional, the text derives much of its flavor from the afternoons and evenings I spent listening to their reminiscences and recollections. I am wholly grateful for their cooperation in those early stages of research, and their stories continued to serve as inspiration throughout the writing and editing of this book.

I would also like to thank Mehray Etamadi for her assistance and inspiration.

I am deeply indebted to many guides, and of them I most warmly thank: Ginu Kamani for her fire and relentless electricity with which she ignited (and continues to ignite) me; Micheline Marcom for drawing my gaze to the infinite wonders hidden in book after book, and for the conversations and her steadfast belief in the sanctity of *the work*; Cristina Garcia for first recognizing there was a book hidden somewhere in the random pages I handed to her that spring long ago, and for her encouragement, connections and excitement that have made these last two years a joyful journey rather than a nerve-racking one. I am forever grateful.

Of friends, there are too many to list here. In the years spent writing this book, a few were omnipresent whom I'd like to thank: Keenan for reading and understanding and with whom I look forward to a long literary friendship; Blaine and Brent for their presence in the house and in my heart; Odiaka, who was a fan from the beginning and an excellent harbor during the storms of doubt; Saneta and Helen for reminding me to take my time. And Erika—who knew my sister would have such wide-eyed stares?

The warmest love to my parents, Kamran and Fereshteh. Your support and love brought this work to life. *Merci.*

ABOUT THE AUTHOR

Laleh Khadivi was born in Esfahan, Iran, in 1977 but left with her family in the aftermath of the Islamic Revolution. *The Age of Orphans* is her debut novel and the first in a trilogy about three generations of Kurdish men.

04/09

DATE DUE